The Ghosts of Oxney Bottom

All for a Secret

E. N. Huddleston

For SW and KW, my world

The Ghosts of Oxney Bottom
"All for a Secret"
by
E. N. Huddleston

1

Autumn 1781

This time, Flora felt sure, her Father and sister were going to kill her.

She knew without a doubt that it had taken her Father some time to arrange the dreadful meal she was currently missing, and she knew too that with all the local smuggling activity along the coast Captain James Reed's time was probably quite precious. Flora adjusted the grip on her horse's reins as she led him across the cornfield.

"Come on, you poor old boy, let's get you home," she murmured, nuzzling her head into the black stallion's neck, enjoying the earthy smell of him.

"They probably think I'm being late on purpose," Flora muttered to her horse. Well, this time they would be wrong - not that she would mind foregoing this dinner. Her eyes flickered to the sky. It was almost dusk, and clouds formed on the horizon. Perhaps Captain Reed had eaten his fill and had already left.

She could but hope.

She and her sister had had a "talk" about the goodly Captain and the dinner her Father had tasked Margaret with arranging. Whenever she was to be scolded, or made to do something she didn't want to, it would always involve Margaret sitting her down for a "talk". At her right, the horse suddenly dropped his head. Flora stumbled a little. "Pudding!" she cried. "Be careful – you almost pulled me over!"

Margaret had come to her bedchamber only a couple of days ago, not bothering to knock on the door or announce herself in any way. Flora supposed that, after all, her older sister had had years to hone her motherly skills towards herself and her brother, it was unlikely she would start acting any differently now and afford her just a little privacy. Flora was unsure what she might have been doing in her chamber by herself that she didn't want Margaret to know about but, she mused, she could have been doing *something* and it would be nice for Margaret to knock and be invited in every once in a while, instead of assuming she could just enter whenever she chose.

"We need a talk," Margaret had announced, seating herself on Flora's bed, knotting her hands, nervously. The younger sister sat at her dressing table, combing out her hair. She had been at the stables and there was straw tangled in the lengths. She watched her sister in the mirror.

"I'm thirty," Margaret began, "and I have spent the last twenty years, since our Mother's death, caring and looking out for both you and your brother."

"Yes... I know..." Flora's brushing slowed as she wondered where this conversation was leading.

"I will have no suitor come to call on me now, to ask Father for my hand in marriage."

Flora turned to face her sister. "I'm sorry," she said. "Do you want to be married then?" Her eyes widened in sudden understanding. "Oh, Margaret. Do you... wish that things had been different? Do you regret those years, just caring for Stephen and I?"

Margaret looked hurt. "No, of course not. But I do wonder what would have happened if Mama hadn't died, if I had married and gone on to have children." She plucked at a loose thread on her gown. "But I didn't marry and I didn't have children. And now it seems Stephen is taking his time finding a wife so, well, Father has had me arrange an evening meal for you with a Captain James Reed of the Middlesex Regiment. Our Father and his were at school together and now he is garrisoned at Archcliffe-"

Flora dropped her brush to the floor. It landed bristles up on the rug, bits and pieces of straw caught in the hog hair. "I beg your pardon?" she said, staring at her sister in horror. "What are you talking about? Oh," she said. "Oh, I see – now *you* are deemed too old, this is Father trying to auction *me* off like a prize cow at a cattle market instead, isn't it? Well, you can tell him that I shan't be going."

Margaret got to her feet and crossed the room to her sister in a rush. "You will go," she said, holding Flora's hands in her own. "You must - you're twenty – grown up. Almost." With this, she gave a half smile. "I know you don't act like it much of the time – still sneaking into the kitchen and helping yourself to Mrs Merson's sweetmeats and pastries when you think no one is looking."

"Well, I-" Flora began.

"And spending time with the tenants when it's really not becoming of you anymore."

"Mr Barns has a litter of kit-"

"And, running around the countryside, by yourself no less, at all hours."

"That is not true!" Flora exclaimed. "I'm always with Pudding and I'm always back before dark." She gave an involuntary shiver. "I don't want to be whisked away by witches or scared to death by the ghosts hereabouts."

Margaret folded her arms across her chest. "Forget about witches and ghosts, silly girl. This is exactly what Father and I mean: it's beyond high time you were married and producing an heir for Father. You need to face facts, Flora. This is real life and you can't spend it as though in one of your adventure books. You need to grow up, and quickly, be the young lady you were born and bred to be.

"Now, Father has asked me to arrange this meal with Captain Reed for the day after tomorrow, on Wednesday. You *will* be there!"

Flora took a breath and shook her head. "No."

"Yes. And you *will* dress appropriately." Margaret pointed at Flora's newest gown which was not yet put away and was still hanging on the armoire, "Look, that will be perfect," she said, taking a tress of Flora's hair between her fingers, "The peach colour will bring out the highlights in your hair."

"Prize cow," muttered Flora through her teeth, picking up her hairbrush. "My, what a lovely rump *this* one has."

"Flora!"

"Well." Flora picked the straw from her brush and rolled her eyes. "What shall we talk about?" she asked. "Aside from being a soldier, who even is this man? Where is he from? Oh, my heavens, how *old* is he?"

Margaret turned her back to her, making her way for the door. "I don't know all the details, maybe these are the things you can ask him about when you meet. I can tell you that, like our father and his, he was educated at Westminster and that he is thirty-two."

"Thirty-two! But... that's... he's old enough to be my father!"

"Oh hardly." Margaret spun around. "You know, Flora, Father was originally thinking of inviting Lord Buttersmere - he's looking for a new wife and he's not a day under seventy. So really, you should think yourself lucky!"

That much was true. Only last year cousin Anna on her Father's side had been married off to a sixty-four-year-old gentleman and she not quite nineteen at the time.

The thought of marriage to anyone – old or young – made her feel quite unwell. She went back to brushing her hair, pulling at the tangles angrily. "But Margaret, I don't *want* to settle down or to be mistress of my own home," she argued. "Where is the fun and excitement to be had in organising servants and managing a household? I don't *want* to be like you and take tea with the ladies every day of the week, or shop the catalogues for silks and satins that I don't even want to wear!" She threw her brush down into her lap. "I want things to stay as they are," she'd finished. But Margaret wasn't having any of it. "The date is set," she'd said, her face fixed in a way that bore no further argument. "And that is final."

Flora came back to the present and led her horse from the field into the lane, her house coming into view as she continued up the dry mud track.

Some people had described her home as desolate and bleak but she loved it. At this moment, in the twilight, the silhouette of the tower to the left and crenellations on the roof made it look more like a castle than ever. When they were children, she and Stephen had liked to pretend the house *was* a castle and that they were princes and princesses in the time of King Arthur. They'd spent many a long day slaying dragons with wooden swords, rescuing fair maidens or being pirates bound for the New World.

"Pudding, come on boy, you can do it, we're almost there." She patted the stallion on his shoulder and gazed ahead of her as they turned in through the open gates of the driveway.

At the rear of the property were beautiful gardens with topiary hedges, partèrres and a tree-lined avenue leading to a decorative raised pond. Beyond the gardens grew a thick haunted woodland of oak, yew, wych elm, and others, and buried deep in the woods, among the crumbling gravestones of previous residents of Oxney Court and forgotten by most, was the historic chapel of St. Nicholas.

St Nicholas's was so ancient that Flora thought it was probably built before time began; made of flint several feet thick it was all but a ruin now with the windows gone and boarded, the thatch down in most parts and the few remaining walls looking like one more strong gust of wind would topple them to the ground. She was banned from going near the chapel, Margaret declaring it dangerous, so of course Flora went there anyway. Beside her, Pudding snorted and plodded on unevenly.

The last time she had been to the chapel must have been well over a year ago and she'd gotten quite a scare, she remembered now.

Despite it being springtime the woodland had been dark and gloomy; the thick, leafy canopy letting in only a little sunlight, and when she looked up only a bare few patches of blue sky could be seen between the tall gnarled branches. The ground was soft underfoot with a carpet of bluebells and snowdrops. Humming to herself, she decided to pick a bunch of the wild-flowers for Mrs Merson to put on the kitchen windowsill. A way into the woods, the flowers bleeding sap onto her hands, Flora suddenly noticed how eerily quiet it was. She stopped humming and slowed to a halt, her head on one side, listening. With no sounds of animals scurrying in the undergrowth and no birdsong sounding among the trees, she could be the only living thing with a heartbeat in the woodland right then. Often-times when she sneaked out here, she would glimpse a squirrel trotting from branch to branch, or a rabbit would stop in front of her, too timid to do anything but stare until she had passed. Not today, though. A chill came over her and goosebumps marched over her arms, up the back of her neck and gathered on her head, prickling her scalp. Flora looked around her, hoping to spot at least a butterfly or bumble bee, but there was nothing.

Then, suddenly, she froze. There *was* a noise, she was sure of it... a little way off in the distance, near the chapel. Flora frowned. It sounded like metal rattling and chinking against metal. Like the chains of prisoners clanking together. And still, over that sound she could also hear a supernatural moaning. Within moments the moaning crescendoed, turned to a piercing shriek, a blood-curdling wail like someone was being mutilated right there in the woodland. Flora had dropped the flowers, wiped the sap off her hands onto her gown and fled the forest never, so far, to return.

Now, she and Pudding had made it to the courtyard and on seeing her, the stable-boy came running across to meet her. "Good day, Ned," she said, handing him the reins, "he's done himself a mischief, will you tend to him or get Willie to?"

"Of course, Mistress," replied Ned, leading the big stallion away.

And now here she was - home. She was dirty and dishevelled, and at least two hours late. Yes, her father and sister were definitely not going to be happy with her. Flora turned back towards the house and, knowing what was coming, took a big breath, straightened her spine and headed for the front door.

She barely made it into the hallway before she was met by Margaret who was wringing her hands in impatience. "Oh my, Flora, where on earth have you *been*?" Not waiting for an answer, she continued, "Luckily, we still have some time; Captain Reed is still here, although he and Father have finished eating and are in the drawing room. It's not too late for him to meet you, even if it's only in passing." She drew a breath. "Molly!" she called. "Goodness, where is that girl? MOLLY!" Flora's maid came running from the dining room. "Mistress?" she inquired.

"Molly, fetch hot water and a wash-cloth at once and assist Mistress Flora to make herself presentable. I will help. Come girl," she took Flora by the elbow and led her away. "Up to your bedchamber, quick as you can." Molly curtsied and hurtled away as Flora, still being led by Margaret, and none too gently, ascended the stairs to her room.

"It wasn't my fault," insisted Flora when they were inside and she had shaken Margaret's grip from her arm. "I was on my way back from the clifftops when Pudding threw a shoe. I had to walk him all the way back home. Ask Ned if you don't believe me."

"It's not that I don't believe you Flora, it's just that this is so typically *you*. Do you know, Father's heart almost gave out over dinner when you still weren't back. I was extremely worried about him."

"I'm sorry." Flora cast her eyes downward.

"Oh, you're always sorry," Margaret blustered in exasperation. "I see you've stolen your brother's breeches again," she continued, helping Flora out of the garments.

"I didn't *steal* them!"

"Did Stephen say you could have them?"

"No, but-"

"Did he say you could enter his bedchamber and help yourself to them?"

"Not exactly, but-"

"Then you stole them. Again." Margaret pursed her lips as she helped Flora out of her chemise.

"Breeches are so much easier to wear when riding," said Flora, sulkily.

"That may be so but – ah, Molly, thank you. Help my sister get the smell of horse off her skin, will you, while I brush these tangles from her hair."

In a much shorter time than it usually took to dress, Flora was on her way downstairs again, wearing the peach silk dress with her hair up anew and her Mama's diamond and emerald pendant at her neck.

The sisters made their way to the hallway. "Don't be nervous, he's very nice-looking," whispered Margaret into Flora's ear.

"I'm not nervous," she whispered back. "He could be the nicest-looking man in the entire world – I still won't marry him."

"You will do what's b-."

"Captain Reed." Jenkins' unwavering voice interrupted the sisters' argument. "May I announce Mistress Flora Harrington." Eyes already lowered, Flora curtsied and extended her hand.

"Ah. *At last!* Delighted to meet you, Mistress Harrington," murmured the Captain, brushing his lips over the back of her hand.

"And you," she replied, raising her eyes, and wishing he would let go of her. She gently pulled her hand away and forced a smile to her face; they had only met seconds ago, and already she felt annoyed by him – she hadn't liked the 'at last' he had added to his greeting, she hadn't liked the fact his grip on her hand was more forceful than it needed to be and she hadn't liked the fact she'd had to be the first to remove her hand from his.

No, Flora thought, I don't like you at all, Captain Reed.

2

To meet the younger Mistress Harrington was certainly worth the wait, thought Captain James Reed. He reluctantly let go of her hand as she tugged it away and appraised her with his eyes.

She most definitely was a bonny creature; her skin appeared smooth and was the colour of unblemished cotton with no imperfections that he could yet see; the pupils of her eyes were wide in the candlelit gloom, the iris's a green almost identical to the emerald she wore at her throat and flecked with gold the shade of fresh honey. Her hair was dark and the candlelight picked out highlights of reds and golden browns. She wore it piled high on her head and fine tendrils of curls escaped the confines of the mother-of-pearl combs she wore, framing her delicate high cheekbones. He saw the nose was small, straight and with an ever-so-tiny upturn at the tip, and her lips, James swallowed, her lips were full and beautiful and he could well imagine how they would feel on his... mouth. She was short in height, barely up to his shoulder, and her figure petite; the waist tiny in its corset but the milky skin of her chest peeping above the low neckline of her attire only invited him to imagine what bounty lay beneath the silken material of her gown.

"Captain Reed. I must apologise for my lateness, please do forgive me." He noticed she spoke clearly and eloquently; there was no hint of nerves or giddiness in her voice although she must surely know why he was invited here today. "I was out riding and my horse threw a shoe," she continued.

"I'm sorry to hear it, my lady. I hope you weren't injured during the incident?"

"Oh, not at all, though I must confess my legs are paining me a little after the long walk back."

"So come," said Margaret, "let us go back into the drawing room and sit a little while. The staff will bring tea and sweet pastries."

"Lord Arthur," said Captain Reed offering a bow to Flora's father, "Please, lead the way."

The gentlemen in front, Margaret took Flora's arm and moved her mouth close to her ear. "I'm glad you're behaving and being polite."

Flora tutted. She whispered back, "I *can* act like a lady if the need arises, you know."

"Where did you ride to?" asked the Captain, offering Flora the chair nearest the fire.

"Just to the cliffs overlooking St. Margaret's Bay. I watched a couple of ships heading into Deal then, as I turned back, Pudding threw a shoe."

"Pudding?" The Captain tilted his head and gave a crooked smile, all the while looking her in the eye. "That's a strange name for a horse. Why is it called Pudding?"

"His proper name is Plum Pudding," replied Flora taking a sip of the tea which had arrived. "His coat is so black that in a certain light it looks almost purple, like plums in a pudding."

Captain Reed snorted with derision. "Plum Pudding. Ha! How amusing."

Flora smiled, sweetly.

She regarded the Captain over the rim of her tea cup. At a glance, he was quite good-looking, she acknowledged, certainly not offensive to the eye. But looks weren't everything and she had felt more than a little uncomfortable under his gaze when they had very first met.

His eyes were a pale but piercing blue and, as he had first appraised her, she felt as though she may as well have been standing in the hallway wearing nothing but the skin she was born in – his gaze had burned through her gown and undergarments right down to her very flesh.

"Margaret," she said now, feeling a sudden and irresistible urge to be away from him, as though she were in danger, despite the fact her father and sister were in the room with her. "I'm afraid I am feeling rather fatigued after having walked all the way home. I wonder if I may be excused?"

Margaret shot her a look that no one aside from her saw. She would be in trouble later, she knew. But she would explain to Margaret her urgent need to get away, and all would be well between them again.

"Of course, my dear."

Flora stood and curtsied to the Captain. She did not want him to touch her hand again – a curtsey would have to do and blast convention, she thought. A round of goodnight wishes followed her to the door. Flora stepped through and Jenkins closed it behind her.

It was all she could do not to run to her bedchamber.

3

"Aye, yer nothin' but a scurvy bastard," the young man laughed good-naturedly, pushing a heap of coins and a battered deck of cards across the table towards his opponent. "One more game," he said. "Last one – my word to yer, Sir."

Fin Dawkins pocketed the coins and cards then finished his beer in one long gulp. "Nine games in a row I've beaten yer now," he said. "Why would ye want to put yersel' through more humiliation?" He cocked a wink at his friend. "I can't, it so 'appens; I've a need to get back to the yard – the MaryAnna won't build hersel'."

"Aye, I s'pose" replied Dobbin, ruefully. He rocked his chair back on two legs. "Don't s'pose ye'd see me right with another pint, would ye – what with ye not 'avin' to pay: yer Da owning the bloody inn an' all!" Fin just shook his head in mock despair and threw some pennies on the table before calling his dog over and leaving.

Outside, it took his eyes a moment to adjust to the brightness of the day after the gloom of the inn. Deal town was busy as always. With his dog following close at his heels, Fin weaved his way between an ensemble of ne-er-do-wells propping up a wall and a group of children playing a game in the dirt of the road. Two high-class ladies passed him without even noticing he was there and in contrast, a gaggle of servant girls with shopping baskets on their arms giggled as he moved out of the way to let them pass. Fin dodged horses and dogs, drunkards and layabouts, and people with jobs running errands or on their way to business meetings.

Out of the main street the crowds thinned, and Fin made his way towards the beach and the boatyard. The noise of a busy town quietened and instead of hearing carriage wheels, the buzz of conversation and the shouts of street vendors, he could hear the sound of waves rolling into shore and the crunch of pebbles beneath infrequent footfalls. The smell of the streets changed too, now instead of the stench of horse shit, piss and the occasional waft of food, the air smelled cleaner; of brine, seaweed and fish.

At the boatyard, the MaryAnna was all but finished, with just another couple of days hard labour she would be done. Fin collected his tools from under the tarpaulin beneath the boat's upturned hull and began finishing off the sanding he'd started during the week. He lost himself in the rhythmic, repetitive movements, the dog curled up on the beach pebbles next to him.

He wanted to get as much of the boat finished today as he could – he'd be busy tonight; there was a shipment of tea and wine due in and he and his friends would be needing to unload the barrels and crates. As the cargo wasn't legal, it would need to be moved and well hidden from the beach front.

The last few weeks had been busy for Fin and his friends; with the nights getting longer and the weather due to turn for the worse soon, they were bringing in as much contraband from the continent as was physically possible. The houses and taverns with hidey-holes and secret passageways were filling up almost as quickly as Fin's men, and other smuggling crews, could move the goods out of the county. Tonight's haul would have to be taken from the beach and into his most secret and isolated store.

Fin was woken from his reverie by a company of soldiers stumbling along the shingled beach-front path towards him. The dog raised his head, gave a disinterested sniff and settled back down. Fin continued sanding and watched the six soldiers with half an eye.

They were all clearly drunk – they looked a mess with their red coats unbuttoned and their black boots dirty with dried sea salt.

"*Seven wise men with knowledge so fine,*" one of them began singing. "*Created a pussy to their design.*" Now the rest joined in. The two men in front appeared by far the most worse for wear. "*First was a carpenter,*" they continued. "No, no, no," corrected one of the others. "*First was a* butcher."

They continued arguing amongst themselves, swaying as they walked, knocking into each other and causing one or other of them to push the offender upright once more. "*Third was a tailor, tall and thin, by using red velvet he lined it within.*" Fin rolled his eyes.

He'd be in for a good payment once the MaryAnna was finished; word of his boatbuilding skills was getting around and he was beginning to have more work than he could manage alone. He ran his hands over the hull, and felt the smoothness of wood under his skin. No splinters. Good. He lifted the tar pot onto the lit brazier near where his tools were, and whistled at the dog to move. "Ye'll get hot tar on yer if you don't," he smiled, giving the creature a scratch behind the ears.

It might be time to start thinking about employing an apprentice, he thought. Dobbin was without work, but in Fin's opinion, he liked the beer too much. As much as he loved him like a brother – they'd been friends since childhood – Fin knew he was unreliable. He'd probably put the rudder on the bow or something daft. He began the task of weather- and water-proofing the boat, the soldiers near enough now that he could hear their footfalls on the shingle path. They all six would be in for it tonight if they made it back to barracks like that, he thought, brushing a layer of tar on the boat.

A soldier's punishment for public drunkenness was lashes, so he'd heard. They'd got to the final verse of the bawdy song and were too far gone to even try and hide the fact they were drunk now. They passed a bottle of rum back and forth between themselves, drinking deep, beginning to sing the same song over again and stumbling into one another. Whoever was metering out the punishments today at the barracks would certainly be suffering from an aching arm tomorrow, after the whipping that lot were going to get, thought Fin. The soldiers were almost upon him now, their bawdy song forgotten somewhere in the fourth verse, now they were just talking, loudly, believing themselves to be speaking in whispers.

"I heard there's £100,000 of the stuff hidden around this place," one was saying. "Gin and wine... wool... tea."

Fin's ears pricked up, his actions slowed as he stirred the tar in the pot.

"Oh aye?" another soldier answered with a laugh. "*One hundred thousand pounds? Where is it then, tell me that. I mean, that's a lot of drink and wool to hide in this pisspot town.*"

"They reckon there's tunnels under here somewhere," slurred the first. He moved his arm in a wide arc to demonstrate the whole of Deal and spun around, tripping over his feet, landing heavily on his arse.

The rest of the soldiers laughed uproariously. "Be quiet and help me up, you bunch of giddy harlots!"

Fin watched as the soldiers assisted their counterpart back up on his feet. "Where did you hear that – about a raid?" asked another. The soldier squinted his eyes and touched his nose in a need-to-know gesture. "Can't tell you," he whispered loudly, "but the smuggling bastards'll be in for a shock when a hundred cavalry men and a thousand infantry stampede the town."

Keeping an ear open in case the soldiers said any more, Fin slowly finished tarring the part he'd been working on. But they had lost their thread when the mouthy one had fallen over and were now talking about the local harlots and the best inns hereabouts for whores.

Fin carefully extinguished the brazier – he definitely wouldn't be using it again today, not after what he'd heard – packed up and put away his tools and called his dog over.

Fin walked back into town, chewing his lip, thinking, absentmindedly fiddling with three one shilling coins in his hand. The town was still busy and it didn't take him long to find what he was looking for.

The boy looked to be no more than ten years old, an urchin,

dressed poorly in nothing so much as rags. He had dirt covering his skin and the Lord God only knew *what* in his hair. He was sitting on the doorstep of a tavern. He'd seen many young boys on his way through the town, but this was exactly the sort he'd been looking for. Fin made his way over to where the young boy sat and hunkered down in front of him. "Hey, lad," he said kindly.

The boy looked up, his face a picture of distrust. "A shilling to ye for each o' the men ye get to meet me at The Star within half an hour." Fin opened his hand away from the lad so he couldn't make a grab for the coins he showed him.

The boy's demeanour brightened immeasurably. "Aye, mister. All right."

Fin said, "Fetch me Tad Walker, you'll find him at the chandlers near the green."

"Tad Walker," repeated the boy.

"And Dobbin Croft. He'll likely be in any of the taverns on the main street." The boy nodded. "Last, William Miller – ye'll find him working at the smithy up by The Black Swan. You know it?"

"Aye, sir," the boy said again, standing up.

Fin felt sorry for the lad – he had no doubt he would do his bidding for the three shillings he'd promised. He hoped the boy would spend it wisely. Fin dug in his money pouch and pulled out a penny. "This fer now," he said, flicking it at the boy who, against all probability, caught it deftly in his small fist. "And the rest when ye bring me my men." The boy grinned and set off at a run.

Still mulling over what he'd heard the soldiers saying, and how it would greatly impact on his less legal business, Fin set off to The Star. There was nothing to be done until his men showed up – he may as well have a beer and something to eat while he waited.

*

Fin was only a couple of swallows into his potato pie when the boy came through the inn door at a run.

"I found 'em all, sir," he said, sweat running from his hairline and making tracks in the dirt on his face.

The door banged opened behind him and William came barging through. Fin handed the boy one of the shillings. "The others are following, lad?"

"Aye."

"Then here's the rest of yer wages. Be sure ye aren't lying to me now."

The boy took the coins Fin held out to him. "I ain't lyin', Sir. Thank you, Sir," he managed before bolting out the door.

Minutes later Tad and Dobbin arrived together. "Where's the fire?" asked Dobbin.

"I've bin askin' him that since I got 'ere." William nodded toward Fin. "Come on, lad. Spill."

"Let's get some beers and I'll tell ye what's happened," replied Fin, leading the way to the group's usual place in the tavern.

The table at the back wall was the one they always used. It was away from flapping ears and prying eyes. It was a good spot to do business. Sukey the waitress brought over four tankards of beer, planted a flirty kiss on Tad's cheek and then left them to it.

Fin said, "I was working on the MaryAnna, when this bunch of soldiers 'appened along..." He told them what he had heard.

At the end of Fin's tale Tad was shaking his head in disbelief, as was Dobbin. William said, "Could jus' be bullshite. I mean, a hundred cavalrymen and a *thousand* infantry?" He pulled a face. "I don't know."

"Aye, could be bull," conceded Fin, "but what if it ain't?"

William wiped the beer from his lips thoughtfully. "We need a plan. In case."

"Shall we tell the others – John Snelling, Ike Stupples and the likes?" asked Dobbin, mentioning other smuggling gangs in the area.

"Aye, but not 'til after our haul is safe." Fin continued, "and I've been thinking on that."

Tad said, "Ye got a plan?"

"Maybe. See what ye reckon. So, we've a shipment due tonight as ye well know. We'll gather up everythin' we 'ave already stashed 'ere at the inn and put it in the yard round the back. When the boat comes in tonight, instead of *unloadin'*, we'll load it - fill it with as much contraband as we can get on it and send it back to France."

The three other men nodded. "Aye," said Tad, nodding slowly. "But we won't get everythin' on that one boat – 'tis only a littl'un. There'll be stuff left over."

"That we'll stash in the bell tower at St Margaret's again. The sexton is happy to oblige for a share o' the profit, and it's a good place to hide it."

Tad looked disappointed. "Apart from the stairs."

"We'll put the lighter stuff there – the wool, silk and such yea like."

"Aye," agreed William. "As a plan it's all right for now. I can't think of anythin' better. Can any of yous?" He looked around the table. Dobbin and Tad shook their heads. "Then we best drink up and get on wi' it, lads."

4

Dobbin, Tad and William met Fin down at the beach at just before midnight. Tonight the moon was a small silver disc in the sky, illuminating a sparse amount of foggy clouds as they climbed across the blackness of space. Only a few stars were close enough to be seen. It was autumn and the temperature at night plummeted from how mild it still was during daytime hours. The four of them were dressed in long woollen overcoats that reached down to their calves and each wore a cocked hat. Behind them, most of the town was sleeping - there was a faint background hum of a few voices coming from the various inns and taverns still serving, and the occasional clop of horse hooves and once, there was the grind of carriage wheels on dirt road.

"Is the cart ready, Tad?" asked Fin, pushing his cold hands deeper into his pockets for warmth.

"Aye. Both 'orses 'arnessed and the sack barrow hidden under some tarpaulin." Happy with this answer, Fin nodded.

They stood around in silence, each looking into the distance for the boat lantern that would let them know their business associates were on their way. William pulled his pipe from his pocket and tamped the tobacco down, lighting it with a striker and tinderbox. Once it was alight, he sighed with pleasure. The tide was in and the sea calm – bubbles of surf almost reached their boots as the waves rippled inwards. Fin's dog wandered the extra couple of feet to the water's edge, dipped a toe in the surf and hurried out again, back to his master.

"That were 'ard toil this day," said Tad. He was speaking of the barrels, kegs and crates they had already moved from their hideaways onto the cart.

"Aye – ye need muscles for this work," agreed William.

"Why's Dobbin 'ere, then?" asked Tad, playfully. Dobbin threw him a look that was missed in the darkness.

"Look!" whispered Fin loudly. "Over there – I think I see a light."

The four of them squinted into the darkness and Fin pulled a spyglass from his pocket. He said, "get the cart ready – he's signalled, 'tis the one we're waiting fer."

Tad went back up to the cart and manhandled the sack barrow down to the beach. William and Dobbin used their boots to sweep and kick as much shingle and as many pebbles as they could away from the short wooden launchway. The little boat bobbed its way nearer, the yellow lantern light on the deck flickering and picking out the silhouettes of the two sailors at the helm. Within minutes the boat was close enough to land.

"Salut!" called the sailors, jumping over the side and splashing into the cold sea water up to their knees. "Ça va?"

"Salut Jacques, Guillaum!" responded Fin. "Il ya un problème."

All six men hauled the boat up onto the pebbly beach. The two sailors wore deep frowns as Fin described what he had heard the soldiers saying. He went on to explain his new plans for this cargo. The two Frenchmen understood his concerns and assisted the men to load more of the crates and tubs from the cart back into the boat. With all six of them working it didn't take long to get the boat loaded to capacity, but there was still plenty of goods left over on the cart.

As much as possible, Fin's men had left the lighter crates containing the wool, silk and bales of lace on the cart.

"All right," he said now. "Dobbin and Tad - yous take the cart to St Margaret's of Antioch - stow what ye can in the bell chamber. William will stay behind wi' me." William was a big man standing just shy of 6' 2". He was large in gut, having a thirst for beer and being always hungry for pie. At almost thirty-six, he was also the oldest of the four, having nearly ten years on Fin and Dobbin and almost fifteen on Tad. Fin was worried his bulk and the obvious difficulty he'd seen him have when climbing any stairs would slow the other two down. "Off you go, lads, William and me, we'll meet yous at The Bottom." He turned to the two sailors and thanked them for coming over. "I'll send word when we know fer sure the cargo is safe to come back," he finished, waving them off.

As Tad and Dobbin climbed to their places on the cart rig, Fin and William headed back through the town and to The Star. The inn was still serving, though quietening down from how it had been. An occasional shout or howl of laughter could be heard from inside. William and Fin headed to the stabling round the back of the building to prepare their two horses for a late night ride.

*

The horses were asleep in their stalls, snorting and snuffling quietly as they breathed. "Sorry, me fellas, ye've work to do" Fin whispered. His own horse, Diamond, half opened an eye, and Fin fussed her velvet nose. "Aye," he said, ""I'd be asleep too, if I 'ad the choice. But ye want nice tasty oats, an' straw to keep ye warm, so ye 'ave to work fer it. Like me." Once his and William's horses were both saddled up they led them out into the yard. Diamond gave a shiver and tossed her head. "Aye, tis cold, I know, but ye'll soon warm up when we get goin'."

Both men mounted their horses and took their reins in their hands. "Ready?" asked William, taking a sip of something warming from the hip flask he always carried.

Fin nodded. "Stay 'ere, boy," he told his dog. "Ye've no need to come."

The dog slumped down on his haunches and looked thoroughly miserable. "Oh, all right. C'mon then. Those big brown eyes get me every time." The dog jumped to his feet, tail wagging and thumping against the stable yard door.

"Yer a soft-hearted fool," said William with a smile.

"I know it."

They started at a walk through Deal then broke into a trot as they left the town and moved into the countryside. It was nearing three o'clock in the morning and the cold of the night made their breath mist on the exhale. The dog ran on ahead, stopping sometimes to look behind him and make sure his master was still following. The white of the mutt's coat caught the moonlight and he shone like a little four-legged ghost in the darkness.

"Go on," said Fin to the dog. "Ye know where we're headed." The dog bolted off into the trees and William and Fin turned their horses left into the undergrowth, following him at a sedate walk.

The woodland was thick although over time Fin, his men and their horses, had trampled a path between the yew, oak and wych elm trees. Moonlight had lighted their way up until now but could no longer pierce the thick tree canopy overhead, and the men relied on their horses to lead them where they needed to be.

After a time they could see the soft golden glow of lantern light between the tree trunks and, moving closer, they could just make out the shape of a horse cart and a ramshackle building a few yards in front of them. They brought their horses to a stop and Fin whistled between his teeth, the sound like the call of an owl. An answering whistle came from just ahead.

When Fin and William reached him, Dobbin was puffing and sweating, "We've done the most of it. Tad's jus' finishin' the last couple o' crates." He nodded towards the run-down building.

"Did ye see anyone?" asked Fin, climbing down from his horse.

"No one and nothin'."

"Didn't need the chains, then?" Fin walked into the old chapel and surveyed the scene. The interior was lit by two lanterns and the light shone on the men's stash. Boxes and crates, casks, barrels and tubs were stacked tidily against the least damaged wall.

The dog jumped up on a crate and looked pleased with himself. "Glad to see ye made it," Fin smiled, rubbing the creature's back and making him do a joyful little dance of pleasure. "Ah, damn, there's more 'ere than I thought there'd be," he said now, looking around. "I'm wonderin' if it's safe to leave it all."

"I think tis a chance we 'ave to take," William replied. "Is only us four know of the place, tis out o' the way, almost derelic', and never used." They each looked around at the gaps in the roof, the missing walls, the windows – those that were left – boarded with planks.

"Aye," agreed Tad. "We could get a local lad out to guard it, but that'd mean someone else learning of it…"

"And it don't take much fer word to get around," agreed Dobbin. He rubbed his dirty hands down his breeches and reached for his overcoat. He had been working in shirtsleeves but now the graft was over he was already chilled. "We've 'ad one scare in three or more years, that's good odds we'll not 'ave another afore this lot is shifted."

Fin pondered. It was Tad and Dobbin who'd had a scare a year or so since, he remembered. Out here, checking inventory to en- sure the place hadn't been found and that nothing was missing, one of the mistresses from the big house over the way had come through the woods. She'd been humming and picking flowers, by Dobbin's account of it. The two had watched her for a while and although she didn't appear to be following a plan of where she might be going, in a haphazard way that was worrying for the men, she was still heading towards them.

Tad picked up the heavy length of chain used previously for securing some boxes, and started to rattle it. Dobbin joined in, making a low, moaning noise. Seeing the young mistress stop in her tracks as she listened, Dobbin changed the moaning to a high-pitched, ear-piercing scream.

"Somethin' bite yer balls?" Tad had asked Dobbin, incredu- lously. "How in Hell did ye manage a scream like that?"

"It worked, didn't it?"

Indeed it had Tad had to agree: the girl had dropped her

flowers and bolted for home.

"Aye, yer right, they're pretty good odds. Let's leave it," Fin decided now. "We'll check on it whenever we get the chance."

5

Flora was rather pleased with herself – she had managed to avoid her sister better than ever over the last two days. To do this she had devised a plan – she would get up early, take breakfast in the kitchen with Mrs Merson and the servants, and then go out with Plum Pudding for the day. So far she'd visited St Margaret's at Cliffe, Walmer and had almost made it into Deal but had changed her mind – her riding attire attracting the attention of most people she passed.

She had been to see some of the tenant farmers' families, too – Mr Barns out near Ringwould was her current favourite; the six tabby kittens were getting bigger by the day. Flora loved the feel of them walking over her arms and hands - the soft velvet pads of their paws and the needle-sharp claws when she dangled a skein a yarn in front of them. Mr Barns had offered for her to take one home but Flora knew she would be pushing her luck with Father and Margaret if she did that – cats were for keeping vermin down, not for keeping as you would a lap dog.

The first evening after meeting Captain Reed, Flora had avoided her family by forgoing dinner and claiming a headache. The next evening, she had had a 'stomach-ache' and had retired to bed early. Today she wasn't so lucky as Margaret was waiting impatiently in the hallway for her to come back from her ride.

"You can't avoid me for ever," the older sister said, meeting Flora at the door.

"I haven't-"

"Do not even *pretend* to me that's not what you have been doing."

Flora sighed. "All right, sister, you have caught me."

"Come," smiled Margaret who could never stay angry at Flora for more than a few minutes. "let's call for some tea." Flora allowed her sister to loop arms with her and lead her into the sitting room. There was a fire in the grate for which Flora was thankful – the weather was turning, there was a definite nip in the air even during the day now. They sat in the high-backed armchairs with an occasional table between them, and within seconds Dot the maid brought tea. Flora assumed it had already been ordered when her sister had spied her through the sitting room window as she was on her way home.

"First," Margaret said, pouring them both a cup, "you have a letter from Stephen."

She nodded to the table and Flora only now noticed the sealed document on the table next to the sugar tongs. Her eyes lit up. She missed her brother dearly. They had been exceptionally close when they were young children, playing together outside in the summer months and in the house when it grew colder. They had adventures where one was a damsel in distress, or a knight, or a princess. She was heartbroken when Stephen went off to join the Navy and could scarcely wait until he came home.

Flora fidgeted – now she'd seen the letter she could hardly tear her eyes away from it.

"I can see you're desperate for news of our dear brother," spoke Margaret. "But first we *need* to speak about Captain Reed."

"Dreadful man." Flora shuddered theatrically. "I won't marry him no matter what you and Father might say, Margaret. I mean it, I'll run away before I marry him."

"Silly girl. Where would you go?" Not waiting for an answer to such a ridiculous statement, Margaret continued. "He was very taken with you. He was sorry you left so abruptly."

"Surely I should be very 'taken' with him also, if I am to marry him?" voiced Flora.

"You know as well as I that that isn't important." Margaret reached across the table and took one of Flora's hands in hers. "My dear, time is moving on - you *need* to be married, Father *needs* an heir. I don't like to think of such things but Stephen is abroad, there are wars and skirmishes around every corner of the globe, it seems, and anything could happen. God forbid." She crossed herself. "We are not like others of our status, with houses in London and other cities, we have... less choice over who we marry as there are less suitable and eligible gentleman in our circle. You know," she continued, letting go of Flora's hand now and refilling her teacup, "many of the young men are off at war, either fighting in the army or the navy, those that are left behind are either unfit or, well, old."

"Lord Buttersmere." Flora murmured.

"Exactly. Which is why we had to find you someone, and sooner rather than later."

Although she could understand the reason for her Father and sister to want to marry her off, the whole idea still make her sick to her stomach. Flora replaced her tea cup on the tray.

"Tell me, dear sister, what is it you dislike so about Captain Reed."

Flora felt herself blush; this was the conversation she had been dreading for the past two days, but for Margaret to understand, she needed to tell the truth.

"I..." she began. "He... Oh, my heavens... Margaret, he was simply awful! When we very first met, he took my hand and I had to almost tear it away from him..."

"I think he was probably captivated."

"He made me feel so uncomfortable in his company."

"I believe he found you to be of the substance young men dream, my dear."

"He *undressed* me with his *eyes*, Margaret! It was like... as though... truly, it was like I was *naked* in front of him!" Flora felt the tears welling in her eyes but she refused, absolutely refused, to let that man make her cry.

"That is because he finds you so attractive, my love." Margaret looked kindly on her sister, but her words cut through her heart like a knife. "I'm sorry Flora, but Father wants you married – the sooner the better. He has said that you are left with two choices – Captain Reed or Lord Buttersmere."

Flora looked aghast. Now the tears did fall, and she could not help it. One of these men was old enough to be her grandfather, and the other…

Really, she had no choice at all.

6

Captain Reed brought his horse to a standstill and looked out over the clifftops and onto the English Channel. The water was deep blue with crowns of white surf far out beyond the harbour. To his left he could see the coves and bays of St Margaret's and to his right, The White Cliffs of Dover, the Norman castle dominating the skyline and presiding over the town. He watched, transfixed, as a multitude of ships navigated the Straights on their ways into England or on their ways out - to Europe, or places farther afield. Seagulls wheeled in the fresh air, flying high above him.

He had grown up in Windsor, some twenty miles west of London, and had always enjoyed the hum of the small market town. As an adult he had seen a great many places in Britain and a great deal of foreign lands too but, by Lord, he didn't think anything could beat the Kent coast for beauty... except Mistress Flora Harrington.

Never in his life had he seen such a beautiful young woman. Just thinking about her or tasting her name on his lips gave rise to a stirring in his groin. Mistress Harrington was his obsession.

Since meeting her, albeit for not very long - he simply could not stop thinking about her; while eating his meals he would see in his mind's eye the delicate way she had eaten her sweet pastry; whilst drinking his ration of beer he would see her daintily sip the tea from her cup. Even grooming his horse reminded him of the sight of her hair – what would it look like loose, he wondered. Was it curly or straight, was it long enough that, when she was naked, it tumbled over her breasts in their entirety or did it fall short and expose her no doubt delicious nipples? Captain Reed dismounted and let his horse have a taste of the lush grass. Even something as simple as this reminded him of her; the green of the grass, the emerald of her eyes. Would they look into his when he was undressing her?

He knew he was smitten but he really couldn't help himself. There had been women in the past, of course – plenty of them and many of them beautiful - but none with half of the beauty of Flora Harrington.

The sound of horse hooves running at a gallop in the distance interrupted his daydream and he viciously cursed the rider. He wondered whether enough time had elapsed since their last meeting to keep up decorum and try and get to see her again. The older Harrington sister and the old Lord himself were both as desperate for him to marry Flora as he was. He felt sure it would take no more than a polite note thanking them for their hospitality to encourage them to offer another invitation.

In the far distance he could just see the cursed rider who had broken into his earlier reverie. They were pushing their horse to a gallop for all it was worth. The rider's hair was loose and he could catch a hint of reds and browns in the lengths of it, and the horse itself was a big stallion with a coat so black it looked purple in the autumn sunlight like… plums in a pudding.

"My God," he said aloud, all but throwing himself upon his horse's back. "It's her. It's Flora."

*

For a fleeting moment, Flora thought she heard a voice calling to her. But the wind was whistling past her ears and the drumming of Pudding's hooves on the ground made her believe she must be mistaken. Besides, she was on the clifftop, pushing Pudding in a gallop they were both enjoying. Who could possibly be calling her all the way out here?

At South Foreland, horse and rider drew level with the lighthouse and Flora slowed Pudding first to a canter, then to a trot, and then to a walk. They stopped in front of the building and Flora dismounted – they could both do with catching their breath. She sat on the grass, the dampness of the cold earth soaking through the breeches that she had 'borrowed' off Stephen again, and pulled his letter from the pocket.

"My dearest Flo", she read for the umpteenth time. "I write with such an abundance of news, I scarcely know where to begin. I suppose I should start by telling you that I am well. This in itself is something akin to a miracle as, once more, I have seen, and indeed been party to, warfare of the first degree.

"Yes, dear Flo – The Dolphin was called up to fight under the command of Vice Admiral Sir Hyde Parker, and I have once more seen first-hand the horrors of war as we fought at the Battle of Dogger Bank. It makes my heart hurt when I recall the pain and suffering those Dutch cannons wrought on my fellow seamen. And now I will speak no more of it, suffice to say that war is a terrible beast, and one I find I have not the stomach for and want no further dealings with."

How dreadful, she thought. Poor Stephen; the sights he must have seen and the things he must have had to do. Absent-mindedly fiddling with the ends of her hair, she continued reading.

"This brings me to my second piece of news and I feel sure you will be best pleased with this tidy snippet – I have decided that I am not going back to sea. I know, of course, that Father will be sorely disappointed in my choice, as will Margaret but, as you alone know, my dearest Flo, being a part of the British Navy was not a life I ever enjoyed and that was a fact even before the ugliness of war showed itself to me. I am now much looking forward to pursuing my passion which, as you know, means my painting and art."

Their father would indeed be cross, but the reason Stephen joined the Navy in the first place was to get away from him.

Stephen had always been a disappointment to their father. As was the case with Flora, there was no love lost between them. Margaret always maintained that their father loved them and that he hadn't always been a curmudgeonly old goat, but in her twenty years Flora hadn't seen much evidence to the contrary.

"So, dearest Flo," Stephen's letter continued, "my final and most wonderful piece of news which I know only you will fully understand, is that I am in love. Yes, I am wholeheartedly, passionately and completely in love and the very best news of all is that, at long last, I am well-loved in return! Myself and my sweetheart, whom I shall call 'S', will be settling in the colonies – we know of a small town overlooking the mountains in North Carolina - and I cannot be any happier! My only wish is that you were here to see how utterly transformed I am from the sad, desolate and lonely man I have been up until now."

As it had the first time she'd read this news, Flora's heart soared for her brother. She knew it had never been easy for him - to find someone with the same preference as he to love…

"And so what of you, dearest Flo?" his letter continued. "I received word from our sister several weeks since telling me the news from home. She writes of the usual: Father and the estate, but she also gave over much of her correspondence in telling me that she and Father have found you a suitor!

"Oh! What exciting news indeed; my littlest sister is to be wed! I only wish that I could be there to see you and give you my love and support in person. Alas, it is not to be. Of course, I need not remind you, dearest Flo, that this news bodes well for Oxney Court and all it holds, as it lies wholly now with you to ensure Father gets the heir which he so desperately wants."

Flora gritted her teeth as she reread this last paragraph; it read as though the marriage proposal was already accepted, the date of the wedding set and the invitations not only sent but replied to as well. Stephen had said he'd heard about her "suitor" several weeks since, now she found herself wondering just how long her Father and sister had been conspiring on this enterprise. She felt hot tears stinging her eyes once more, and once more blinked them away.

"I should tell you that I have already written to Father and to Margaret and told them a rather watered-down version of my news in respect of 'S', but, of course, it is always you, dearest, to whom I tell all – as when we were but children, there still remains no secrets between us. My dearest Flo, I wish you and your sweetheart the love and happiness that I have at last found with 'S'."

There was nothing else of any consequence in Stephen's letter – he hoped that he would hear from her soon, and signed off.

"Mistress Harrington."

Flora jumped at the sound of her name and hurriedly returned the letter to her pocket. She was horrified to see it was Captain Reed who had spoken. She looked wildly around her – she was alone on a clifftop at least a mile in any direction away from anyone else. She rose hastily to her feet. The Captain held out his hand and offered a small bow. She had no choice but to give him her hand once more, and once more he continued to keep it in his well beyond what was considered polite.

"I thought I saw you several minutes ago heading towards the village over the way. I tried to catch up but lost you when you went behind the copse." He looked intently at her with his strange, piercing blue eyes.

Disconcerted, Flora answered him. "I stopped off so Pudding could rest before we ventured home."

"Ah. And is he? Rested?"

Flora turned her eyes to the horse who was happily ripping at the grass with his teeth. "I believe so."

"Then come." Captain Reed caught Pudding's reins and handed them to her. "Let me see you home."

Unable to decline his offer through sheer good upbringing, Flora took the reins from the Captain's hand and they started walking their horses across the clifftop.

Captain Reed frowned. "You appear to be wearing... breeches."

"They belong to my brother. I borrow them to ride in."

The Captain looked Pudding over. "And you don't ride side-saddle." At this he seemed truly shocked, possibly more so than at the fact she was wearing gentleman's attire.

"No. I find it more comfortable to ride as a man does." Please Lord, she prayed silently, let this put him off me. "You don't approve?" she asked, hopefully.

"It's certainly unconventional," he replied through tight lips. And something he would absolutely put a stop to once they were married. God Lord, you could see the shapeliness of her legs under the buckskin. They left next to nothing to the imagination and he would be damned if he would allow her to go around dressed like that where other men might happen to see, and want, her. Thank the Lord she was wearing a suitably long coat, which at least covered her derrière.

"A lovely day for a ride," he said.

"Yes."

"Should we…? Ride?"

"Yes, I think so." Flora stopped Pudding in his tracks and mounted the very large stallion seemingly without any effort. As she did so, the Captain saw some parchment float to the ground. He quickly picked it up. "Mistress Fl-",

She turned toward him. "Yes?"

Quickly, the Captain pocketed the paper. "Never mind. I was going to offer some assistance, but I see you don't need it."

"No," replied Flora. "I don't need any help from you. Thank you."

They set off in silence. Flora was feeling angry that even before they were married – she shuddered at the very thought – she couldn't enjoy some time alone without him being there. Captain Reed was feeling ridiculously tongue-tied, like a virgin on his first trip to a brothel. All he could do was cast surreptitious glances her way, noticing her hands on the reins, her legs astride the saddle, savouring each movement she made and storing all memories in his mind so that he could replay them later, in the privacy of his bed.

They reached the drive at Oxney Court and Flora stopped Pudding at the gates. "Thank you for seeing me home, Captain Reed," she said, politely. "I hope you have a pleasant ride back to Dover." With that she nudged Pudding to walk on, leaving the

Captain no choice but to turn tail and head back from where he'd come.

7

Deal was a small but thriving town, the narrow streets - many too narrow to drive a cart through - boasted all manner of businesses; bakers, chandlers, coopers and anyone else you might need. There was a wheelwright to fix your carriage or cart, a smithy to make your horseshoes and no end of inns, taverns and alehouses. As well as beer, wine and gin, these establishments offered meals for varying budgets.

Fin's father's inn, The Star, was on St George's Road and was one of the larger hostelries. It served good, basic food and had stables around the back. Inside, below the stairs, the cellar was large and Fin had built shelving to hide the entrance to further storage rooms and passageways. Upstairs, aside from the private bedchambers for Fin and his father, there were several other rooms that his Da let out to weary travellers to rest in before they headed the seventy or so miles to London, or caught a ship to the continent.

Fin was headed to The Star to meet his men and grab a pint and a pie before starting on his latest boat. The MaryAnna was finished and the buyer so happy with her that he had ordered another just like it. Not only that, but he had spread the word of Fin's superior skill when it came to boat-building and four more boats of varying sizes and designs were on order with him.

This was lucky, he was thinking, as he manoeuvred his way between the busy crowds in the street; he hadn't seen any contraband into or out of the town for nigh on three weeks, since he and his men had hidden all they could over at Oxney Bottom. The lack of smuggling money was a disappointment but not a crisis – he made enough money to live on from his boatbuilding, but the haul couldn't stay hidden forever; the sexton at St Margaret's was making noises about his bell chamber being full, he and his men needed to send word to their French counterparts to get the stuff brought back over and they needed to offload the goods hidden at Oxney Bottom. He'd called a meeting to see what views the others held on the situation.

It was market day and the crowds were thick. Not only was he having to avoid men, women and babes but also cows, pigs, ducks and any other manner of livestock as the farmers drove them through the cobbled streets. Fin's dog followed close at his heels, paying no heed to the other animals he encountered except for a cow, which he gave a good, long sniff before giving a tentative wag of his tail and leaving the strange creature to be led away.

Market day always brought in more crowds – the wares available to buy included everything from pots and pans to silk and lace. Most of the latter gotten through smuggling. Women stopped to gossip with their friends, their babes running rings around their legs. Men slapped each other heartily on the back when they bumped into a friend or neighbour. Soldiers mingled between the crowds, easy to spot in their bright red coats.

Fin contemplated the issue of his hidden stash of smuggled goods. It had been secreted away for a fair few weeks now and no one had heard anything about a raid on the town. Fin had paid a couple of young lads a few farthings each to keep an ear to the ground, an eye open, and to let him know if they heard any whispers or gossip pertaining to sightings of cavalrymen or extra infantrymen in the town, or anything else that might seem out of the ordinary. So far, all the boys had taken their money and happily reported no news.

At The Star, Fin made his way through the throng of drinkers to his table at the back. He saw that William was already there, a pint and a pie in front of him, his pipe lit and casting more smoke into the already cloudy atmosphere. He spied Tad at the bar, one hand on a tankard, the other on Sukey's arse. He and the barmaid had been courting for a while now and made a good-looking pair.

Sukey poured Fin a tankard of beer. "Dobbin's late," she said, "asleep somewhere, ye reckon?"

Fin pulled his watch from his pocket. It was a fine, silver piece, ornately engraved and one of the first things he had bought with the proceeds of his smuggling. Perhaps he should give it to Dobbin and buy himself another, he thought as he checked the time. "Probably," he answered the barmaid. "He'll be late fer his own funeral, that one." He wiped a moustache of beer from his lips and indicated the table at the back wall. "C'mon Tad, put yer lady down for now. We'll sit while we wait."

The three of them sipped beer and ate their fill of good food. William finished off Tad's meat pie and lit his pipe again. Time rolled on. At last, almost an hour after they had agreed to meet, Dobbin came bowling through the front door and barged his way breathlessly to the table.

"It's today," he gasped. "One o' the boys 'as seen a whole lot o' mounted soldiers up the way." He motioned for Sukey to bring him over a beer. "And I seen Ike Stupples on me way over 'ere; he's on his way to spread the word and asks that we do the same." He took a large draught of the beer Sukey handed him and gave out a loud belch.

"Tarnation!" said Tad. "Them drunken arses was right all along. A thousand-"

"Is there a plan?" interrupted Fin. "What else do we know?"

"Jus' that." Dobbin called over for another tankard of beer. "At least a hundred mounted soldiers will be hittin' the beach tonight, the infantry… They want to seize all the goods they can get their 'ands on. Oh, and they're goin' to be armed, of course."

This was a massive disappointment. Fin didn't own a gun or a sword and as far as he knew neither did the rest of his little crew. William might, he supposed, but he'd never seen him with either weapon. "Anythin' else?" he asked now, his mind whirring already, formulating plans and discarding them even before they were fully thought out.

"Aye. Ike and 'is men are goin' to round up everyone they can to try and stop the soldiers from gettin' into the town and striking the buildings. He's goin' to post guards everywhere and whosoever sees 'em first will let the others know."

"We'll be there as well then?" Fin looked at his friends, they nodded their agreement.

"What'll we use as weapons?" asked Tad, his eyes wide with both fear and excitement.

Fin said, "Whatever ye can lay yer hands on, lad."

8

Even the dog seemed to be on tenterhooks – he looked from his master to the road and back again, seeming to sense that something unusual was about to happen. His tail, usually wagging, stayed resolutely tucked tight between his legs.

Fin had tried to leave him at the inn, but the dog was having none of it – whining and following him each time Fin tried to walk away. In the end he'd had no choice but to relent and let him come. He fussed the hound on its head, absent-mindedly, both of them staring up the road towards Dover.

Men who boated across the English channel to take out goods such as wool from the Romney Marsh sheep and those, like Fin, who remained on dry land and took goods in such as tea, and even those who, for a couple of bob and a nod of the head, lent their horses to be used in the operation, they all lined the beach at regular intervals looking for a sea of red coats.

Almost all the men were armed, Fin saw. A few did have guns or swords and Fin hoped against hope that they wouldn't need to use either weapon. Most men had picked up what they could find on the way or already had in their hands – farm labourers carried pitchforks and scythes; sailors, fishermen and boatmen carried knives or heavy chains; anyone who owned a horse – which was most of them – carried at least toe knife and still others held ordinary carving knives borrowed from their kitchens or pokers taken from beside their home fires. Fin himself held a mattock iron he'd found in the stables at the back of The Star. What it had been doing there he couldn't say but, as makeshift weapons went, he could have done a lot worse. The chisel ends had razor sharp edges which would cause a nasty gash if met with flesh or, if swung side-on from the handle it would likely brain someone if the iron head met with a skull.

Fin wasn't a violent man and he tended to stay away from those that were. Some of the other smuggling crews used violence and threats in their business but not him and his gang. That wasn't to say that Fin wouldn't put up a fight if need be – he had in the past and still had the scars to prove it.

The dog laid down at his feet now, head up, ever alert. The beach-front was lined with men from Sandown in the north to Walmer in the south, each ready to give the shout if the soldiers, once given the order to mobilise, came into view by the coast road. Where possible, a man stood at the corner of every street leading to the beach ready to sound the alert if the troops came via the London road, and some were stationed at Walmer itself, keeping a look out up the main Deal to Dover road.

The weather had turned overnight, also. From a fresh autumn day yesterday with clear, crisp blue skies, today the sky was grey as dirty steel, and rain was hammering down. Fin hunkered down on his haunches and wiped a hand the length of the dog's back. A stream of water left the animal's hide and joined the puddles on the ground. "Told ye to stay at 'ome," Fin told the dog. "Ye could be curled up in front of a nice, warm fire now."

It was a miserable wait – Fin's hat kept the rainwater off his head but the way the wind was blowing meant his face was soaked and raindrops ran into his eyes, down over the planes of his cheekbones, and into his mouth.

Time passed and nothing happened. Fin began to wonder if anything would come of Ike Stupples' information. He was freezing cold, soaking wet and fed up with the wait. Suddenly, a cry went up from his left – mounted troops, and plenty of them, had been seen approaching from the coast road at a canter.

This is it, he thought. Fin hefted the mattock-iron in his hand.

*

Almost as soon as the cry went up, the town closed down. Those still in the inns and taverns were shepherded outside into the torrential rain and the innkeepers shut the doors behind them, bolting them fast. Shopkeepers hustled their customers out into the street, locking the doors and barring the windows. The streets were momentarily busy with people running every which way to get back to their homes before the soldiers arrived. Men and women jostled each other, the rain ran in torrents on the cobbles, mixing with the horse shit, and rendering the surface both slippery and smelly.

A woman looked about her, calling for her children. "Tabitha, Jacob, where are you?"

The girl, Tabitha, arrived at her mother's side, her clothes and hair sopping wet. "Jacob's there, Ma," called the girl over the sound of the rain. The boy peeked out from behind a cooper's barrel, an advertisement for the shop it stood outside. Swiftly the mother grabbed him by the arm and dragged him towards her. "Get 'ere," she said, and gave him a clip round the ear as she led him away. The market vendors packed up their wares, loaded their carts and horses and skedaddled, leaving trestles and tarps where they fell. The town grew quieter, save for the drumming of rain on roofs, and rushing in gulleys down the roads. The animals brought to market that day and not already secured ran freely through the streets – pigs snorted, cows bellowed and a herd of geese and ducks tottered away, wings flapping, honking and quacking, as fast as their feet would carry them. Within minutes, it seemed, Deal was a ghost town.

And then, mere moments later, over the noise of the rain, the sound of a hundred mounted soldiers split the air.

The soldiers hit the menfolk *en masse* from the coast road. They rode in, raising their swords and striking whosoever was in their way. They were headed for the town and the houses along the sea front – the word was there were tunnels below those homes and this is where all the contraband was being hidden. The infantrymen followed on foot. A few townsfolk that were mounted managed to cut the soldiers off by standing in front of their horses, trying to deny access to the houses but, whilst the men of Deal had the advantage in numbers, the soldiers won out in weaponry. Shots were fired and shouts of anger and defiance turned to howls of pain as the soldiers battled through the crowds, slashing with swords, using their horses to slam into people, knocking them to the ground, trampling them where they lay.

Fin had lost sight of his men from the very first – he'd seen William pull a soldier from his horse and punch the man in the face, knocking him out cold – he just hoped that the three of them were uninjured and managing to hold their own.

Fin heard horse hooves behind him and span round to see two soldiers homing in on him. He stood his ground, the mattock iron at his side. It was easier to swing it upwards when needed than to hold it aloft and wait to strike. One soldier levelled with him and raised his sword, Fin swiped it away with the mattock, loosening the soldier's grip on the weapon but not enough to make him drop it. The second soldier was holding a gun Fin saw, alarmed, and was aiming for his chest. Fin didn't know an awful lot about guns but thought that at a bare six feet or so between him and it, the chances of the musket ball hitting its intended target were pretty high. He stumbled backward, swinging the mattock across himself, still warding off the sword blows from the first soldier but his eyes remaining on the one holding the gun. The rain continued to beat down on them. The sword swung through the air and knocked Fin's hat to the ground, rainwater hit him in the face, he swiped a hand across his eyes hoping to clear his vision and now he could just see the soldier's finger tighten on the trigger in readiness to shoot. Fin slung the mattock for all he was worth at the soldiers and turned, scrambling to get over the wall behind him. He got one leg over and was trying to find purchase for the other, but the flint was shiny and slippery from the wet.

He felt a blow on his lower back and cried out in pain, then another blow landed on his right arm just above the elbow. The soldier fired, the musket ball exploded into his shoulder, bringing with it a whole new level of pain. Again, Fin cried out, but by then he'd made it - he was on the other side of the wall where he fell, headfirst, his skull meeting the brickwork with a resounding thud.

9

Fin came to with a cough and a splutter. He was on the ground, his clothes soaked through, his face to one side with his mouth in a puddle of rainwater. The band he used to tie back his long hair was missing and his wet hair fell in ribbons over his shoulders and in his face. He tried to move but the effort was too painful. He laid there, his mouth turned away from the puddle but his breathing still ragged. For a second he wondered what had happened, then the faces of the soldiers who had cut him down came to mind and he remembered all too well. Fin tried moving his legs again and managed to bring his right knee underneath him. He tried pushing up with his arms and a blaze of searing hot pain hit him everywhere. He fell back to the ground with a grunt and laid there, unconscious once more.

*

Still the rain fell, and Fin was swimming in the sea. He'd headed away from the beach and was out of his depth. An enormous beast, part octopus and part fish, tangled its tentacles around him and pulled him under the choppy waves. He threw his arms around, fighting the creature as best he could but it had him in a tight grip, a tentacle wrapped around his right arm, one around his waist and still another feeling its slimy way across his face… Fin started, and began to beat the creature away in earnest. Pain ambushed him. At his head, the dog yelped in fright and backed away. Fin awoke, realising the hound had been licking his face, trying to wake him with his tongue, lapping the rainwater from the stubble on his chin. "Oh, good boy," he murmured. "I'm sorry. Good boy." The dog came back to him, tentatively wagging his tail. Fin stretched out a hand and stroked the dog's head. It took an almighty effort, but this time Fin managed to pull himself into a sitting position, his back against the wall he had scrambled over last night.

Had it only been last night… just a few hours ago? he wondered. He listened hard, between his ragged breaths and the dog's almost constant worried whines he could hear only the sound of the rain still falling, and drip, drip, dripping from the roofs above him, splashing into the puddles where he sat.

"C'm'ere, good boy," he told the dog again. His voice was a bare, rasping whisper at the back of his throat. The dog wagged his tail. Fin shook his head to try and clear the fuzziness in front of his eyes and a flash of pain ripped through his skull. He reached a hand up to assess the damage. There was an egg-sized bump on his head from where he'd landed on it when he'd fallen over the wall, but worse was the pain in his shoulder, arm and back. Just moving a couple of inches to adjust his position on the ground caused a sheet of white agony to pass in front of his eyes. He really had come off pretty bad, he thought.

He remembered the feel of the sword striking across his back and arm and used his good hand to feel behind him. Touching the wound area was tortuous. He sucked the air in between his teeth, grimacing. The sword edge had hit its target well – blood oozed from the wound when he touched it and he could make out the coppery smell of it. Now that his senses were clearing, he noticed his coat and shirt were soaked both with rainwater and blood and, looking down, in the early morning light he could see the puddles near where he now sat were tinged with red. He tentatively touched his shoulder and once again pain like nothing he had ever felt before ripped through him, sending a dizziness to his head, almost making him lose consciousness once more.

Fin waited a while for the dizziness to subside, but his thoughts remained foggy - like mist slipping through his fingers when he tried to grasp them. He tried to get to his feet but the pain was too much, he slumped back down again onto his left side and tried inching his way across the ground hoping he was going in the right direction for a gateway that lead back onto the road. Over the sound of the rain, he could hear a horse nicker not too far away, and poultry clucking in the street the other side of the wall. Inching along he could now see a break in the brick-work - at least he was heading in the right direction, albeit at a snail's pace. At the gateway he peeked through.

Dawn was breaking, the streets were clear of people but clothing, tarps and improvised weapons lay abandoned on the ground, silently telling the tale of last night's skirmish.

Over in the distance he saw the fuzzy shape of the horse, a chestnut, very much like his Diamond. She had her saddle on but it was loosened and hung to one side like the rider had slid over on her and then fallen off. Fin made smooching noises and she raised her head, saw him, and sauntered over in the way only a horse can. "Good girl," Fin rasped, using the gatepost to try and pull himself up.

The pain was tremendous – the whole of his right side felt as though it was being stuck with thousands of fiery needles. He took hold of the horse's reins and grabbed the back of her saddle and then realised; there was no way he'd be able to climb on. Keeping all his weight on his left side, Fin loosened the lea-thers so the iron stirrups were as long as they could be. With a massive effort and a great deal of pain, he got his left foot in the stirrup. The horse, perhaps sensing that all was not quite right with her new rider, remained perfectly motionless allowing Fin to scrabble for purchase on her saddle. At his feet the dog whined quietly, feeling his master's pain. Fin realised he wouldn't be able to straighten the saddle and would have to manage the ride as best he could. He tried to ready himself for the agony he knew was coming by taking a deep breath, but that only caused more fiery pokers to shoot through his body. Feeling exhausted, fuzzy-headed and dazed, he hefted himself crossways over the horse, one foot in the stirrup, the reins in his hand and his good arm slung around the beast's neck. The horse moved off at a sedate walk and Fin felt the wounds to his torso stretch open further.

His head filled with fog. "Ye know where to go, boy," he muttered to the dog.

And then he was out again.

Unconscious.

10

The entire night raid had been an unmitigated disaster. Fifteen of his men wounded - including one losing an eye to the pointy end of a fire poker – and next to no contraband to show for it. Captain Reed paced his quarters like a caged animal. They were supposed to have seized a hundred thousand pounds worth of smuggled goods but instead the townsfolk had somehow discovered his plan in advance. They had sold up, used up or hidden elsewhere the majority of the stuff, and his company had come away with only several crates of tea, a few tubs of wine and some bloody, cursed *lace*. Altogether, everything they had seized measured up to around a thousand pounds – a mere bloody tenth of what they should have recovered.

He paced the room, back and forth, bed to desk, desk to bed and subconsciously balled his hands into fists. Someone knocked at his door. "Go away!" he all but screamed. Unless they had come to wake him up from what was surely just a cursed nightmare, Captain Reed didn't want to know.

He decided now that the whole unfortunate debacle was the fault of Mistress Flora Harrington; if he hadn't met her, if she hadn't cast a spell over him, if she would only leave his senses alone for *five damned minutes*, then he would have been better able to plan the raid and ensure its success.

Even now, after the whole fiasco, he couldn't get the sight of her out of his head. Now when he thought of her she was in breeches, her legs shapely, her coat short, the outline of her derrière looking like two round, ripe melons just waiting to be cupped in his hands.

"Leave me," he groaned to the Flora in his head. "Leave me be.

Please!"

Because of her he hadn't properly planned for this raid, giving himself only a couple of days to prepare his men. The written order to strike whenever he felt it appropriate had come down from on high weeks since. He'd briefed his men on his plans and what to expect but hadn't given any time-frame and now he wanted to find out who had warned the townsfolk of it. When he found who was responsible, he would personally lash them to within an inch of their life. After that, he would put the loose-lipped bastard on guard duty until the regiment was posted elsewhere and then he'd have him put on guard duty there as well.

Of course, saying all that didn't take away from the fact that it was he himself who should have planned things better; *he* should have struck sooner, perhaps planted a spy to see for sure where the smugglers hid their goods. At least the bastards had also paid some little price – there had been many reported injuries from last night, some more serious than others, although no deaths on either side.

Again, he paced from bed to chair, chair to window, window to desk. His eyes fell on the invitation from Lord Arthur Harrington that had arrived last week and was now laying nonchalantly on his blotter; ...*we should be delighted to invite you to afternoon tea when Flora will be playing the pianoforte for your pleasure...*

And *that* was why his raid had failed.

Captain Reed wheeled round and punched the wall. "Damn you, woman!" he growled. "Damn you! Damn you! *Damn you!*" On each curse he thumped the wall again, harder than before. On the fourth punch, his knuckles split and blood smeared the brickwork. He sucked the blood from his hand and then Captain Reed slumped to the floor, holding his head, feeling dejected.

11

Flora didn't know what was wrong with her lately, just that it was something more than a general malaise. She hadn't any appetite – even Mrs Merson's rout drop cakes couldn't cheer her, if anything they stuck in her throat and threatened to choke her. Neither was she sleeping – she'd lay awake all night, tossing and turning, then fall asleep just as dawn was breaking and Molly came to get her up ready for the day ahead. Nor could she find any joy in anything – not her books, not her drawings - even Mr Barns' kittens held little interest for her; she hadn't been to see them for days. She felt a strange sense of fear when she thought about leaving the house or grounds and the further afield she thought of going, the heavier seemed the stone she felt she was carrying in her guts.

She and her sister were both in the drawing room, each sitting in a chair near the window catching the morning light. Flora was sketching and Margaret was ostensibly working on her needlepoint. The room was silent save for the ticking of the clock on the mantle and the sound of pencil strokes on paper.

"You're very quiet," Margaret said.

Flora didn't look up. She was sketching the glass on the table next to her, trying, and failing today, to catch the light and reflections as the weak sunlight hit the vessel. "Hmm," she said in response.

"I thought you'd be out on Plum Pudding now the rain appears to have let up for the day."

"No." Flora used her finger to smudge a shadow on the paper.

"You've not ridden for days." Margaret lowered her needlepoint and looked to her sister.

"No." Furiously scrubbing at the picture with her finger, Flora continued. "Last time I rode I was intercepted by Captain Reed. He walked me home." She hadn't mentioned it before as she held such mixed feelings about the whole episode.

Had he been lying in wait for her? she couldn't help but wonder. After all, what were the chances he would have just happened across her in the middle of nowhere, and why didn't he go riding the other way, from his barracks at Dover. Flora knew the clifftop path along to Capel-le-Ferne and further, to Folkestone, was just as beautiful as the one between Dover and Deal.

"When was this?" asked Margaret.

"The day you gave me Stephen's letter. Which, by the way, is lost, because of him."

Margaret put down her needlepoint and picked up the hand bell next to her. She shook it and within seconds Dot appeared at the door. "Tea, Dot, please."

Still drawing, Flora expanded. "I took the letter to the cliffs to read it again. Captain Reed appeared out of nowhere and startled me. When I returned home, I realised that I no longer had it."

They discussed where she could have left it – Flora thought probably at the lighthouse - it was the last place she remembered having it for definite.

Margaret said, "It's likely on its way to France and beyond now, the wind has no doubt taken it up from where you dropped it, and whisked it away over the sea."

Flora scrubbed out what she had drawn, took up a clean piece of parchment and began again. "Probably, yes."

"I received a lovely note from the Captain thanking us for our hospitality," Margaret said, nodding to Dot to enter the room with the tea tray. "So, I have invited him to tea next week. I have also said you will play the pianoforte for him."

Flora dropped her pencil to the floor. It rolled under the table. "I beg your pardon?" she said, feeling quietly outraged.

"Now don't be cross, dear. It won't be a fancy do like the dinner you missed," Margaret gave a tight smile. "Just a few little cakes and pastries, some nuts and fruit and tea."

"And I'm to play the pianoforte?"

"Yes."

Flora left the pencil where it lay and put her drawing down on the table. "I think I will take a walk," she said. "I feel I need some air."

*

Shortly after the conversation with her sister, Flora began another sedate lap around the kitchen garden. A tea and pianoforte afternoon. She shook her head. Mind, she supposed, at least all the while she was playing the pianoforte she wouldn't have to speak to the Captain or see his strange, intense, ice-blue eyes staring at her and scrutinising her every movement.

She left the kitchen garden and made her way to the bench seat overlooking the partèrre and sat down. Water from last night's downpour soaked through her gown and petticoats and she couldn't care less. She was trying to come to terms with the fact that if she didn't take Captain Reed as her husband, she would end up wed to Lord Buttersmere. The thought of being married to either of them filled her with dread. One small mercy was that Captain Reed was relatively young and at least therefore much better looking than the old Lord. Once married, her main job would be to produce an heir and although she had no idea as to the mechanics of this task, she did know that to get with child, one needed to lay with a man.

Flora stood again, and shuddered. Her damp clothes adding to the cold shivers she felt on her skin just thinking about it. How could she possibly even consider laying with ancient Lord Buttersmere? His children from his first marriage were older than she was. No, that was altogether out of the question. There was nothing for it but to try and get to know, and even like, the Captain.

Margaret had previously said that he might possibly be

posted away, maybe to the Colonies if the war there continued. Perhaps she could stay here, in Kent, while he was off fighting abroad. Perhaps, if he did go to the Colonies, he would be killed in battle. A tiny thrill went through her at the prospect and then a cloud of self-disgust enveloped her; how could she even think such a thing? "Oh, my heavens," she muttered aloud. He was turning her into someone she no longer recognised and they were not yet courting, let alone wed.

Her thoughts had carried her to the very edge of Oxney Court gardens and now she wandered alongside the perimeter where the lush grass lawns met the woodland.

She and Stephen had played here for hours as children – far enough away from the house to make as much noise as they liked, yet close enough that they could run back in minutes if necessary. Like the time they had been playing pirates and Stephen had tripped over and cut his knee on a tree stump; they had run back so she could clean and bandage the wound before Margaret found out about it and banned them from playing there. She wondered now, a smile on her lips, if he still had the scar.

They had loved play-acting out here, she remembered. When they were pirates she would capture him and make him walk the plank, or in a different game, she would rescue him from a briar-covered tower. At least now it sounded like her dear brother had found true love with the 'S' of his letter.

Although their relationship meant he would sire no heir, Father would not know that; it was their secret – hers and Stephen's alone. But their Father, not knowing, would keep on at him about it until he was made miserable once more. No, Flora decided, as she had saved her brother in their games of pretend when they were young, so she would save him now in real life – she would save both his happiness and his reputation.

Now she had made up her mind she felt better than she had in days. Flora walked more resolutely along the path. She *would* marry Captain Reed. And perhaps, once married and made a mother, it would not be quite as bad as she imagined – she could throw all her love on their child. Flora stopped in her tracks and smiled for what seemed like the first time in a lifetime. Yes, that is what she would do, and she would do it for Stephen, for hi-

"Oh, my heavens," she cried as something hurtled out from the woods and almost bowled her over. Shocked, she looked down at her feet.

"Where on earth did you come from, little pup?"

12

The dog ran in circles around her legs, barking, his eyes smiling, his tail wagging feverishly. Flora looked about her for its owner – on a very rare occasion, people had stumbled into the woods or gardens not realising it was private property. When she was a child Father had shown them off the land with one of his guns, nowadays it laid with Cyrus or Old Bill to escort them from the grounds.

"Where is your master, little pup?" she asked the dog. The creature turned another circle and barked once more.

He did have a master, Flora was sure. He appeared in good health; his coat – mainly white but with splodges of tan and black – was full with no signs of bald spots or flea bites, he looked well fed - even having a slight pot belly - and his eyes were bright and sparkly.

"Go and find him," Flora said now. She threw her arm as though throwing a stick but the dog wasn't fooled and just sat at her feet.

"Woof," he said.

Flora reached down tentatively to fuss him. He certainly seemed friendly enough, he was now rolling around on his back, all four legs in the air. Flora chuckled. "Silly boy." She turned slowly on the spot, searching again for any sign of an owner and listened hard, her head on one side. There was no sound of anyone calling him, either. Maybe, she wondered, he was lost. She started away and the hound bounced back up onto his feet, and this time gave out a whine.

"What is it?" she asked. "What are you telling me?"

The dog moved off towards the woodland, then stopped and

turned to look at her. "That's right, pup. Off you- Oh!" He'd bounded back to her again, knocking into her legs, turning in circles, tail wagging furiously. Flora raised an eyebrow. "What?" she repeated.

Again, the dog trotted towards the woods, stopped, turned, sat down and looked at her. "Woof," it said again.

"You want me to follow you?" asked Flora. The dog stood and wagged his tail. "Woof."

Unable to help the smile on her face, Flora took a breath and sighed it out. "All right. Come on then."

The dog led her further into the woods, stopping every so often to turn back and make sure she was still behind him. The woodland floor was wet from yesterday's rain and the red, gold and yellow autumn leaves already fallen from the trees had turned to mulch. Her boots were going to be ruined by the time she got home. Wood pigeons coo-coo'd in the treetops and a squirrel ran across a fallen log to the left of her. "Look, pup – a squirrel." The dog ignored both her and the creature, intent on leading her wherever it was he wanted to take her. Flora found herself venturing further and further into the Oxney Bottom woods and, she confessed to herself, after feeling so out of sorts for the past few days, this walk was doing her good. She took a big breath of cool air into her lungs. The woods smelled damp, the trees still wet from the downpour yesterday. The way ahead was well lit as most of the leaves were fallen, and the bare branches gave the autumn sun room to shine.

"Where are you taking me?" she asked the dog again. "All the way to Deal, it looks like," she answered herself with a smile, stepping over a clutch of golden toadstools.

"Woof," the dog barked, and ran on ahead faster than he had been up until now. Flora picked up her pace and followed him. She could tell now they were heading towards the old St Nicholas's chapel and she slowed her steps a little, remembering what had happened last time she had gone near there. But, this time there was no eerie silence. And then there was the dog, which absolutely, definitely wasn't a ghost dog - she knew this for a fact as she had touched it and it just felt like, well, dog. It hadn't faded away at her touch, or disappeared in a puff of smoke. He definitely wanted to show her something so Flora kept on following. The ground beneath her feet changed, the mulchy leaves now interspersed with broken bits of flint and stone. She watched her footing, looking carefully for masonry that had fallen from the building and been washed this way by years of rainstorms. The dog came back to her and wagged his tail.

"Is this what you wanted me to see?" she asked him, arriving in the small clearing where the chapel was. "I've seen it before, pup. Many times." The dog sat by the broken down doorway and looked at her. "Don't tell me – woof," she said, laughing. The dog wagged his tail, his mouth open from the walk, his pink tongue lolling out to one side.

Flora took a walk around the building, stepping over broken walls, moving bits of cast off flint and wood from the broken window boards out of the way with the toe of her boot. The place was in an even worse state than she remembered. This had been her and Stephen's hide-out for one gloriously long hot summer when they were children… until Margaret found out and banned them from ever coming here, too.

Now the dog moved into the broken doorway, obviously waiting for her to follow. "I don't want to go inside, pup," she said. "It's too dangerous." But the dog stared at her beseechingly, his tail now thumping slowly on the broken flag-stoned floor just inside the doorway. Flora relented on a sigh. "All right, pup, you win. I'll poke my head inside, but I'm not going all the way in and you can look at me with those big br- Oh, my heavens! What on earth is all that?"

*

Immediately forgetting any danger she might be in, Flora stepped inside. She could see piles of boxes, crates and small barrels stacked neatly along the back wall. She went in further, watching where she walked, stepping over flint and bits of broken wood. Weak midday sunlight lit the chapel better than a lantern but still cast deep shadows in the corners of the large room. The boxes all appeared to be unmarked giving no clue as to what might be inside each one. She walked alongside them, carefully running her hands over the wooden casks and spied a pile of rags in the farthest corner. The floor was wet, boggy earth and moss showed in between the broken flagstones and the whole place smelled damp and mildewy. Next to her, the dog whined and moved to the pile of rags, laying down at the side of them. He pawed at the material and the rags moved. Flora gave a cry and took a step back. A voice came from under the tattered material. "Good boy," it said, sounding extremely weak.

"Oh, my heavens," Flora breathed. Not a pile of rags, but a man.

All sense of propriety gone, Flora rushed towards the shape lying on the ground. The dog wagged his tail. The man began to cough – the sound raspy and breathless - and in between coughs he moaned in pain.

"Sir, are you all right?" asked Flora, and then admonished herself. Even from the several feet between them she could see that the man was quite clearly not all right. His clothes, what she had at first thought were rags she could see now, were decent quality – the shirt white linen, the overcoat warm wool and the boots without holes.

"Water. Please." The man tried to raise himself up but the pain he was in seemed too much for him to manage. He fell back again, his head resting against the wet flint wall. "Water," he said again between rasping bouts of coughing.

"Sir, I have none." Flora looked about her for a water flask or anything similar, not expecting to see one and not being disappointed when she didn't.

"There." The man pointed in the vague direction of one of the small barrels stood on one of the crates. "Wine."

Flora picked up the barrel and took it to the man. He was young, she saw, probably not a great deal older than her. His hair was long, a dirty blonde colour and untied. It was wet and hung over his shoulders and in his face. She handed him the tub of wine and he struggled to remove the cork stopper. Eventually, and in obvious discomfort, he lifted the tub to his mouth and pulled the stopper out with his teeth. Wine rushed from the barrel and the man caught what he could in his mouth as it ran a torrent over his face and chest. He dropped the barrel and laid back against the wall, wincing as he moved.

"What happened to you, Sir?" asked Flora.

"Big raid," the man began, "in Deal… last night… shot… here." He pointed to the area of his shoulder.

"Shot?" Flora cried. "Are you a… criminal. Oh." Before he could answer she realised just exactly what he was, and what all the barrels and crates meant. "You're a smuggler."

The man nodded. And winced again with pain.

Flora looked at the dog, curled up at his master's side. The dog looked back at her, his chin on the man's leg, his eyes huge. He wagged his tail once, twice.

"Well," she said, "let us not worry about that for the moment. You clearly need some help. Your dog fetched me from over the way and made me follow him here. I will go back home and fetch you some water… I shall be back shortly."

The man looked her in the eye and tried to smile. "Thank ye, My Lady."

*

Flora got to the doorway and turned to see if the dog would follow, but it seemed that now he had found help for him, he was going to stay at his master's side.

She set off for home at a brisk pace, her speed hindered by the confining stomacher she wore. She tore the article from the front of her gown and carried it instead. At least now she could run a little easier.

A flock of wood pigeons was startled into flight, their wings beating in time to her footfalls in the mulchy woodlands. Soon enough, the trees thinned a little as she reached the perimeter of the woods and she could see the grassy expanse of lawns up ahead. At the very edge of the tree-line she stopped, turned and replaced the stomacher, just in case someone happened to see her in her state of undress. Walking as briskly as the constrictive garment would allow, Flora entered the avenue and passed the raised pond, the partèrre and the topiary hedges. She carried on, past the drive which led to the stables and went around the back of the house into the kitchen garden.

"Everythin' all right, Mistress Flora?"

Flora jumped. It was just Old Bill, snipping at the herbs. Flora slowed to a more lady-like pace. "Oh, yes, Bill. Everything is fine. Thank you." She was aware of him watching her fast-retreating back, a puzzled frown on his face.

Flora entered the house through the scullery door and went on into the kitchen. "Good day, Mrs Merson. Dot."

They both curtsied. "Mistress."

She continued out into the hallway, up the stairs to her bed-chamber. Once there she finally stopped. The injured man had said he was shot – he would need bandages. Flora threw open her armoire and, finding nothing suitable, went instead to her clothing cabinet, pulling open the drawers. There, she found a chemise and a cotton petticoat. She slung them on her bed. What else would she need, she wondered. Oh! Scissors. Hurrying again, she let herself into her sister's room, thankful that Margaret was out taking tea with her friends and shopping the catalogues, no doubt talking a lot of old nonsense. In Margaret's room she pulled open more drawers until she found embroidery scissors, needles and thread. What else? she wondered. Water? Food? And something to carry it all in.

On down the hallway and Flora let herself into Stephen's room. She knew there wasn't much left in it – he had taken al-most everything with him when he'd joined the navy, but he surely should have a bag around here somewhere. Flora opened cupboards and drawers and eventually found a hessian carry-all.

On her way out of Stephen's room, she literally ran into Dot, carrying an armful of laundry. "Oh, Dot," Flora said, "would you please run over to Ned and ask him or Willie to ready Pudding for me." The scullery maid nodded, curtsied again and went on her way.

Her next stop was the kitchen. She was pleased to see Mrs Merson busy over at the butcher's block with her back to her, Flora sneaked on tiptoe into the pantry. The shelves were filled all kinds of treats and she quietly heaped some bread and cheese, some left over rout drop cakes, some meat and a few apples in her arms.

"And what are you up to, Young Mistress Flora?" Mrs Merson's voice came as a surprise. Flora spun around to face her. An apple fell from her hands and rolled across the floor, stopping in between the cook's feet. Mrs Merson bent and picked it up with floury hands.

"I'm… going to have a picnic!" Flora answered. "I thought I'd do some sketching over near the pond, so I helped myself to some bread and cheese. You don't mind, do you?"

Mrs Merson took up a cloth and wiped her hands. "No, I don't mind. But I can't help but wonder how many of you will be on this picnic?" she asked, seeing how much food Flora had balanced in her arms.

"Just me."

Mrs Merson shook her head in disbelief. "Well, in that case, I'm glad to see you've got your appetite back, Mistress Flora. Would you like me to get Dot to bring some tea down for you?"

Oh no, thought Flora. She'd just asked Dot to run to the stables. Why should she need Pudding if she were only going to be at the end of the garden? This one lie was turning into two and growing quite rapidly. But then, she thought, feeling more exhilarated than she had for weeks - this is what life is all about; fun, excitement, perhaps even a little bit of danger, not spending her time like Margaret – taking tea with ladies who pretend to be your friends and then gossip about you behind your back, not selecting gown patterns and materials from catalogues only to have those 'friends' snigger at your choices when your back was turned.

"Actually," she said now, "I think I would like a flask of sweet tea to take with me… and perhaps one of water, too."

*

The journey back to the chapel was made much quicker thanks to Pudding. She rode at a trot and once there, dismounted and tied the horse's reins to a tree, letting him forage among the leaves on the woodland floor. The dog came to greet her when she got to the door, his tail wagging. He ran back to his master, then back to Flora, then back to the door again, fast enough to make Flora's head spin.

Inside, the first thing she noticed was that the man had tried to move – he was now a little more upright - leaning to the left, propping himself up on his elbow and arm, his long legs straight out in front of him. His eyes were closed, his long hair, curly at the ends, still falling about his face and shoulders. She could see the faint movement of his chest rising and falling beneath his unbuttoned coat, but his breaths were quieter than they had been. Flora wasn't sure if that was a good thing or not – was he recovering or dying? She stepped forward, placing the bag of supplies on the floor near him.

"Sir," she whispered. "Sir. I have water and food for you."

The man started and opened his eyes. Confusion was apparent on his face. He frowned.

"You've been shot," Flora reminded him. "You're at St Nicholas's chapel at Oxney." Though how he had got all the way here from Deal was anyone's guess – surely he hadn't walked, not with his injury.

Flora knelt beside him. "Here. Have some sweet tea." She unfastened the flask and held it to his lips. He stank of the wine he'd spilled over himself earlier and Flora almost felt drunk just on the fumes.

The man covered her hand with his own as, between them, they held the flask to his mouth. "I'm Fin," he said, and took another swallow of the warm, sweet liquid. "Phineas Dawkins."

"Oh." She hadn't even considered what his name might be.

"I'm Flora. Harrington." She removed the flask. "I live in the big house beyond the woods. Oxney Court."

Fin struggled to move himself more upright, taking all of his weight now on his buttocks. He lifted his left arm and moved the hair from his eyes. Flora couldn't help but notice a large purple bump on his forehead. The skin around his eye was blackening already.

"What happened last night?" she asked. "You mentioned a raid."

"Aye. Mounted soldiers and infantrymen – hordes of 'em. Came over from Dover way to confiscate this stuff." He nodded his head in the direction of the boxes and crates. "They was armed wi' swords an' guns. Got me good, m'lady, with both."

"Both?" Flora was shocked. "You have sword wounds, too?"

"Aye. Me back an' me arm."

No wonder then, thought Flora, he'd looked to be at death's door when she'd discovered him.

"I have brought needle and thread, water for cleaning the wound." She corrected herself. "Wounds. And something to make bandages from. Are you able to remove your coat so I might look?"

Fin took a shuddering breath. "I might need some help, m'lady."

"Here, let me." Flora carefully pulled the coat off his left shoulder and the sleeve off his arm. The right side was more difficult as that was where the majority of his pain was. Eventually, and causing as little discomfort to him as possible, the coat was off. Now she could see that his shirt was almost entirely covered in blood – the back and sides, the right sleeve. He really was quite badly injured.

"I think, Sir-"

"Fin."

"I think, *Fin*, you will need to move a little more so that I can clean these wounds. Are you able to lay on your front, do you think?"

"Ah, 'tis a good question." He almost smiled. "Well, we'll see, won't we."

Flora said, "I'll make some bandages."

She pulled the chemise and petticoat from the bag and began tearing the material into strips. That done, she readied a needle and thread. When she turned back to him, Fin had removed his blood-soaked shirt and was laying face down on the broken flag-stone floor, his coat bundled under his head as a makeshift pillow.

Flora blushed – she had never seen a semi-naked man before, covered in blood or not. She couldn't help but notice that his skin was smooth and the muscles of his shoulders and back well-defined. His hair lay partway across his body and strangely, to move that seemed more intimate than tending to his wounds. "Your hair," she said. "It's in the way."

He lifted his uninjured arm and moved the length of it to one side. "Sorry."

On closer inspection Flora saw the sword injuries to his back and arm were not too deep. Of the two, the one on his lower back just above the waistband of his breeches was the worst. Both wounds were gaping open and oozing blood but she thought he had been saved from mortal harm by the thick woollen coat he had been wearing. The gunshot wound was a different matter – it was small, circular where the shot had entered, and judging by the lack of blood on the front of his shirt she felt sure that the musket ball was still inside. It would have to be removed but she really wasn't sure she would have the stomach to go prodding and poking inside the poor man's – *Fin's* – shoulder to pull the shot out.

Flora opened the flask of water. First, let's deal with the cuts, she thought, running the liquid over the wound, making Fin flinch. Maybe tending to these would strengthen her stomach. "This will hurt," she said, lifting the needle in her fingers, the black thread trailing behind.

She put needle to skin and Fin winced. "Are you some kind of healer? he asked.

"No." Flora laughed. "Not at all. My brother was quite the

clumsy oaf when we were children. If anyone was going to fall over, fall down or trip up, it would be Stephen. I was always having to bandage him up."

"And how many stitches 'ave ye done in the past?"

Flora thought. The answer was none but should she lie, to put Fin's mind at ease? She answered, "Hmm, how many have I done? So far… one."

Despite his pain, Fin looked over his shoulder at her. "One, ye say?" The look of horror on his face made Flora smile. "Yes, this one. My sister is deft with a needle I, not so much. She threw my sampler away as it was so shockingly bad."

"Ye gods." Fin laid his head back down, burying his face in his coat.

"Perhaps you should have some more wine?"

"Aye, perhaps I should."

Flora left the needle and thread resting on his back and went to the back wall of the chapel.

Fin lifted his head again and watched her as she selected a tub of drink.

She was a rare breed this Flora Harrington, he thought. She couldn't be very old, perhaps nineteen or twenty, but she let herself be led out here to come across a wounded criminal and then she returned to the big house over the way to fetch things to help him. Aye, not many a young girl of her social standing would do that.

Flora returned with the wine and uncorked it. Fin took several large swallows.

"Ready?" she asked. Fin nodded.

She needed something to distract him while she sewed him back together, the alcohol could only do so much. "Tell me about your dog," she said, stitching carefully, "he's very clever. What's his name?"

"He doesn't 'ave a name, jus' Dog. He found me while I was at the yard about a year ago and 'asn't left my side since. He was a mess when he found me – skin an' bone, fur all matted, but he eats his fill now and his coat's got better over time with a borrow of my horse's brush ev'ry now an' then."

"And does your horse have a name or is it just Horse?"

"Aye," Fin chuckled, then coughed, "she's Diamond."

"My horse is called Plum Pudding. He's outside, you can probably hear him raking in the leaves." Flora continued stitching – he would have quite the scar when healed. "Tell me, Fin, what do you do when you're not smuggling and hiding your ill-gotten gains on my Father's estate?"

He tried to turn to look at her, to gauge how serious she was. Flora put a hand on his back. "Be still," she said, smiling.

"I'm a shipwright, down in Deal. Sometimes I used to help my Da run his inn, but I'm too busy nowadays."

"How does he manage without you?"

"I've four brothers, all older. Three of 'em are married with babes but the next youngest, Thomas, is on is own so he works with me Da now."

It was ironic, but Flora fell into silence while thinking how easy this Fin was to talk to. Not like with Captain Reed.

On their way back from South Foreland that time, hardly a word had passed their lips. He hadn't asked her anything – what she liked to do, her dislikes, anything about her family… She realised, of course, that conversation was a two-way exercise and that she hadn't spoken to him either, but she just found he made her so very uncomfortable with his eyes that were constantly on her somewhere – her hands, her face, her body. He'd grown decidedly thin-lipped during the extremely brief exchange they'd had about her wearing Stephen's breeches, she recalled, and it had been glaringly apparent that her wearing breeches and riding astride Pudding displeased him greatly. Marriage to Captain Reed was going to mean a whole new way of life for her she was just beginning to realise, and she was going to hate every single minute of it; it was obvious that he was not going to allow her to be herself – he would expect her to be nothing more that Mrs James Reed, there only to run his household – wherever that might turn out to be – dress up, look pretty and perform, with good grace, her marital duties…

"Ye gods, that hurt!"

Flora came back to the here and now with a jolt. She had pulled the thread too tight on one of Fin's stitches. "Oh, my heavens, I'm so sorry."

"Maybe yer sister was right to throw your sewing thing away," he grumbled, good naturedly.

Flora couldn't help but smile. "Be careful, Mr Dawkins, I have another wound to sew yet – I might use twenty stitches where only ten is needed!"

"Ah, I'm asking ye nicely right now, m'lady, please don't make me suffer any more."

"Here. Have some more wine, lie still and be quiet."

Silence fell between them but, thought Flora, it was a nice *comfortable* silence. She continued stitching and soon noticed the silence was punctuated every so often with soft snores. She smiled – the wine had done more than its job.

The wound to Fin's back was sewn up and the twenty-two stitches neat – Margaret, she thought, would be proud if she saw them… save the fact they were on a half-naked criminal, of course. Flora slightly moved Fin's arm so she could continue with her task, and he didn't even stir.

She couldn't imagine doing anything like this for Captain Reed. Also, she imagined him to be a bad patient. In her mind's eye she saw Captain Reed where Fin was, but as she sewed he complained, whined – *are you finished, hurry up, you're hurting me*. She paused in her suturing and shook her head to try and clear her thoughts.

She *must* stop berating the Captain if they were to be married. She must settle herself and give him a chance. Perhaps it was true that they had got off on the wrong foot but really, she thought, wasn't it she who was to blame for that? First, she had been extraordinarily late for their first meeting and second, she had felt annoyed at him appearing out of nowhere during her ride at the cliffs. She supposed, as she continued with the last few sutures on Fin's arm that, if it were the other way around, she too would have been fed up if the person she was meeting with a view to marrying was almost two hours late and, as for finding her on her ride, the cliffs is a wide expanse perfect for beautiful views of the Straights – he was tasked with finding as many smugglers as he could, so why *wouldn't* he be there, keeping an eye on the comings and goings of the ships and small boats in the channel?

Yes, she could see now that it was *her* who had been in the wrong. When she got home today she would carefully choose which music she would play for him when he visited later this week.

The suturing was finished and Fin was still asleep. She could see his breaths were even from the rise and fall of his back, and he was still giving out small snores on occasion. The skin on his back was stained with blood and the gunshot wound had a circle of red around it. It seemed a shame to have to wake him but the wounds needed covering with the bandages she had made.

"Fin," she whispered. "Mr Dawkins. Wake up." He stirred, opened his eyes and she could see they were a warm hazel colour with flecks of green radiating from their centres.

"M'lady? Flora?"

"You are all put back together, sir. But the wounds need bandaging. Can you sit up?"

He did as he was bid and took her warm hand in his cold one. "Thank ye," he said in earnest, although more than a little drunk. "I would likely 'ave died if it weren't fer ye."

"There's still time yet," she replied seriously. "Let's get these bandages on, shall we?"

13

F in was awoken by someone shaking him and calling his name. "Aye," he said. "Aye, I'm awake." He opened his eyes and was disappointed to see it had been Dobbin doing the shaking and not the young Lady Flora. He was also disturbed to find his head still hurt, possibly even more than it had yesterday. He was freezing cold too, despite being wrapped in the tattered remains of his coat.

"Dobbin," he said. "Ye found me then."

"Aye, after a time. We thought ye'd gone 'ome but yer Da said he'd not seen ye."

Fin indicated the boxes and crates near him. "I wanted to make sure all this was safe. I found an 'orse and got Dog to lead us over." He sat up.

The injuries to his back and arm felt much better for being clean, stitched and dressed.

"There was a girl," he said. "Flora. From the big house over the way." He thought about her. She'd done a good job. She hadn't fainted at the sight of his injuries, she had got her hands dirty with the blood, dirt and whatever else had been on him. Flora had been gentle when cleaning the wounds and had applied the bandages well – not so tight they hampered his breathing, yet not so loose that they would slip down in a few hour's time and become uncomfortable. Almost as soon as she had finished patching him up, Flora had left him with a bag of supplies and a promise to return tomorrow to check on him.

"I never knew young women from big houses was like that," he said.

"They ain't," Dobbin replied, reaching for a tub of wine.

"But," continued Fin, "she was so easy to talk to, wi' no airs or graces, and even a sense o' humour. And, she is beautiful, Dobbin. I don't think I've seen anyone so beautiful in my life." In fact, he was surprised that she hadn't been married off already. Or, he suddenly thought, perhaps she *was* married – he had hardly been in a place to have noticed a wedding band on her finger when they'd met. Not that it mattered from his perspective of lowly shipwright-cum-smuggler, although right now he was scarcely in a position to fight off any put-out husband who might happen along wondering where his young wife was and what she was up to with an injured smuggler. He helped himself to a few mouthfuls of water from the flask Flora had left – his throat really was quite sore and his head was pounding.

Dobbin rolled his eyes and broke open the wine. "She'll be after somethin'" he said. "She'll tell the authorities an' another hundred soldiers'll be beating-" he looked at the hole where the door should have been, "You know," he finished. "Or, she'll blackmail us."

Fin snorted. It hurt his head. "Blackmail us for what? She's rich anyway."

"Well, I don't know. But why would a young Lady bother hersel' wi' the likes of us?"

Fin thought this over. He didn't know either but he was just grateful that she had. He changed the subject. "What 'appened to Tad and William, are they all right, were they hurt?"

Dobbin tipped more wine down his throat and sat on the floor next to his friend. He offered across the wine. Fin declined. "William is all right - 'ardly a scratch on 'im. Tad took a good 'ard whollop on the 'ead. Sukey's lookin' after 'im at one of the rooms at The Star."

"And everyone else? Was anyone killed?"

"No. No deaths. Injuries all round, though – I 'eard as one of the soldiers got a fire poker in the eye, and some o' the others got broken bones, that's all."

Spying the bag of supplies Flora had left, Fin opened it. There was more than he expected - a half loaf of bread, some cheese, a couple of apples and several little cakes the likes of which he'd never seen before. He hadn't even realised he was hungry until he started eating, then it turned out he was ravenous.

"You hungry?" he asked Dobbin, offering him a hunk of bread and some cheese. At the smell of food, Dog lifted his head, gave a big sniff and was rewarded with a bit of cheese. Fin saw there was a flask containing the rest of the sweet tea she'd brought for him. He felt he needed water and was exceedingly grateful to find another flask of that, as well. He'd drunk an enormous amount of wine yesterday and he was, in general, a beer drinking man. Now, probably because of the amount of alcohol he'd thrown down his neck, his head ached, his throat was sore and he had a raging thirst.

He drank half the water down and he and Dobbin sat in silence, eating the food Flora had left. He hoped she would keep to her word and come again tomorrow.

Fin looked around at the boxes and crates lining the wall. "'Tis lucky we moved all this stuff over 'ere and kept the other lot in France," he said.

"Aye."

He chewed on the bread. "'Tis lucky I overheard that soldier sayin' about the raid, as well."

"Aye." Dobbin took another huge swallow of wine. "'Tis lucky you was rescued by young Lady whatsername."

Grinning and coughing, Fin jabbed Dobbin in the ribs with his elbow. "Aye."

14

Flora had left the house early that morning. The weather was poor, with a constant, miserable drizzly rain that simply would not let up. The temperature had fallen still further and she dressed as she preferred – in her brother's breeches, with boots and a warm riding jacket.

She had brought more things for Fin – one of her own velvet ribbons to keep his hair from his eyes, more water and a thick plaid blanket to try and keep the chill off him. Of course, depending on how his wounds were and how he was feeling, he might be thinking of journeying home.

She expected 'home' was somewhere in Deal, but wondered how he would get there – he certainly wasn't fit enough to walk, especially in this dreary weather. Maybe she could take him back on Pudding, but Pudding was a big horse and she didn't believe he would be able to mount him without pulling at least some of his stitches out. Perhaps they could make a staircase out of some of the crates hidden in the chapel so that he might climb onto Pudding, but that presented the same problem – he wouldn't be able to move the boxes without pulling his stitches, and they would be too heavy for her to move. Pondering on this conundrum kept her busy as she rode the stallion at a trot through the woods. The autumn leaves covering the woodland floor were boggy with drizzle and Pudding's hooves left deep impressions in the ground.

As she came through the thicker trees into the clearing by the chapel, she was surprised to see another horse standing by the ruined walls. Flora brought Pudding to a standstill, a frown on her face. Whose horse was it? *Had* Fin managed to walk all the way home and then return with the creature? Had it been here all along – hiding out of sight among the thicker tree trunks? Was it Fin's – the one that had brought him out here in the first place? She remembered him telling her that his horse was called Diamond. The one standing nonchalantly next to the wall was piebald, the name just didn't suit it.

Flora felt torn – should she turn back, go home and perhaps return later? Or should she go on into the chapel? Pudding gave a snort and pawed at the ground. He wasn't a one to enjoy standing still. "Shh," said Flora, patting his neck. "I'm still trying to decide what to do." But Dog answered the question for her; on hearing her voice he ran out of the chapel towards her, barking with delight. Well, it was no secret now that she was here so she may as well go in, she decided. Flora dismounted, leaving Pudding to roam free - he would come back when she called - and followed Dog into the chapel.

Fin was where she had left him yesterday but sitting up against the wall, his tattered coat around his shoulders. He looked paler than he had yesterday but gave a brilliant smile when he saw her.

"Flora," he said. "M'lady. You came back."

"Of course," Flora replied, "and you appear to have another visitor." She cast her eyes to the man sitting next to Fin. Unruly dark curls slipped the confines of his ponytail and framed an impish face, with wide blue eyes.

Fin said, "This is Dobbin-"

"Robert," interrupted the stranger.

"Dobbin," argued Fin. "No one but yer Ma calls ye Robert."

Dobbin shrugged and grinned, looking more impish than ever. "'Tis true." He stood and held out a hand to catch Flora's. "Dobbin Croft, my Lady. Pleased to meet yer acquaintance."

"Flora," said Flora.

"Aye, I know. Fin's bin tellin' me of ye – and of what ye did fer 'im." With this, the impish smile faded and he looked at Fin. "He's my oldest friend, and I thank ye fer yer help yesterday."

Flora smiled. "You are welcome. And today I have brought

more water and a blanket. It's getting colder," she continued, looking at Fin, "and you don't appear well enough to go elsewhere." As though to prove her point, Fin barked out a cough. "That doesn't sound good," Flora said. "How do your wounds feel?"

Fin coughed again. His head was still pounding, his throat felt on fire and now he had pains in his stomach. "They feel fine, but 'tis sore where the musket ball hit me."

"May I look?"

Fin sat forward and let go of the coat which fell around his waist. Shocked, Flora was barely able to suppress a gasp.

The bullet hole looked so much worse than it had yesterday – the edges were an angry red, surrounded by a circle of purple, and yellow pus filled the centre. "It's inflamed," said Flora. "We had a horse catch itself on a broken fence last year – this looks the same."

"Can ye do something?" asked both men together.

The horse had been declared too ill and lame to save and had been killed, but she didn't want to let Fin or Dobbin know this. "The musket ball needs removing," she said decisively. "Because of how inflamed it is it will hurt very much and I don't have anything to relieve you of the pain".

"Wine?" asked Dobbin, already heading for the casket he'd opened earlier.

"That will make him pass out well enough if he drinks enough of it." Beside them, Fin writhed in discomfort. "Or, of course! My Father has laudanum at home! Do you have a knife or something similar I can use to remove the shot?"

Dobbin shook his head. "I carry no weapon, my Lady."

Thinking, Flora bent and covered Fin with the blanket she'd brought, wrapping it around his shoulders, mindful of the injury. She gently touched his forehead with her hand. He was burning up with a fever. That made her mind up. "All right," she said, "there's really nothing else for it but for me to ride home and get what is needed. Wait here. Dobbin, please keep a close eye on your friend and give him plenty of water to drink."

She made for the doorway and Dobbin laid a hand on her arm to stop her. "Why are ye doin' this?" he asked quietly. "Why do ye care?"

Flora looked about her at the injured man laying on the floor, at the crates, caskets and tubs lining the far wall. "I like tea as much as the next person, Mr Croft."

*

She rode back home deep in thought. She might have made an easy quip to Dobbin about her reasons to help Fin – you couldn't live along the south Kent coast and not know about the contraband flowing to and fro across the channel. Most people along the coast from Kent to Cornwall had a hand in the smuggling in some way – perhaps they didn't actively cross the sea to bring in tea and wine or to take out Romney Marsh wool, but when they bought it on the sly from John Brown at the local tavern, or Mary Mason at the market, they would be paying a fraction of what it cost legitimately at the grocer's. She was aware from conversations overheard in the kitchen that tea was especially sought after as it was ruinously expensive. It was known that less honest servants would save the leaves, dry them, roll them and sell them on. This was just as illegal as smuggling the product in the first place. But aside from all that, and her easy answer, Dobbin's question had been valid – why *was* she assisting a couple of criminals who were hiding contraband on her father's estate? Flora rode up the drive to the house.

Since she was a small child she had never, ever been able to leave something (or apparently *someone*) that was injured or hurt in some way – she had found countless birds that had tried to fledge too early and had fallen from the trees or roofs. Sparrows, pigeons, and once, a blackbird, had all been nursed by her with varying degrees of success. Also, she thought, turning into the stable yard, this was likely to be the very last chance she would ever have to do something exciting, spontaneous, daring... perhaps even dangerous.

If, no, *when* she married Captain Reed, she would probably be lucky if she was even allowed to ride anywhere alone again, let alone in breeches and to a long forgotten and abandoned chapel. And then there was this, Flora admitted, helping Fin Dawkins, a criminal, a smuggler, was something that neither her father or her sister would approve of in any way. She felt this was her last hurrah before being handed over to the Captain. And speaking of which, she had kept to her word – last night she had chosen a few pieces of music to play for him on Sunday. She had given no thought yet as to what they would speak about but, she still had just over two days to consider that.

She arrived at the stable yard and slid expertly from Pudding's saddle. Time was pressing – poor Fin looked to be suffering but putting a brave face on it. She had noticed him shivering when she had wrapped the blanket on him and the cough he had sounded dry and painful.

Again, Flora sneaked the back way into the house. Both Mrs Merson and Dot were in the main kitchen, she could hear pots and pans being rattled and Dot being admonished for something. She crept into the pantry and helped herself to some honey to help heal the wounds, putting it carefully into the bag she'd brought with her from the chapel. She tiptoed out and into the main hall. Her sister was with friends in the sitting room – she could hear voices laughing and talking, and teacups rattling on saucers. She crossed the tiled floor as quickly and quietly as possible but heard Clara Patrick say to Margaret,"Is that your *sister*, crossing the *hallway*, in *breeches*?" Margaret called her. Flora held the bag behind her back and poked her head around the door frame. "We are having tea, dear sister. Why don't you join us?"

"Thank you, but no. I… need to… brush Pudding."

"That is what your groomsman is for, dear girl," tittered Clara.

Flora held the bag out in front of her. "Not when I have the brush," she said, and left them to their tea and gossip and fits of giggles.

"Oh, my heavens," she muttered on her way upstairs. "This is what I've got to look forward to."

15

It was frightening to see just how much Fin's condition had deteriorated in the short time she had been away – his cough was worse; dry and hacking and bending him double during particularly bad bouts. He couldn't stop shivering despite being wrapped in both his coat and the blanket she'd brought previously, yet his face and torso were shiny with sweat.

Flora had heard the story of her mother's death from the influenza outbreak of '61 too many times to count and she feared the parallels of Fin's symptoms. A short while ago, on her instruction, Dobbin had mixed a few drops of the laudanum with water and had Fin swallow the contents.

"How are you feeling?" she asked him, setting the rest of what was needed on the floor nearby.

Fin grinned stupidly and took her hands in his. "Flora, Flora how I adore yer," he slurred.

Oh dear. "Yer like an angel," he continued in a murmur. "A vision come to me in my hour of need, with yer beautiful hair and yer emerald eyes... An' yer a picture... in... breeches." He coughed long and hard, then his eyes rolled back in his head and he gave out a snore.

"Come, Dobbin," said Flora, suppressing an indulgent smile, "help me lay him down."

The two of them manhandled Fin out of the blanket and coat and laid him on his front on the floor, his head to one side, his long hair damp with sweat.

"All right. I think we're ready." Flora's hands were also sweating, she wiped them down her breeches and said a silent prayer for Fin's recovery. "Please pass me the letter opener, Dobbin." A letter opener was all she could risk laying her hands on back at the house. Her father was in the library when she'd returned so she had sneaked into his office. The laudanum was on a shelf alongside decanters of whiskey, brandy and rum. She swiftly helped herself to the bottle and saw the letter opener, blunt edged but with a good point, laying on the blotter on his desk. It would have to do – she couldn't risk going back into the kitchen to get a knife. She looked more closely at the bullet wound in Fin's shoulder. Doing anything with it was going to be messy. She needed to try and find where exactly the shot was located before poking the steel blade into his flesh to retrieve it. She felt around outside the hole, hoping to feel the bullet beneath her fingers but all she managed was to free a lot of pus from the wound.

Dobbin gave her a look. "Better out than in, aye?"

Flora nodded. "Could you pour some brandy on one of those bandages – quite a lot – I'll use it to wipe this away." Dobbin did what was asked and handed the cloth to her. "I've an apology to make to yer," he said.

"Oh, yes?" Flora wiped the wound. There was nothing else for it but to poke a finger inside and try to gauge where the shot was.

"Aye. Me and Tad was 'ere last year, we'd just brought some goods in…"

Having her finger inside another person's flesh was probably the single most disgusting thing she'd ever done, but she could feel the musket ball underneath her fingernail about two inches deep into the wound.

"… we saw yous walking in the woods and scared ye off so's ye didn't find us."

"What?" Flora removed her finger from the hole and wiped it and the wound again with the brandy-soaked cloth. "That was you rattling chains and screaming?"

"Aye. We didn't want ye to find the haul."

Flora took up the letter opener and carefully inserted it where her finger had been. Gently, gently, she pushed it in until she felt the tip touch the shot. Carefully, she manoeuvred the tip under the shot and brought it to the surface. Once it was out, Flora checked it over – it appeared to be whole. She wiped the entry site again. "You gave me such a fright," she replied to Dobbin.

"Aye. That was the idea."

Flora slathered honey on Fin's wound and motioned for Dobbin to pass her more material bandages. She laid a honey-soaked cloth against the wound and, in silence, she and Dobbin wrapped a bandage around Fin's shoulder, Dobbin lifting Fin when necessary and she, wrapping carefully. At last they were finished. There was nothing more to be done now, save hoping for the best and praying to God that he recovered.

"So, you three are the ghosts of Oxney Bottom?" she asked, tight-lipped and cross.

"Aye," he replied. "Aye. I s'pose we are, at that."

16

Captain Reed had arrived punctually, smartly attired as always, in his uniform, with his hair knotted and powdered. He again held her hand to his lips for longer than necessary but she had been expecting that. Once more, he could scarcely tear his gaze from her and, once more, she had prepared herself.

Once everyone was seated, Flora took her place at the pianoforte and stretched her fingers. She hadn't played for weeks and she hadn't practised for today - it would be nothing short of a miracle if she didn't strike any wrong notes. Across the room, Margaret looked encouragingly at her, her Father looked bored, and Captain Reed tried to hold her gaze, his eyes like ice chips, his mouth a straight line. Flora looked away and began to play. Her first piece was a Mozart sonata which she was confident she knew like the back of her hand.

For a whole host of reasons this afternoon's production was proving to be infinitely worse than she could ever have imagined, not least because of the range of emotions she had experienced over the last two days.

When she had visited the chapel on Saturday, she had been pleased and relieved to see that Fin had been much improved – his colour was back to normal, aside from the black eye which was now a putrid yellow colour, and he was no longer sweating and shivering. He still had his cough but even that sounded better and wasn't causing him to double over in pain. He was mortified at his behaviour the day before while under the effects of the laudanum, and apologised over and over again.

"That is a strange brew, that laudanum," he said again. "I

meant no offence at what I said. Will ye ever forgive me, m'lady?"

Flora smiled. "You are forgiven. You know, of course, that Dobbin found it hilarious."

"He would. He has no sense of propriety. I'm sorry."

"Please. Stop apologising. I'm just immensely glad that you have made such a good recovery. We were lucky to have been able to treat the inflammation so quickly else I'm afraid to think what might have happened."

"Aye, and I can't thank ye enough for that, either."

"I can't stay for long today." She fussed Dog along the length of his back and he wriggled appreciatively. "I need to prepare for a tea party that my sister and Father have arranged that I must attend." Suddenly, the sun went out of her eyes and she looked crestfallen. "The guest is the man that I am to marry, so you see, it's quite important that I be there."

The man she was to marry? Fin's heart almost stopped. It was as though those words had torn it in two, which was ridiculous – what had he expected, that he – a boatbuilder-cum-smuggler – and she, a Lady, would have a future together? He took a steadying breath.

He was cross with himself. He had let her get under his skin, quite literally, through no fault of hers. She was just a kind, decent human being doing a kind, decent thing. But that didn't take away the feeling of abject dejection that he felt. He slumped against the wall, minding his shoulder, his hair falling like a curtain across his face.

"Oh," said Flora, pulling something from the pocket of her breeches. "I brought you this but keep forgetting to give it to you." She held out the thin black velvet ribbon in her hand. "For your hair," she continued, needlessly.

He took it from her with a smile that didn't reach his eyes. "Thank ye, m'lady. For everything."

Flora stood to leave. "As I have said before, you are welcome. You are also welcome to continue to use the chapel to store your goods – no one comes here, it should be perfectly safe. But," she had continued, heading for the doorway, "please tell Dobbin that if I happen along, and he tries to frighten me with his chains and wailing, I will personally kill him dead and then he really will be a ghost!"

She finished the Mozart piece and began to play a slow score by Handel. The room was silent save for her music and the occasional chink of china teacups.

Flora had spent Saturday evening writing to Stephen. She had told him of Fin and Dobbin and Dog, how the chapel where they had such wonderful pretend adventures when children was now the theatre for a real live adventure. She wrote of the smugglers' haul hidden away there, and of her healing Fin's wounds, the description of her nursing made as graphic as possible, knowing that Stephen would simply shudder at the thought! She wrote of Dog's cleverness, of Dobbin's impishness, and of Fin.

Then, this morning, she had ridden Pudding out to the chapel, the sky was beautifully clear - an azure blue with not a cloud to be seen, there was a wintry nip to the air that the sun, shining but weak, could not warm. The lawns looked bright and crisp and, in the woodland, the carpet of fallen leaves had dried a little giving a crunch to Pudding's steps as he trotted through them, kicking them up at his heels.

As she approached the chapel she thought it odd that Dog hadn't rushed out to greet them – he always ran around Pudding in circles, barking and smiling, his tongue lolling, so pleased to see them whenever they arrived. Dobbin's horse wasn't in the clearing and neither was he tied to any trees. Disconcerted, Flora slid from Pudding's saddle and left him to nuzzle in the undergrowth. She made her way to the chapel doorway and stepped inside. The cool light through the broken thatched roof showed the place was empty – there were no crates, caskets or tubs, there was no Dog and there was no Fin. He might never have been there at all except in his place was the plaid blanket she had wrapped him in, folded neatly, with bag she had brought supplies in placed on top.

A wave of light-headedness had hit her and she'd felt sick to her stomach. Flora had gasped and sank to her knees against the wall where, only yesterday, Fin had lain. She'd picked up the blanket and shook it out, bunching it to her face as tears fell from her eyes. She hadn't known what she was feeling, just that it was painful and raw and hurt like she had never felt pain before.

She finished the music piece and Margaret called time for refreshments. Dot came in bringing more tea and plates of cakes and sweetmeats. Flora moved to the seat nearest the window and furthest from the Captain. She watched him over the rim of her teacup, unable to stop herself making comparisons between him and Fin. The Captain, speaking with her father, sensed her watching him and looked over, inclining his head, a smile on his thin lips that didn't reach his cold, icy stare. Even when in so much pain from his wounds Fin's smile had been warm, lighting his hazel eyes. She thought of the softness of his skin, the defined muscles of his back, his long dark blonde hair with the curl at the ends. In her mind's eye she saw his mouth, the way his two front teeth were just the tiniest bit crooked, his full nicely shaped lips, and then she thought of the silly little rhyme he had sang under the effects of the laudanum. Her heart somersaulted in her chest and her stomach hatched a score of butterflies which fluttered inside her.

The afternoon passed in a blur, Flora was present in body only, her mind back at the chapel, back with Fin. Twice Margaret had to call her name sharply to bring her back to the present and elicit a response to a question asked of her.

"I wondered," said the Captain, "if Mistress Flora and myself might take a trip around the garden. If you feel it appropriate, of course," he added.

Margaret answered with a barely concealed burst of enthusiasm. "Of course! I shall ask Molly to accompany you."

And so there they were, walking along the avenue side-by-side with Molly walking a suitable distance and out of earshot behind them.

"You know, of course," said the Captain, "that I will be asking your Father for your hand in marriage."

"I know." Flora's heart sunk. So, this was it. He would ask and her father would agree and there would be no getting away from it.

"I feel, Mistress, that you are not particularly happy about this arrangement?"

Flora took a breath. Her chest felt tight enough in her corset and stomacher but now she felt as though her insides were being crushed. "I will do what I have to, Sir," she replied.

The Captain stopped in his tracks and turned so that he was out of Molly's sight. "That is good news as I was hoping not to have to show you this, but I think now, just to ensure our agreement, I will." From the pocket of his smart red coat the Captain took a leaf of parchment and opened it. "A letter," he said, "from your brother. I believe you may have thought you'd lost it that day at the lighthouse?"

"Why, yes, I-"

"It fell from the pocket of those dam-, those breeches you were wearing."

"And you kept it?" Flora was shocked.

The Captain pursed his lips. "Kept it. Read it. Read it perhaps a hundred times more and, on each reading, I believe I saw more *between* the lines than I did *on* the lines." He stared at her. "Would this be true?"

Once more, she felt her heart sink to the very bottom of her stomach. "I-"

"No need to answer, my dear, I can see you know exactly of what I speak. Your brother and you, I think it is fair to say, hold a very closely guarded secret." He carefully refolded the letter and put it back in his pocket. He moved off again, indicating she should join him. "I can only imagine the shock and absolute horror your father and sister would feel if this secret were to be spilled," he said. Flora stopped again and looked at him, aghast. "You won't tell them?" she whispered. "You can't!"

"I can... but I won't... *if* you given me your solemn word that you will be my wife."

Flora's thoughts were in turmoil. He had pulled an ace from his sleeve and there was absolutely nothing she could do about it. If Father and Margaret found out about Stephen, Margaret would be beside herself and their Father would be outraged – Lord only knew what he would do. And what would stop Captain Reed from telling others? She could just imagine the shock and disgust they would be subjected to, could see Louise Kingsley-Turner and Clara Patrick gossiping behind their fans. The news would be all over Kent, their Father's enterprises would come to a halt, his business partners would tactfully refuse to negotiate future dealings. Once more, Flora felt she was left with two choices that really only boiled down to one – risk her brother's reputation and family's good standing, or marry Captain James Reed.

"I will," she replied on a barely concealed sob. "I will marry you."

The Captain smiled. "Good." He checked to ensure Molly wasn't looking and took a tendril of Flora's hair between his fingers. "You look beautiful today," he whispered, close to her ear. "But next time, wear your hair loose. I prefer it that way. Now, take the sullen look from your face and smile; you are to be married."

17

Captain James Reed disguised himself well by wearing silk breeches, a crisp linen shirt, and a civilian frock coat. His hair was in a queue and had not been powdered. He walked with a spring in his step as he headed from Archcliffe on the Western Heights along the busy Snargate Street and into the town. To his right, the marina was busy with ships and boats of all shapes and sizes heading into and out of Dover. News of the recent raid in Deal had made it around the coastline and he would be surprised if any of the vessels were carrying too much of what they shouldn't be right now, but give it another few days, or a week at the very most, and no doubt the bastard smugglers would be up to their old tricks. He continued along the narrow road, dodging seafarers, drunkards and street whores.

Whoring among the upper ranks of the army was quite severely frowned upon – that pastime was good enough for the lower echelons, but if captains such as himself wanted to engage in some tomfoolery outside their marriages then it was expected they should take a mistress. Captain James Reed didn't have a mistress, so tonight, in celebration of his betrothal, a common whore would have to do.

He dodged the street whores and beggars and eventually found himself outside The Bluebird, which looked to be a more upmarket establishment than most of the other inns and taverns he had passed along the way. This was good – there was less chance that any of his men would be there.

Once inside, Captain Reed stood at the bar and ordered himself a whiskey, followed almost immediately by another. He was nearly ecstatic at the thought of his marriage to Flora. Today had shown him that as well as being beautiful, she was also quite an accomplished musician, and he could imagine her playing like that at tea parties and social gatherings at their home, once he'd found one for them. People would be impressed by her, not least because her beauty outweighed anything she might say or do. He could see her on his arm at functions and balls, dressed in colours that flattered her beautiful hair or emerald eyes and he could imagine the jealous stares of his fellow comrades as they wished their wife was even half as alluring.

He turned to face the inside of the inn and ordered another shot of whiskey. Within minutes his eyes lit on a relatively decent-looking woman in her mid twenties. He caught her eye and she tipped him a wink. Captain Reed downed his drink, put the glass on the bar and followed the woman upstairs.

The room was a fair size and the décor passable – he'd certainly seen worse. The woman shut the door behind him and made her way to the bed in the centre of the room. "Good evenin' to yer, Sir," she began, casting off her gown. "My name is-"

"I care not who you are, madam," spoke the Captain, unburdening himself of his breeches and boots. "I care only for *what* you are and what you can give me." With that he grabbed the woman forcibly by the arm and all but threw her face-down on the bed.

Captain Reed closed his eyes and conjured a picture of Flora to his mind. It didn't take much to see her in his mind's eye; she was almost all he saw these days. Now, here, in this gloomy room he saw his Flora with her long dark hair and milky white skin. He saw her perky breasts and grabbed one of the whore's in his hand, pinching the nipple to full bloom.

His Flora was pure and untouched, it had been a while since he'd had a maiden and he was looking forward to deflowering her, devouring her and teaching her how to pleasure him. He spat on his hand and rubbed it over the whore's slit and pushed himself roughly into her. This whore beneath him could hold no comparison to how Flora would feel around his cock. Just the thought of her tight, velvety newness was enough to make him shoot his load. He grunted, pumping every last drop of himself into the woman. James laid for a moment, thoughts of Flora slowly ebbing from his mind as he came back to the here and now. He disentangled himself from the young girl and rolled away from her. The whore laid there, still, next to him. She'd had men like him before – forceful, bestial - she'd learned it was best not to move a muscle until they said she could. After a while, the Captain reached to his coat and pulled out her payment, throwing it down beside her.

"Be gone," he said.

Silent as a ghost, she gathered her clothing to her and went.

18

The Star was busy as usual. Men who had finished their day's work sat at the tables or stood shoulder to shoulder at the bar, laughing, joking, the sound of their voices carrying across the low ceilinged room. A few women accompanied them – come to bring their husbands home but then finding themselves caught up in the reverie, until they remembered why they were there and then pulled their spouses to the door by their coattails.

At the back of the room, at their table sat Fin, William, Dobbin and Tad, with Sukey taking a five minute break and sitting on Tad's knee.

"Fin!" shouted William. "Ye Gods! FIN!"

Fin came to with a shake of his head. "Sorry." He placed a card on the pile in front of them and even Sukey raised an eyebrow.

"A deuce?" asked Tad. "Are ye mad?"

Fin looked at the cards face up on the table, and then at the cards in his hand. Laying a deuce was definitely a mistake. He pushed the coins away from himself. "Too late now," he said, and threw his hand down on top of the coins.

"What's up wi' ye, lad?" asked William, kindly. "Ye've bin off yer game for days and days now."

"He's in love." Dobbin scooped the cards up and began shuffling them. "I ain't complainin' though – I've surely won a pretty penny thanks to Mistress Flora."

Sukey playfully pulled at Fin's ponytail as she got to her feet to return to the bar. "Phineas, somehow, some way, go and see her."

Fin sighed. "How?"

"We could get a message to her, me an' Sukey," put in Tad, helpfully. "Get her to come here."

Fin threw him a look. "Bring a Lady *here*?" While it was true that as well as being his home, The Star was by no means the roughest inn in Deal, he looked around him at the comings and goings; the loudness of the clientele, the men shouting, laughing, swearing – one of them quite literally being dragged out the door by his wife.

Tad followed his gaze and looked defeated. "Aye, p'raps yer right."

"'Ave ye bin back to the chapel?" asked Dobbin.

"A fair few times, aye. No sign of her ever 'avin' bin there."

William said, "Cheer up, lad. As says the Bard - 'tis better to 'ave loved and lost than never to 'ave loved at all." He patted him gently on the shoulder.

Fin winced. His shoulder still hurt considerably. He'd already been to the barber surgeon and had him cut the stitches out a few days since. While the scars were neat and the injuries healing well, the wounds to his back, arm and shoulder were seriously hampering his work. Whereas before he could easily lift small boat frames with help, now he found himself struggling. The repetitive movements he used to lose himself in such as hammering and sanding, were now the bane of his life. He was behind on the order that he'd got from the owner of the Mary-Anna and Lord only knew when he'd even begin to be able to make a start on the bigger boats. The difficulty completing the vessels meant he was losing out on payments and running out of money.

While lying injured in the chapel, Fin had asked Dobbin to contact Jacques and Guillaume to pick up the haul both from St Margarets bell chamber and the chapel, and ship it out as soon as possible, but aside from that the four of them hadn't dared to move any shipments in or out of the country since the raid. After the attack, the town *seemed* to revert back to normal, with the general comings and goings of the soldiers stationed nearby in Dover, but Fin wasn't entirely convinced that it wasn't just a ploy to lull everyone into a false sense of security while the powers that be planned a better and bigger attack.

When the three of them had shown up on that Sunday afternoon, he'd been unable to help them move anything of any worth due to his injuries and, while he might no longer be stitched and bandaged, knowing the difficulty he was having at the boat yard he felt sure he would not be able to pull his weight shifting the contraband, either.

He could only hope that the pain would subside and his injuries would heal quickly letting him get back to the life he had before. He cast his eyes to the bar and watched his brother pour a tankard of ale. To end up like Thomas, working behind the bar at his Da's inn was probably his worst nightmare.

"What will ye do, about Flora?" Dobbin asked now, all serious.

"Nothin'. There's nothing' to be done. I just need to forget her." That was easier said than done when every time he moved the pain in his right side reminded him of her. He stood up. "I'm done fer the night. I'll see yous tomorrow. C'mon Dog."

*

In his room at the top of the inn, Fin lit a couple of candles and readied himself for bed. Dog curled up on his blanket on the floor. Under the covers but shivering from the cold, Fin took the velvet hair ribbon that Flora had given him out from under his pillow and held it in his hand.

"Stupid," he told himself.

He could hardly concentrate on anything for thinking about her. He played the length of velvet through his fingers remembering the gentle touch of her hands on his skin as she was tending to his wounds. He thought back to the last day he had seen her – the wintry sun through the open thatch of the chapel roof was just strong enough to pick out the reds and golds in her hair and turn it almost auburn in the light. The shadows had turned her emerald eyes a deep sea-green.

He and Flora together made for a wonderful daydream. In it,

he had them living in one of the cottages near the middle of town. He was a successful shipwright and Flora was a wonderful mother to their two, no, *four*, babes. In the evening they would sit by the fire talking and laughing, perhaps reading to each other, telling the little ones stories.

Fin bunched the ribbon in his fist. It was a fantastical day-dream and stood as much chance of becoming a reality as people walking on the moon. Not least because of the fact she was due to get married. Fin leaned over and blew out the candles. He closed his eyes. He knew they would never be together – the Lady and the boatbuilder-cum-smuggler – but, please God, to see her one last time, to say a proper goodbye.

He replaced the velvet ribbon beneath his pillow and slept on both that, and a prayer.

19

A commotion downstairs brought Flora out of her slumber. It was gone midday and she was still in her bed. Molly had been in at daybreak as usual and had only just managed to open the window drapes before Flora had sent her away.

She'd laid on her side, gazing out of the window at the blue, cloudless sky, the seagulls circling overhead and shrieking as they were prone to do. After a while and with a tremendous sigh, she had rolled over with her back to the view and had laid there thinking about Captain Reed, her upcoming wedding, her life being married to man with so few scruples as to blackmail her into marrying him. She thought too, of Fin the boatbuilding smuggler, and his gentle ways, and then she began to overthink her whole situation until she found herself utterly exhausted by all her thinking, suffocated by thoughts of her no doubt dreadful future, and had fallen into a fitful sleep with dreams haunted by nightmares in which Captain Reed would cover her face and chain her to a chaise and refuse to allow her to breathe until he said she could.

She could hear Margaret downstairs ordering the servants to be careful and to fetch the brandy. Her interest piqued, Flora slung on a gown and made her way down the stairs.

Such a sight met her before she had even made it to the landing – her father being as good as carried by Jenkins and Margaret to a seat in the hallway. His clothing was dishevelled, his periwig was in his hand and his colour was high. Margaret didn't appear to fare much better – she had lost a shoe and her hair, usually worn up with jewelled combs, was down and in one big tangle.

Flora flew the rest of the way down the staircase. "Oh, my heavens! Whatever has happened?" she asked, helping Margaret to a seat near the clock.

Her sister choked on a sob. "We were robbed! On the way back from Dover!"

"Bloody highway robber!" swore Lord Arthur Harrington, "waving his bloody pistols in our faces, forcing us out of the carriage."

"He took everything." Margaret tentatively touched at her mess of hair. "Father's money, his gold watch. He took my seed pearl necklace, my rings, even my hair combs."

"And what of him?" asked Flora, "Did you see where he went?"

"No, he jumped back on his horse and rode off towards Deal." Margaret sobbed. "I'm never travelling alone in the carriage again."

Flora relieved Dot of the brandy bottle and refilled the glasses. "You weren't alone this time and it made no difference."

"But what if Father hadn't been there and I *had* been alone. What then?" She shuddered. Flora also felt shivers of unease crawl up the skin of her arms.

"I am due in Deal tomorrow. I promised Clara that I would help her with some embroidery." Margaret took Flora's hands in hers. "Will you come with me? Please?"

Flora couldn't think of a worse way to spend an afternoon, but she knew Margaret would have done the same for her had the situation been reversed. She squeezed her sister's hand gently. "Of course I will," she said.

20

The next day bloomed bright and dry and brought with it some wonderful news – a messenger had arrived bearing a note from Captain Reed. *My dearest Flora,* it had began, *it is with deepest regret that I write to inform you that I am being immediately sent overseas to assist my comrades out in the Balearic Islands. I am unsure when I will return but please, rest assured, I will return, and when I do, our wedding will go ahead…*

He had asked that she begin making preparations for the big day and signed off with the words *Your own, James.*

Again, Flora found the idea that despite his promise the Captain might not return run quickly through her mind, but this time she felt hardly any guilt at the thought - only a large portion of hope.

The sisters were due at Clara's at midday and Flora decided to pack her drawing supplies. She wasn't particularly talented at drawing people but Clara had two young children and Flora thought she might, with the lady's agreement, practice on them.

She dressed well in a cream gown with a pink flower print pattern. It wasn't something she would chose to wear ordinarily, but she knew how spiteful Clara could be and she didn't want to let Margaret down.

As they waited in the hallway for the carriage to arrive Flora couldn't help but notice her sister gradually turning paler and paler. She took her hand. "It will be all right," she said, reassuringly. "It won't happen again."

Margaret chewed at her lip. "You can't know that."

"No, I don't. But it is highly unlikely, don't you think?" She rummaged in her bag. "And if it does, I'll stab them with this," she finished, brandishing a pencil like a sword, eliciting a small smile from her sister. "En guard!"

Margaret gave a laugh, the worry lines on her brow disappearing.

"Here's the carriage," she said, taking Flora's hand. "Put away your rapier and let us go."

*

Flora seldom went anywhere by carriage – the last time she had been in a carriage was to a summer ball out at Whitfield, she had no girlfriends to visit like Margaret did and if she did go anywhere she preferred to ride, if possible. She found the carriage to be claustrophobic and uncomfortable – shaking her very bones as the wheels travelled over the uneven dirt roads, falling into ruts made by other carriages that had travelled the same route before them. She and Margaret took their places next to each other in the vehicle, each minding their gowns so the other didn't sit upon it. Inside the vehicle, gloomy with its dark wood and red painted interior, it was a tight fit.

"I'm sorry the wedding might be put back until later in the year," said Margaret.

Flora rearranged her skirts. "Hmm."

"You don't mind? I thought you'd be pleased to be wed, to get it out of the way."

"It's the marriage I'm not looking forward to, sister, not just the wedding itself."

She thought of all the preparation that would be needed – the gown, the guest list, the food, the seating arrangements; cousin Sarah would need to be seated at the opposite end of the room from Aunt Elizabeth as they didn't get on and sparks would surely fly if they were within ten feet of each other. Fortunately, Margaret excelled at arranging balls and celebrations and she hoped to be able to pass as much of the planning and preparation over to her as possible. If she had any say in it she wouldn't lift a finger to assist towards this awful union. She planned to get up on the day, get dressed, arrive at the church, say what needed to be said and that be the end of it.

The carriage rumbled along the Dover to Deal road, spilling the ladies sideways into each other on occasion when the wheels fell into a particularly deep rut.

"I think it wise to get everything ready as soon as we can – the gown, guest list and so on so that when your Captain returns, we can pick a date almost immediately and then send out the invitations."

Flora sighed. She had felt happy and carefree when she had first received word of Captain Reed's- James, she reminded herself, of *James's* - posting this morning, but all this talk of her future with him had put her back in a black mood. "Do whatever you think is best, Margaret," she said. "I shall leave the whole arrangement in your hands."

The carriage travelled up the hill and down the other side into Walmer. The fields either side of the road were muddy and awaiting a new planting season. Flora thought of what would happen immediately after she and Capt-*James*, were married.

At some point during the evening of their wedding they would be expected to leave the celebration and go off to lay together and seal her fate. The sight of James's cold blue eyes came to her, the thought of those eyes appraising her and seeing parts of her that no one else ever had brought chills to her skin. She thought of being kissed with his hard, thin lips and she shuddered. After the nakedness and the kissing came something more. She knew that much, but didn't know what the something more actually was, and she had no one to ask. Her sister had never lain with a man; all the female servants at home were unmarried although she could never, ever have asked any of them for advice on such a delicate matter, and speaking with any of Margaret's friends was also out of the question. She supposed she would just have to wait and see, let James lead the way. If anything was expected of her when they laid together she felt sure he wouldn't shy away from letting her know.

The carriage passed through Walmer and made its way into Deal. Clara lived at the far end of the town and they would have to travel the entire length of the coastal road to get there.

"You never asked how Father is after yesterday's fright," Margaret said. "He's still rather shaken up, you know."

Flora turned to her sister and faced her head on. "Margaret, I am truly sorry that you both had that terrible experience yesterday but I find myself still feeling quite unsympathetic towards Father. I am still so very cross with him."

"Cross? Why?"

Flora's eyes flashed. "For arranging this wedding! I hope he is happy about the whole thing because I tell you now, sister – once that wedding band is on my finger, I will never be happy again." Finished with her outburst Flora turned as best as she could on the bench seat and looked out of the window. Did she feel better for venting her frustration onto Margaret, no, she realised, now she just felt awful for upsetting her.

They were alongside the beach front now and Flora gazed out at the sea. It was such a clear match for the sky today that it was difficult to say where the one ended and the other began.

It was busier here, only a few hundred yards from the centre of town, and the carriage driver slowed the horses to a walk. People dodged the vehicle as they went about their business. She moved nearer the open window and breathed in the briny air. There was much to see along near the waterfront – fishing boats were pulled up on to the beach with the fishermen selling their early morning catch from trestles set up on the pebbles, smaller row boats lined the beach, some upside down, a dog ran around a boat that was being worked on by a man in shirtsleeves and Flora moved forward in her seat, her head almost completely out of the window. The dog was white with splodges of tan and black, and that man was Fin.

21

Fin had started work at first light but, following the pattern of the last few weeks hadn't managed to get much done. The pain he felt whilst working was both troubling and wearisome, affecting everything he did – lifting, sawing, hammering or sanding. He had given more serious thought to finding an apprentice but didn't think that would make much difference – yes, it would take some of the physical strain off him, but he'd been doing this job since he was first apprenticed at thirteen and showing someone else the ropes would take years and would slow him down even further. As if struggling to work physically wasn't bad enough, he still found his thoughts constantly on Flora almost to the point of taking Tad and Sukey up on their offer of getting a message to her. Fin nudged Dog out of the way and moved round the boat carcass he was working on. If he did see her again, he didn't believe it would achieve anything – once more he ran through the scenarios in his mind.

Flora received word from him... and then what? She had already said she was to be married, so she probably, more than likely, almost definitely, wouldn't even respond. Or, she responded by telling him she had done him a kindness and now she was to be married so leave her be. Or, finally, she responded, they met, they said their proper, final goodbyes... would that be enough for him to forget her and move on with his life? He doubted it. Fin picked up the hammer and began working on the bow end of the boat. Before Flora, he had been able to lose himself in the rhythm of the work but nowadays the repetitive banging of metal on iron just spelled out the name Flora on each hammer blow. He moved round the small boat checking for bits he'd missed and Dog followed, finally laying himself down on the cold pebbles. "What to do, Dog, eh?" he muttered and the dog looked up at him with his head resting on his paws.

There was a time Fin used to enjoy his work – the craftsmanship of it, the smell of the timber, the changes in the wood from rough to smooth as his work progressed. Nowadays he could find little joy in anything – his stomach felt in a knot constantly and he could feel his heart beating harder and faster each time Flora made her way to the forefront of his thoughts. He stopped hammering and stood straight to stretch his back. Dog jumped to his feet expectantly.

"I'm not goin' anywhere," Fin told him. "Ye can take a wander if ye will, but this is taking double the time it should so I shan't be accompanying ye any time soon." Dog shook himself and wandered up the beach to the road and Fin took up his hammer again, starting back where he had left off. *FLOR, RA, FLOR, RA, FLOR, RA*, went the rhythm. *FLOR, RA*. And then Dog was at his side, barking, his tail wagging.

"What's the ma-" Fin looked up in time to see Flora's face at the carriage window as the vehicle drew level with him. His eyes widened, as did Flora's. He saw a dazzling smile light her face. He dropped the hammer and it landed on his foot. He didn't even notice. He had just enough time to return her smile before the carriage passed him by and, once more, she was gone.

Fin could hardly believe it. He watched the carriage trundle down the road until it was lost from view. The smile she had given him had been bright enough to light a dark room and he stood leaning against the part-built boat, his own smile an echo of hers.

22

A t long last he heard hoof falls in the dry autumn leaves and the slip and creak of material against a leather saddle, and then a shadow fell across the chapel doorway. Flora stepped over the threshold and Fin was at her side in an instant. "Mistress, I mean M'lady. Ah, Flora. I'm glad ye thought to come. Ye Gods, I've missed ye."

Dog bounded over, jumping up, his tail beating a tattoo on the broken down door frame. Flora laughed. She was overcome by both their greetings. She wanted so very much to run into Fin's arms but twenty years of 'proper' upbringing held her back. "I've missed you, too," she said, laughing. And now, seeing him, seeing the look of joy on his face, she realised that she had indeed missed him more than she thought it possible to miss anyone. "Have you been back here since you left?" she asked, hanging decorum and dropping to her knees to fuss Dog who had now rolled onto his back for a belly rub.

"Aye, several times. 'Ave you?"

"Yes. We must have just missed each other. Why didn't you get a message to me? I would have come sooner."

Fin fell to his knees beside her. "I wanted to. Ye'll never know how much I wanted to, but I didn't think it would be fitting," he said. "Why didn't *you* leave a note?"

Flora frowned at him. "A note? Well, because, I-"

"Ye didn't think I can read." Fin finished for her, a smile on his face. "I can. And I can write, too. Look." He took one of her hands in his own and looked into her eyes. With his rough, shipwright's fingers he slowly traced the letter F in her palm and Flora felt herself falling into the depths of his warm hazel eyes.

Without breaking his gaze, he followed the F with an L. "I 'ad a few years schoolin'," he said, tracing the O of her name. "The rest of my learnin'..." he continued, on to to R now, "'as come from books." Finally, he traced the A. He closed her hand over the letters he'd made and helped her to her feet. She felt her heart lurch in her chest and butterflies take flight in her stomach. She felt light-headed, faint, giddy, euphoric. "I need to sit down again," she whispered.

Fin rushed to the wall and picked up the blanket that she'd brought weeks ago and had never taken back. He spread it on the ground and helped her sit. Dog nudged himself in between them, his head on Flora's leg.

"Should I get ye some water?" Fin asked, a smile playing on his lips, "although I'd have further to go than you did, fer me."

She smiled back and realised he was still holding her hand in his. It felt nice. She tried not to move it for fear he would notice and take it away.

"I think I will be all right," she said. But would she? she wondered. She had never felt such a depth of feeling for someone in her life before. A shadow fell across her face and she felt tears brimming in her eyes. Damn you, Captain James Reed, she thought, and damn you too, Father.

He saw the tears form in her eyes, balancing on the edges of her long dark lashes, saw the smile vanish from her face. "What is it?" he asked. "What's the matter?"

Flora plucked at the knee of her breeches. "I was thinking of the man I am to marry. He is a Captain in the army and has been posted away."

Fin released her hand. "Ah. And ye miss him."

He was surprised to see her look aghast. "Oh, my heavens, no! I am pleased. I don't want to marry him. Heavens, I don't even like him! My Father and sister have arranged it all. You remember I said before that I was meeting him and that I had to leave early in order to do so?" Fin nodded, a frown on his face. "That was only the second time I had met him formally."

"But-," Fin was confused. In his world you met someone, fell in love, or got them with child - a situation certainly not unheard of – and you married them.

Flora's face fell further and the tears that had threatened to fall now spilled over her lashes. "He's a beast, an utter pig, and..." She faltered. Fin was so easy to talk to. She felt she could tell him anything, but if she shared the fact James was blackmailing her, she would have to tell him how, and she couldn't do that to Stephen; his secret was hers, and now James's, for the two of them to keep.

She was clearly upset, Fin could see she was fighting an inner battle - there was something more she wanted to tell him but wouldn't, or couldn't. He once more took her hand in his and gently stroked his thumb across the back of it. "And yer Father and sister know this? They know how ye feel?"

Flora sniffed. "I certainly haven't kept my opinion a secret from them. But, you see, Father needs an heir and here I am," she indicated herself with a flick of her free hand, "his prize Angus, auctioned off to the man with the best prospects and the highest regard."

Despite the seriousness of the situation, Fin couldn't help but smile at her simile – a prize Angus Flora most certainly wasn't. "So, where is 'e now, this captain?"

"He's been sent to the Balearic Islands, to Menorca, until the siege there is over."

Suddenly, she turned to face him, an earnest look in her eyes. "Can I tell you something? Something I can't tell anyone else?"

Taken aback at her sudden ferocity, Fin nodded. "Aye, what ye tells me won't travel further. Ye 'ave my word."

Flora took a breath. "I hope he dies there," she said, and the tears fell faster from her eyes. "I hope he gets shot straight through his black heart and never comes back."

Fin squeezed her hand. This Captain must really be a brute; Flora was kind, gracious, gentle, she would put others before herself. Hang her upbringing, he knew in his heart and soul that if Flora saw even a beggar in distress she would stop to help him. She had helped him, a smuggler, after all.

He held her hand while she cried, softly. He wanted so much to wipe her tears away. No, he wanted to kiss them away, but that would be wrong; if he kissed her tears away he would end up kissing her and although the man she was due to marry was, in her words, a pig and a brute, she was still his.

"Oh, my heavens," she laughed minutes later, embarrassed and frantically wiping at her tear-stained face. "Please excuse that outburst, it was unforgivable of me."

"'T'ain't unforgivable, it's how ye feel. Ye say he's a beast… perhaps he deserves what ye hope of him."

"Perhaps he does, but let's not speak of him any more."

"Aye, all right, but one question more – what do yer friends think of this? Is this situation… normal… for ladies such as yer-sel'?"

"I have no friends," Flora said, giving Dog a fuss behind his ears. "I care not for the things ladies such as my sister do and the company they keep. They are all…" She frowned, trying to think of a way to explain herself. "It's as though they are all having a big competition – who can have the best, most expensive dress, or jewellery. Who has the most servants, whose house is the biggest. I do not want any part of that. I would rather spend time by myself, drawing, riding out on Pudding, reading."

Fin was taken aback. Who could survive like that, with no friends and no one to talk to? He and Dobbin had been best friends since they were children. They had laughed together, sometimes even cried together, often fought each other, regularly got drunk together and had always kept each other's secrets for almost as long as he could remember.

"Do you ride Diamond for fun?" Flora asked now, bringing him back to the present. He shook his head. "Not often. I don't have the time – between boatbuilding and smug- ye know," he gave an embarrassed smile. "When I do have time to meself, I like to read. I like to lose myself in the pages, in the story."

"As do I." They spoke of their love of books, both admitting to enjoying the smell of new ink on new parchment, they spoke of Flora's drawing, of riding along the clifftop paths, of Fin's enjoyment of his friends' company. Eventually, Flora glanced up at the doorway. The light was beginning to fade. "I should go," she said. "It's beginning to get dark."

"Aye." Fin was disappointed, but certainly didn't want her riding home alone in the dark, and it wasn't as though he could do the gentlemanly thing and escort her to her door.

At the broken doorway, Flora stopped, turned to him and looked shyly up between her lashes. "Will you be here tomorrow?" she asked.

There was no question of him not being there. Fin nodded. "One o'clock. I'll be 'ere."

23

The letter was waiting on one of the hallway table when she got home. Flora snatched it up and carried it to her bedchamber. It was another letter from Stephen and received so soon after she had written to him she hoped it didn't bear any bad news. She broke the seal and sat on her bed to read it.

"My dearest Flo," it began. "I could hardly believe my eyes on reading your last letter! We always knew the chapel was a magical place and thus it has been proven. What an exciting adventure you had!"

Flora smiled – exciting indeed, and now Stephen didn't know the half of it.

"The people you met and Dog, of course, sound like characters in one of our stories from when we were children. To think our chapel was being used by smugglers to hide their supplies! Tell me more – what happened next? Did Master Fin survive your operation (and I thank you for the gory details of that, my dearest sister), and what of Master Dobbin, and Dog?"

Flora pulled her legs up under her and propped herself against her pillow. Stephen's letter continued with a word of warning -

"Please have a care," he wrote. "If Father or Margaret get wind of your adventure I would hate to think of the punishment they would wrought on you: Needless to say, Master Fin *et al* would be found and handed over to the authorities and I should imagine you yourself would never be let out of their sight again until the day of your marriage."

At the word marriage, Flora's heart fell into her stomach. Stephen's letter continued.

"My news from this wonderful country across the far side of the globe, is that indeed I have left the navy!" This would be why his letter got here so soon, thought Flora, no longer did it have to travel ship to ship to find him. He continued, "'S' and myself have found a beautiful piece of land an hour's ride outside Rayleigh and have employed some men to build us a cabin to our own specifications. The land lies just south of the mountains and there is a lake not a stone's throw from where our front door will be. We will have views of open countryside that you could not even imagine in your very wildest imaginings! And the air here is so fresh and clean it feels as though you can bathe in it."

Flora sighed with happiness for her brother. He had painted a picture of an idyll lacking in her life.

"Our cabin will have two bedrooms and a sitting-room-cum-kitchen which is how they do things here, in this new country. But the best part, dearest Flo, is that 'S' has insisted an extra room be built upstairs with windows on three sides so that I might have a proper studio to use for my art! My only wish now is that you will be able to visit sometime and see this beautiful land and our wonderful home with your own eyes."

He closed with another warning – "Please do take heed, darling sister, do not do anything too reckless or, if you do, be sure that Father and Margaret do not learn of it."

Flora carefully folded the letter and put it safely in her drawer – she had learned her lesson from last time and would only read letters at home in future.

Today had been a truly wonderful day – spending time with Fin and making an arrangement to meet him again tomorrow, and receiving a letter from her dearest, darling brother. Life could hardly get any better aside from the one big, black blot on the horizon. She remembered how upset she had become venting her feelings to Fin earlier. She had never, ever wished harm on another person and in doing so today felt she had let herself down badly. How could one man so easily change her and turn her into someone she was not. Flora decided to keep him on the horizon – just the very thought of him tarnished anything good she felt. From now on, James could stay in the far reaches of her mind, at the furthest possible distance.

24

Fin was at the boatyard well before daybreak. As it made its way over the horizon, the winter sun cast a hue of reds and oranges on the small boat he was working on. The vessel didn't yet have a name but it did have a skeleton, and Fin had been working doubly hard to put flesh on it this morning. Working doubly hard meant suffering double the pain and while working, and aching, he began to fret about what to do in the future.

Around him, the town seemed to have settled back into its usual rhythm. To those who hadn't been injured in the raid of weeks ago, it was now all just a distant memory. Ike Stupples, his crew, and others like them, had returned to shipping contraband in and out almost immediately - within days - and now Fin decided he'd been cautious enough and it was high time he and his friends did the same – not least because he was beginning to need the extra money his illicit activities brought in. This was a bad time of year all round – for boatbuilding and smuggling alike – the weather was turning unpredictable; one day it could be like today, calm and dry, the next day could be like Armageddon itself had arrived, with howling winds, lashing rain and high waves that crashed onto the beach like they were trying to reach the town itself and claw it and everything in it back into its depths. On a good day a small boat like that of Jacques and Guillaume's could make it across the channel in eight hours, if they hit bad weather and rough waters it could take an aeon and they ran the risk of losing merchandise and even their lives.

Fin cast his eye over his handiwork; she was looking good so far. His hands, when he passed them over her hull, told the same story; the wood was smooth and ready for the next process. He pulled his watch from his pocket and checked the time – ten o'clock – that gave him two hours. He called Dog to his side. "Time to pack it in fer now," he told the hound, "we've an errand to run afore we meet the Lady Flora."

*

Fin made it to the chapel first, which was good; he had a surprise for her and couldn't help the smile from spreading across his face as he thought of it. Within minutes he heard Pudding's steady footfalls in the leaves outside and Dog ran off to find his equine friend and give him a good sniff.

As usual, Flora was dressed in breeches and a long riding coat which served Fin's purpose perfectly. She made her way from the doorway, eyes shining, a smile on her face.

"M'lady Flora," Fin greeted her. "Y'er well?"

Flora nodded. "I am indeed! I received a letter from my brother yesterday, full of news of his new home in the Colonies." Dog came over and demanded a fuss by looking at her beseechingly and raising a paw. "You devil," she laughed, patting his rump and making him wriggle with delight.

"I forgot ye said ye 'ad a brother." Fin fidgeted with something held behind his back.

"Oh yes, Stephen." Flora explained he he had just left the navy and was having a cabin built in the shadow of the Blue Ridge mountains. "I miss him terribly," she continued, a distant look in her eye. "He has always been my best friend."

"Ah, well. I might 'ave something 'ere that might cheer ye." From behind his back, Fin brought out a cocked hat. "A gift. Fer ye."

Flora took the gift and frowned. "It's… a hat."

"Aye, but not jus' *any* hat. This 'ere is special kind o' hat."

Flora looked at him now with her eyebrows raised. "Special how?"

"It can change ladies into men," Fin said.

Flora's curiosity piqued, she asked, "What in heaven's name are you talking about?"

"I can show ye. But, before I do anythin'... Do ye trust me, m'lady?"

Flora looked at him, his deep, warm hazel eyes, his open face. It took less than a second for her to answer. "Yes," she said. "I do."

"Then don't fret," he said, moving behind her.

She felt him gently lift her hair from where it lay loose on her neck and over her shoulders. His touch was gentle, but she felt his hands shaking as he secured it in a bunch with a ribbon from his pocket. Once tied back, her curls fell in a ponytail between her shoulder blades. Fin stepped around to the front of her, took the hat from her hands and carefully placed in on her head, pulling it down slightly at the front so that her green eyes were in shadow. He stepped back, appraising the effect and nodded, happily. "There. Say farewell to Mistress Flora and hello to... Master Francis." Flora reached up to touch the hat.

"Ah, no, don't move it!" said Fin, panicked. "It looks fine. *Ye* looks fine-"

"But-"

"And now fer the second part of my gift to ye."

"Second part?" Flora asked, eyes askew as she tried to look at the hat on her head and then gave up.

"Aye, and fer the second part, again we 'ave need for a small bit o' deceit." He smiled, wickedly, and took her hand. "Come wi' me."

Flora allowed herself to be led outside to where the two horses stood, each nuzzling the leaves at their feet.

"Ye can't take Pudding fer this," Fin said. "He's too recognizable. We'll 'ave to ride double on Diamond."

Now Flora was really intrigued. "Fin, I-"

"Ah, no. Jus' do as I bid ye. Please. And Dog – stay 'ere." Dog looked at them sulkily and laid down on the ground.

"I have no thought as to what you are planning, Master Dawkins," Flora said with a smile of resignation. "But, I do indeed trust you, so this time I'll let you do whatever it is you're plotting."

They mounted Diamond with Flora behind and moved out of the woodland and on to the main road. "Where are we going with me disguised as… Francis?" asked Flora, over Fin's shoulder.

"'Tis a surprise. I ain't tellin' ye. And mind yer hat," he replied, with a smile on his face that Flora could hear in his voice.

They rode on in silence with just the sound of Diamond's hooves on the dry mud track and the birds calling in the trees to the left and right of them. Flora had no clue what Fin was up to but, she found herself a little frightened to admit, she was enjoying the varying sensations of riding double with him with her hands around his waist and her chest sometimes bumping against his back.

As he drove Diamond at a walk, she could feel his thigh muscles moving under his breeches and could tell of the strength in them, his arms rested on hers and again, she could feel his muscles tense and relax as he expertly used the reins to drive the chestnut where she needed to be. The whole experience was giving her a strange and yet not unpleasant feeling low down in her stomach.

For his part, Fin was glad they had fallen into a companionable silence – he didn't trust himself to speak, thinking his voice would be nothing but gravel in his throat if he tried to get a word out at the moment. Flora's legs so near his and her tiny hands around his waist was torture enough, but to feel her pert little breasts bumping against his back on occasion was almost enough to drive him insane with want for her.

He reminded himself, as he was having to do more and more often lately, that the lady behind him was another man's would-be wife. He'd had more than plenty of conversations with himself about this – late at night when he couldn't sleep for thinking of her, or when at work, in the times he didn't need to concentrate, and images of her came to his mind.

Time and again he'd had to remind himself that, despite her down to earth demeanour and even the breeches she preferred to dress in, Flora was still a Lady and he was nothing more than a common shipwright-cum-smuggler. To even share a friendship with her was more than he should have allowed from the outset; he was setting himself up for heartbreak.

He knew it, but he couldn't help it.

She was spellbinding to him.

But, he asked himself for the millionth time, what would come of it all when this pig, this brute of hers returned from where he had been posted? Once more Fin put the future to the very back of his mind – if he didn't think of it, maybe it wouldn't happen. Maybe, as Flora had hoped, this captain *would* come off worse at the hands of the people he was fighting.

Fin was not a man to wish ill on anyone and could understand completely why voicing her thoughts on the matter yesterday had caused Flora such upset, but in this instance, and especially if this *gentleman* was as heinous as she had said, he felt wont to agree with her.

They had made it to the outskirts of Deal and Fin drove Diamond onwards. No one gave a second look as the two young men rode in between the crowds in the narrow streets. At last Fin turned Diamond down a side street and into a stable yard. "This is it, we're 'ere," he said, dismounting and holding out his hand to help her down from the horse.

"Here, where?" Flora asked, looking around her at the several stalls, some empty, most full of horses. Fin called a lad over to unsaddle and stable his horse. "'Ere. Home. The Star," he replied with a grin. "Come and meet my friends."

Flora was stunned into silence as he took her gently by the elbow and led her the back way into the inn.

The place was bustling, rowdy in a good-natured way. Men were laughing and drinking, sitting at tables playing cards, and another group was singing over in the far corner, near the front door.

"The old man at the bar is me Da and the other is Thomas, me brother. But never mind them, come, Master Francis," said Fin, laughing at her wide-eyed wonder. "Let's go an' join the others, aye?"

*

The others were sitting at their customary table at the back of the inn just to Flora's left. Fin steered her over and bid she take a seat facing away from the rest of the folk gathered in the premises. "This is Master Francis," he announced, cocking a wink and a grin at Flora. Dobbin's eyes lit up at seeing her. "'Tis good to see you again Mis- Master Francis."

"And you, Dobbin."

"And this 'ere is William," Fin said, indicating a man of epic proportions with a lit pipe dangling out of his mouth, a fiery red beard and kind eyes. William smiled and inclined his head in greeting. "And," continued Fin clapping his hand on the shoulder of the man sitting next to her, "This is Tad."

The man was no more than a boy, really, and couldn't be much older than Flora herself. He dropped his eyes when she looked at him. "I've to apologise to yer, Mis- Master Francis," he mumbled, fidgeting with the tankard on the table in front of him. "I was wi' Dobbin that day at the chapel. T'was us both what gave ye a fright."

Flora narrowed her eyes at him. "Oh, so *you're* the other ghost of Oxney Bottom?"

He looked at her now with the largest brown eyes she had ever seen. "Sorry to say it, but, aye, that I am." Flora laughed. "You certainly did give me a scare, the both of you, but all is forgiven, Master Tad."

At her elbow, Sukey appeared with a tankard of beer for Fin. She gave a barely discernible curtsey and a dazzling smile to Flora. "I'm pleased to see ye at last, Mistress Flora," she said quietly. "Fin 'as spoken of no one nor nothin' else since ye did 'im such a kindness wi' 'is injuries. An' we all thank ye for that." She looked at the men sitting around the table, the three of them raised their tankards and nodded to Flora. "And we'll drink to that," said William, once more inclining his head to Flora.

"So, enough of all that," put in Fin, a trifle embarrassed.

"What d'ye drink, Francis?"

"Oh, wine if you have any, or port maybe?"

Sukey smiled kindly and touched Flora's arm. "I'll get yer one or t'other in a tankard so it looks like beer… ye don't see many men in 'ere wi' a glass o' port in their dirty paws."

Flora smiled back. "Thank you."

"So, d'ye play cards?" William pulled a battered pack out from his pocket and began shuffling them deftly, his pipe still hanging from the corner of his mouth.

"I play Patience, but I don't suppose that's a game you had in mind."

William snorted. "Patience! Nah, how about we teach ye some stud."

"Is it a gambling game? I, I have no money,"

"I'll lend ye some coins," said Dobbin quickly. Fin rolled his eyes.

William dealt the cards. Flora found it an easy game and one she apparently excelled at – it wasn't long before she had the largest pile of coins on the table in front of her. "Beginner's luck," mumbled Dobbin, but he smiled as he said it.

They talked between hands and laughed at jokes Dobbin made. Between refilling tankards, Sukey often came over and sat on Tad's knee as they played. Flora thought they made a very handsome couple – Tad with his dark hair and huge brown eyes and Sukey with her blonde curls and pretty grey eyes. She couldn't help but notice how Tad often had his hand on the girl, either around her waist, or on her knee, and whenever they looked at each other it was with smiles and adoration.

For a large man, she noticed that William was short on words. He often said nothing at all and when the others laughed out loud he held only a small smile on his face.

Dobbin was a clown, making them laugh with tales and anecdotes and sometimes he only had to look at one of them with his impish grin to start them all off in a fit of the giggles.

Fin joined in with his friends, and made a point of including her or explaining things if they spoke of subjects she knew nothing about – their livelihoods, their smuggling, their families.

Eventually Fin called time on them by saying they had to get back to the chapel or it would be dark by the time Flora/Francis made it back to the big house.

Flora was sad to have to leave. "Thank you everyone," she said on a small bow, in the manner of a man. "It was lovely to meet you all, but now Francis needs to take his leave and head home."

They said their goodbyes and she and Fin headed out to the stables. "I'll take Diamond and you can take this mare, 'ere," said Fin, saddling a beautiful bay. "She's an old girl but a good 'un and she'll be led back behind Diamond and me wi' no bother when we come back later. She's called Beau on account of 'er bein' beautiful. Aren't ye, girl, yes," he continued, rubbing the creature's nose.

They rode at a gallop when they could and arrived back at the chapel just as the light was beginning to fade. Pudding gave a snort to show his displeasure at being left behind with only a mere dog for company.

Flora removed her hat and loosened her hair. "Oh, it's the ribbon I gave you," she said, returning it back to Fin.

Fin took the length of velvet and put it in his pocket. "Aye. I keep it wi' me. For luck."

Flora smiled. "Today was wonderful - I haven't had as much fun since, well, in my whole, entire life, actually."

"I'm glad ye liked my gift." Fin looked at her earnestly. "I was worried about takin' ye to the inn… t'ain't a very fitting place fer a lady."

Flora smiled. "I'm not a lady there – I'm Master Francis."

"Well then, Master Francis, now ye've met 'em, be sure to know – my friends are yours as well."

Such thoughtfulness brought prickles of tears to her eyes. Flora stood on tiptoe and kissed him on the cheek. "Thank you, Fin." She turned, mounted Pudding and set off back to the house, leaving Fin touching the place she had kissed and with his nerves all of a jangle.

25

She had fallen asleep remembering the way Fin's muscles had felt against her legs and arms as they'd ridden to the inn, but had dreamt that Fin was using a deck of cards to build a tower except, every time he went to place the last card on top, the whole structure had crashed to the ground. She had hardly had time to draw breath on waking before Margaret blasted into her room.

"Father is in a red rage!" her sister cried. "I've never seen him so angry."

Flora sat up in bed, momentarily confused. "Father is always in a red rage. What's the matter now?"

"Stephen has left the navy." She waited for Flora's shock to surface. When it didn't she said, "Did you know about this?"

"He might have mentioned something about it in the letter I lost."

Margaret rounded on her and Flora could see their Father's face in hers. "And you chose not to say anything?"

"It was not my news to tell."

"You silly girl. If you knew before he had done it, we could have written to him, perhaps got him to change his mind... All those years, wasted." She sunk down onto the bed, all bluster having left her. "What will he do now? Father won't support him, he has already said that. He will have to find some menial work doing... something."

Flora threw back the covers and got out of bed. She rang the hand bell for Molly to fetch water for her to wash in. "He did mention something about art," she said. "And he'll have his half pay."

"I don't think either of those things will placate Father."

Flora found fresh breeches in her armoire and a fitted jacket. "I don't suppose they will."

In a bad mood herself now, Margaret grumbled, "I can't believe you didn't say anything when you heard. And, we've spoken about this before - *must* you wear your brother's breeches all the time? Could you not wear a gown on occasion?"

"Why?"

"Because you are a young woman!" Margaret spluttered. "Because you are about to be married. Because it is *normal*."

Flora turned to face her sister. About to be married, she had said. Oh, my heaven's. "Have you heard from the Captain?" she asked, heart in her throat.

"No. Why do you ask?"

Flora felt her whole body slump with relief. "Just… curious."

"We need to have a talk about that," said Margaret. "We really must start making plans for the wedding."

"I already told you, sister. I am leaving it all up to you, every last thing - the entire arrangement, Margaret. I will be here for gown fittings, if I must, but that is all. I will turn up on the day because I have to and most certainly not because I want to." Flora threw her clothes on the bed. "Sometimes, no, often, I wish I was of common stock," she said.

Margaret looked aghast. "Why on earth would you wish that? What do you even know of common people?"

"I know they are probably happier that I am. They are not tied to expectations – a common person would not be expected to marry someone they had only met twice and didn't even like. And I feel for Stephen – I suppose the fact that he made Lieutenant means nothing to Father; he is only in a rage because of how it looks to other people. Stephen would have been expected to stay at sea and make it to Admiral. Or die trying." She picked the clothes up off the bed, threw them back down again and glared at her sister. "Do not try and tie me down and bend me to your conformities, Margaret. I will wear whatever I choose and go wherever I want until marriage to that man stops me, and at that time my life will be over anyway!" Margaret's mouth hung agape at her sister's outburst. Flora took her sister by the arms and marched her to the door. "Now leave me, please. Look, Molly is here with my water."

*

Once she was dressed Flora found herself at a loss of what to do. She thought about taking Pudding for a run along the cliffs but a look out the window showed her a dark morning with heavy clouds gathering. Besides, Margaret talking about the dreaded wedding had put her in mind for some company rather than solitude; if she spent the day by herself her thoughts, she knew, would return again and again to their conversation and in turn, those thoughts would inevitably lead to James.

Flora decided she would put her new hat to use instead – she would ride into town under the guise of Master Francis. It would be busy there, no doubt, and full of sights to take her mind off things. She had only previously been into Deal with Margaret by carriage, it might be fun to be a young man in the midst of it all.

She had Ned ready Missy, an old chestnut of theirs, and made her way to the chapel to pick up her hat. Once there, she tied her hair back and carefully placed the hat on her head, being sure to have it as low over her eyes as possible.

She trotted the horse through the woods and out onto the road. Once she had got as far as Walmer the roadway became much busier with people and horses, carts and carriages going every which way. Out in the channel the clouds were gathering and rumbles of thunder could be heard far away, over France. She continued on and headed toward the beach front. The air was fresher here, though she doubted it was anywhere near as fresh and clear as that described by her brother when he spoke about North Carolina, and it was beginning to rain. Spits and spots hit her every so often and the sky was beginning to darken here, too – the clouds now so thick there was almost no break in them.

The weather wasn't yet stopping anyone from going about their business - as she had seen the last time she had happened this way, in the carriage on their way to Clara's, the beach front was exceptionally busy with fishing boats and fishermen and, she stopped Missy in her tracks, there was Fin, in the distance, busy working on a boat.

She slid from the saddle and walked the horse slowly along the road, stopping a hundred yards or so away from where he was working. Dog was by his side, asleep on a piece of tarpaulin on the beach. Fin had his coat hung on a groin nearby and was in shirtsleeves, hard at it sanding the underside of a small boat which was balanced upside down on some trestles. Every so often he'd look up at the sky, no doubt wondering whether to stop working, but then he'd put his head down and get on with it again. Flora sat on the damp pebbles and watched him for a while.

He made for a good sight – his shirt buffeting in the breeze as he worked, the muscles of his arms rigid with tension as he moved his hands back and forth across the woodwork. She wished she'd had the foresight to bring some parchment and pencils with her – he would have made a wonderful study, although the rain was coming on now and she would have had to stop anyway. She was getting more rained on by the minute, but found him mesmerising to watch. She saw with some sadness that every few minutes he had to stop, stand and straighten. He would stretch his back, occasionally reach behind him and rub at the place where the sword had cut him and that she had stitched. The rain was beginning to get heavier and Missy pawed at the ground wanting, no doubt, to get out of it. At the sound of the pebbles moving, Dog looked up and saw them both. He jumped to his feet, barking with excitement. Flora stood and walked the horse on nearer.

"Ye Gods, Dog!" she heard Fin say. "What's the matter wi' ye? Yer barking fit to wake the dead."

"He's barking at me."

Fin nearly fell over himself he spun round so quickly. "Flora?"

he said.

Flora indicated her attire. "Well, some might say Francis."

And then all hell was let loose as lightning filled the sky over the channel, thunder crackled in the distance and the rain fell in torrents. Missy immediately lost her nerve and bucked at Flora's side.

"Shh," she said, digging her heels into the pebbles, holding the horse tight to the bit and rubbing her forehead. "Shh, Missy, it's all right." The horse calmed a little but her eyes were still huge and bulging with fear. She threw her head around in distress and it was all Flora could do to hold onto her. Fin threw his tools down, slung on his coat and ran over.

"Go to The Star," he shouted over the noise of the rain. "Dog'll lead the way. I'll bring the 'orse and meet ye in the stables. Dog, go 'ome."

Flora nodded and handed the reins over. She followed Dog off the beach and onto the road. There was hardly anyone around now – the fishermen had thrown covers on their wares, weighting them down so they were less likely to be blown away in the strengthening wind, people were running this way and that, and Flora and Dog ran through the streets until a few minutes later he led her to the inn.

Flora was soaked to the skin and shivering with cold by the time Fin arrived, on horseback, minutes later. They unbridled the horse and settled her in a stall with some hay.

"Yer drenched through," said Fin, looking at Flora.

"It was fine when I left home," she replied, through chattering teeth. "You're even more saturated than me."

He took her hand. "Come," he said, "Let's get dry."

He led her the back way into the inn and up the stairs. "Where are we going?" asked Flora, shivering all over, her teeth still chattering. Fin opened a door at the top of the stairs. "Here. My bedchamber. Come in, I'll get a fire lit."

Flora looked around her. It was a neat and pleasant room - the bed was made and there was a blanket box at the end of it. Opposite, there was a chest of drawers with a wash bowl and jug on top and a mirror hanging above. One wall was almost entirely given over to shelves of books, there was a desk near the window, a chair by the fire grate.

"Come." He led her across the room and took her hat and riding coat from her, closing the door and hanging the sodden garments as well as his own coat on a hook there. "I need to take this shirt off," he said, about to pull it over his head. "Ye can look away if ye like, but t'ain't nothin' ye've not already seen."

Except it was.

Flora stood and shivered, watching him making up the fire. The last time she'd seen him semi-naked she'd had a task to complete and his back had been a mess of blood and open wounds. She'd noticed the smoothness of his skin but hadn't appreciated it at the time. Now she could see the scars where she'd sewn him up were neat but still red and healing. She watched the muscles under his skin move as he set to using a tinderbox to light the kindling and wood he had laid in the grate.

The spark caught and a soft glow filled the room as the fire took hold. He turned back to her and she couldn't help but see his bare chest, smooth with a light dusting of dark hair across its width and leading down over his stomach.

A strange feeling fell over her, one she could not describe; her heart beat faster and louder under her sopping wet clothes and her stomach released butterflies that fluttered inside her. Goosebumps, not from the cold and wet, spread over her arms and legs and lit on her entire body.

Fin was busy rummaging in the blanket box and at last emerged with a soft woollen plaid. "Ye should take that jacket and chemise off – I'll dry 'em by the fire," he said, holding the blanket up in front of her. "I won't look and ye can cover yersel' wi' this when yer done."

Flora struggled out of her wet garments, the cotton chemise sticking to her skin, all the while watching Fin studiously not watching her. He was such a gentleman, so courteous and so, so *kind*. Flora thought that too short and simple a word to encompass the depth of him. She untied her hair and it fell, sodden, over her shoulders. The goosebumps rose again on her skin and she took the blanket he held. "All right."

Fin turned to her and she let the blanket fall. It pooled at her feet along with her clothes.

"What are ye-?"

She stood up on tiptoe and silenced him with a kiss on the mouth. For a moment, a fleeting moment, he didn't respond, then he took her in his arms and kissed her back.

Flora felt herself falling, her head spinning, as his lips moved from her mouth and began to cover her cheeks, her eyes, her throat. Lightning flashed across the sky and thunder crackled overhead and still she could have sworn she could hear their heartbeats over the sound of it. With one swift movement, Fin lifted her from her feet and carried her to the bed, still kissing her, as he laid her down as gently as could be.

Flora found she had no thoughts, all words had flown from her mind, now she only had feelings and they overtook her. When Fin softly, gently, oh so gently, took one of her breasts in his hand and ran a thumb over the nipple she wondered if she might not explode with pleasure.

As well as their heartbeats and the rain and the storm that was now raging outside, she could hear a soft mewling sound and realised it was coming from her. She ran a hand over his back, feeling the scars she had sown under her fingers, gripped his shoulder as he lowered his lips down over her throat and chest and caught a nipple in his mouth. She had a feeling inside her breeches, between her legs, like her heart had moved from its customary place in her chest and was beating down there instead, and then Fin pulled back and looked at her. "We need to stop, Flora, or I won't be able to stop," he said, and she heard his voice was hoarse, saw his face was pained.

Flora pulled him back down to her and kissed him again, her hand in his hair which had somehow at sometime become loose of its tie and he moaned and said her name and she realized that whatever came next she needed it, and she wanted it, she wanted *him*.

"Don't stop," she said breathlessly. "If you stop now I think I might die from wanting you."

In a deft movement she hardly grasped, he removed his breeches and she had only a swift glance of him before he lay above her again. "I've never seen a naked man before," she whispered, between laying kisses on his chest as he leaned over her.

"Then ye don't 'ave to look."

"I want to."

Fin knelt astride her and she took in the sight of him, his powerful thighs, muscles taught with holding his weight on his knees, the hair on his chest, across his finely toned stomach down to his manhood. She tentatively took him in her hand and he moaned aloud, his head back, eyes closed, biting his lower lip. "Ye Gods, Flora," he murmured. "Let me take ye now. May I?"

She answered by pulling him to her and wriggling out of her own clothing. Fin kissed her again and held one of her hands above her head, stroking her fingers, running his thumb along her palm. His other hand reached down below and he traced those fingers to the very heart of her. She was wet and ready for him and when he slipped a finger inside her she gasped and pulled his hand closer to her.

"I'll be gentle," he whispered, his voice hoarse in her ear. "If I hurt ye, tell me, I'll stop – I never want to hurt ye, Flora, in love or in life." He lowered his body over hers and guided himself into her.

It was pleasure and pain for her, all bound up in one package, and if her mind didn't know what to do with it, her body did and it responded by moving with him, on gentle waves until he couldn't bear it anymore and slid himself from her before it was too late.

"Are ye all right?" he asked.

He felt her nod against his chest. Then heard her give a sob. He was on his knees with her face in his hands in an instant. "What's the matter? Did I hurt ye? Why are ye crying?"

Flora clung to him, her tears running down his chest. "I've never been so happy in my whole entire life," she sobbed.

They had fallen asleep in each other's arms, but not before Fin had been true to his word and set Flora's clothes in front of the fire to dry. She'd watched him as he'd moved about the room, naked and unabashed. His scars were large and still red where they were healing and she could see why they gave him so much discomfort.

She woke, on her back, with one of Fin's legs draped across her own and one of his hands resting just below her breast. She turned her head towards him and his hair, now dry, the ends a mess of curls, fell across his face and she lifted a hand to move it out of the way as she took in the beauty of him – his eyes closed, long lashes casting shadows on the planes of his cheekbones, blond stubble just beginning to form over his strong jawline, the just-barely-there dimple on his chin. She smiled to herself and then the smile slid from her face.

Flora knew, with absolutely no doubt, that if, *when*, she laid with James on their wedding night and they did what she and Fin had just done, it wouldn't be anything like what had happened between them. She imagined James's cold eyes on her. The skin of his hands might not be rough like Fin's, but they would be rough in a different way; forceful, greedy. Would he be able to tell she was no longer a maiden? Flora took a breath and let it out slowly, forcing James to the back of her mind. She said a silent prayer that, for a reason she did not want to put a name to, he really, really wouldn't come back.

Beside her, Fin stirred and opened his eyes. "I dreamt of ye," he said, smiling, taking her hand in his. "I dreamt we was together, like this, and then I woke up and it weren't a dream after all – t'was real." He moved his leg against hers, let go of her hand and cupped her breast in his as he kissed her shoulder, her neck, her throat. "Ye drive me to madness, m'lady," he murmured in her ear. "And I long fer ye again."

It was true; she could feel him against her body getting hard once more, and she felt intoxicated by the thought of him inside her again.

He kissed her on the mouth, moving his lips down to her ear. "Yer skin smells of rosewater and us," he whispered, moving his kisses down to her neck, her throat and down further, to her chest. He took a nipple in his mouth and Flora felt her senses spinning out of control as he gently sucked at it then released it and moved his mouth down further. She gripped the bedsheets in her hands and dug her heels into the mattress.

"I love the taste o' ye on my tongue," he murmured, kissing and licking the very centre of her, moving with her as she writhed and wriggled and arched her back, as he brought her to the brink.

"Feel me," he said, kneeling over her now, taking her hand and placing it on his chest. "Feel my heart beatin' for ye, Flora."

She touched him all over, kneading her fingers into his shoulders, moving down his chest, feeling his nipples beneath her palms, the hair on his stomach, pulling him closer, kissing the places she had touched. Still unsure of herself, she took him in her hand, feeling the size of him, before gently cupping his balls in her hand. This time she guided him into her and he moaned and she said his name and they moved together, still kissing, and it was slow and sweet and sensual and, where he'd brought her to the brink before, almost just the feel of him against her most sensitive parts had her pulling him closer and shuddering to a climax that felt as though every fibre of her being had been set on fire. The feel of her quivering around him brought him to his own climax and he barely had time to withdraw before he came. He collapsed beside her, taking her hand in his and holding it to his heart.

"You kill me, Flora," he said.

"I do?"

"Aye. In a good way," he grinned, kissing her hand. They lay like that for a while, silent, but both comfortable with saying nothing. Then Fin asked, "Are ye hungry? Thirsty?" He jumped up from the bed and pulled on his breeches. "I'll get us something to eat afore the sight of ye there, naked, in my bed, makes me want to take ye again." He left the room and immediately came back in looking shamefaced. He plucked his shirt from the floor and pulled it over his head. "Forgot," he said by way of explanation, and left the room again.

*

Flora slipped from the bed and pulled her own chemise from the chair and put it on. It felt warm and soft from being dried by the fire. She padded barefoot to the dresser and took advantage of the wash bowl and water there. She looked at herself in the mirror hanging there – did she look any different, she wondered. Would anyone be able to see just by looking at her, what she, what *they*, had done?

True, her face was flushed, but the room was small and still heated by the fire, and her eyes were bright, but that could just be due to the reflection from the window. No, she thought her secret was probably safe.

She moved over to Fin's collection of books. He had quite a selection – many by authors she'd never heard of but a fair few by Jonathan Swift. She ran her fingers along the spines and noticed all the books were laid out in alphabetical order, by writer. She moved to the window feeling guilty and embarrassed that she had been so presumptuous to think that Fin, just because he wasn't a peer or a gentleman, wouldn't be able to read.

The window backed onto a churchyard and the clock on the spire tower showed it was just shy of one o'clock. The skies were now clear of rain but thick clouds moved slowly across them. It was still hard to believe that mere hours ago they had been caught in a storm and had both been soaked to the skin but, yes, there was the evidence; her brother's breeches hanging by the fireside.

"I've brought food and drink." Fin came into the room holding a tray of three tankards and a plate of bread, cheese and meat. He gently nudged the door closed with his foot. "Beer, wine and water. Take yer pick."

Flora hopped up on the bed, cross legged, covering herself with her chemise. "I'll take the wine. Thank you. Will you be going back to your boat? It's still quite early."

Fin took a slug of beer. "No. I didn't get a chance to cover her – the wood will be swollen. I'll need to wait for it to dry out, an' it's winter – will be too dark to see soon enough." He took a hunk of bread in his mouth and spoke around it. "So, tell me – why were you down at the beach, Francis?"

Flora helped herself to a cube of cheese. "I had an argument with my sister and I felt I needed to get out of her way." Fin gave her a questioning look. "My Father received word from Stephen telling him he is not returning to sea. I already knew, of course, and Margaret was angry with me for not saying something before."

"T'weren't your news to tell," shrugged Fin, simply.

"Exactly! That is *exactly* what I told her but she doesn't see it that way. Then she began picking at me for not dressing like a Lady."

"I like the way ye dress," Fin stated. "It shows yer independence. 'Course," he continued with a grin, "I like it better when yer not dressed at all." Flora laughed and fed him a slither of meat. "D'ye remember, when I was layin' injured and ye brought me food an' drink?" Flora nodded. "Them little cake things ye brought - me and Dobbin fought for the last one."

"And who won?"

Fin rolled his eyes. "Dobbin."

"Then I'll have to fetch you some more," she laughed. Then, serious once again she said, "I watched you for a time, whilst you were working. Your injuries are still troubling you, aren't they." It was a statement, not a question, and Fin looked downcast.

"Aye." He added quickly, "T'is through no fault of yours, Flora. The barber-surgeon, when I went to 'im to get the stitches cut out, said whoever 'ad sewn it in the first place 'ad done a better job than he could've. But it's where they are, see. Everything I do hurts. It's taking twice as long to do any work and, like I said, with it gettin' dark sooner these days I 'ave less time to do anythin' afore I even start."

"What will you do? Can you employ someone to help you?"

Fin explained that by the time he'd shown someone what to do he could have done the same task at least twice. He just hoped that in time, perhaps by the spring when the weather began to improve, his injuries would also have improved to the point they no longer bothered him. "Meantime," he said, feeding Flora the last bit of cheese from the plate, "I've a shipment due in tonight an' I jus' need to hope the weather holds and it don't storm again."

"Will you be storing the goods at the chapel?" asked Flora, tying her hair back off her face.

"Aye, 'tis a good spot – out o' the way. People don't come near on account of the ghosts that are supposed to haunt there."

"You mean Dobbin and Tad." Flora smiled, remembering the scare they had given her. She could laugh about it now. Wretches.

"Aye." He chuckled. "I'm sorry they frightened ye half to death, y'know."

Flora took his hands in hers. "Please be careful when you drive down the main road – there's been a highway robber there."

Fin looked shocked. "A highwayman? On the Dover to Deal road?" He frowned. "I've 'eard of men holding up coaches on the London road, but 'tis rare in these parts. How d'ye know of it?"

"He held up my Father and sister at gunpoint. Margaret was extremely unnerved by it. He took everything he could, but at least they weren't harmed."

Fin looked thoughtful. "Small mercies," he said. "I'll let the others know."

26

Back at home in her fire-dried breeches, Flora ran into Margaret in the hallway. "Where have you been?" the older sister inquired. "Did you get caught in that storm?" She took in Flora's appearance. "You weren't out riding in it, were you?"

"No," replied Flora. "I found shelter until it passed."

Margaret peered at her. "You look different," she said.

Flora felt herself blush. How could she tell? she wondered. What could be so glaringly obvious to Margaret that she herself hadn't seen in Fin's mirror? "Different how?" she asked quietly, afraid to hear the answer.

"It's as though..." Margaret thought. "As though you have a secret," she said at last. "You haven't had more news from Stephen, have you?"

Flora let out a breath she hadn't even been aware she'd been holding. "No. No further news," she lied. "Excuse me but I did get a little wet in the rain and I'm cold. I'm going to get Molly to run me a bath."

"Of course. Oh, my ladies are visiting this afternoon if you would care to join us?"

Flora smiled. "I'll think about it," she said on her way upstairs already.

*

The entire ground floor of the house had been decorated for Christmastide by the time Flora had bathed, dressed and come downstairs. Old Bill had picked the greenest, most fragrant evergreens, and the fattest pine cones he could find, and there were garlands of holly, mistletoe and ivy on every conceivable surface. The house smelled like a forest. As usual, Margaret had made a kissing bough, and it sat on the mantle in the sitting room exuding the aromas of rosemary, orange and spices.

"I don't know why you make one of these every year," said Flora walking over to the bough and sniffing at it. "Although it does always smell delicious."

"That is why I make one every year, dear sister," replied Margaret. "And this year, I had hoped it would have been put to good use with you and the Captain Reed."

Flora's heart lurched into her stomach. "Have you heard from him? Is he back from the Balearics?"

Margaret finished fussing with a table piece of apples, candles and ribbons. "No, I haven't heard from him. If anyone would have received any notice, I would think it would have been you."

Flora arranged her drawing things in front of her – she needed something to do while the other ladies gossiped and embroidered. "I haven't heard from him, either," she said.

"Well then, let's hope that means good news and that he isn't injured or has been captured. Help me turn this chair a little so it's facing more to the fire, please. I can't have Clara or Louisa freezing to death in our sitting room."

The ladies arrived together, by carriage, and Jenkins showed them to the sitting room. "It looks and smells beautiful in here, Margaret," said Louisa, giving up her coat to Jenkins. "Your Christmas decorations always look the best out of everyone's."

The ladies took their seats and Clara said, "you know, of course, that our dear Margaret almost wasn't here to celebrate Christmas this year."

Flora frowned over her parchment and Margaret raised an eyebrow. "Whatever do you mean?" asked Louisa her eyes wide.

With the kind of spiteful glee only Clara could possess, she said, "I mean, Margaret and her Father were stopped by a *highwayman* on the Dover to Deal road! Tell Louisa what happened, Margaret."

Flora remembered how the woman had taken great delight in hearing all about it when she and Margaret had visited the afternoon after it had happened. Now it seemed she was all but revelling in making Margaret relive the whole terrifying experience ostensibly for Louisa's benefit, but really for her own.

Margaret shifted uncomfortably in her seat and picked up her teacup. "We were travelling back from Dover when the driver suddenly brought the carriage to such a screeching halt that I thought I should be thrown out the door." Margaret shuddered, visibly. "The next thing we knew there was a masked man, at the carriage window, waving a pistol in our faces."

Louisa drew in an audible breath. "A pistol? How terrifying!"

"That's what I said: terrifying," put in Clara, eyes wide, sitting on the edge of her seat. "Tell us what happened next, Margaret, dear," she prompted.

"He had us leave the carriage and stand in the road. He ordered Father to empty his pockets and took his money and watch, then he pointed the pistol at me-"

"No!"

"Yes, and made me remove my jewellery. He couldn't wait for me to take the combs from my hair and grabbed them himself with his gloved hands."

"He should be found and hanged," Clara said, decisively.

"What if he had no choice?" put in Flora, noticing that Margaret had turned pale but continuing on anyway. "Perhaps, as no one has heard of it happening since, he did it because he was desperate. Perhaps he has fallen on hard times. It might be that he was forced to do that one single robbery to sell on what he stole." She thought of Fin, of his difficulty when she watched him at the boatyard. "Perhaps an accident or, or an injury befell him, and he can no longer do what he usually does. Maybe it was that or see his family starve."

"I cannot believe you are making excuses for him, when it was your poor, dear sister who he held up at gunpoint." Clara looked shocked.

"Not excuses," said Flora. "Reasons."

"Surely there are other ways to make a living besides robbing people who are just going about their business. And robbing a Lady, too. It's horrifying," said Louisa, reaching across and taking Margaret's hand in her own.

"I agree." Clara refilled her teacup. "No one should put a Lady through such a trauma and expect to get away with it." She looked pointedly at Flora. "For whatever "reason". No, he should be hanged. Beast. Now, I have brought with me the latest catalogue my cousin has sent me from Paris. Who would like to see?"

27

The lightning woke her even before the thunder crashed overhead. It illuminated her bedchamber better than any number of candles could, and rain coursed down her windows; fat, heavy drops battering so hard against it that Flora felt afraid the glass might break. Above her, on the roof, the wind whistled and screamed like a Banshee as it tore around the crenellations.

Flora pulled a blanket tight around her shoulders and padded over to the window. This was just exactly the type of weather that Fin and his men had been praying wouldn't happen. She gazed over at the woodland behind the house, near where the chapel was hidden. The trees were lit every few moments by flashes of lightning so long and bright that there was hardly time for one to fade before another took its place. She didn't think she had ever witnessed a storm so vicious in all her life.

She thought of Fin, Dobbin, William and Tad – due to meet on the beach to take in their shipment of contraband. Surely they hadn't ventured out in this – the beach front was open with no shelter, if they were there the four of them would be baring the full force of it all. And what of the two Frenchmen who were on their way across the channel to meet them? Fin had said theirs was only a small boat, surely it would have been tossed to Kingdom Come in this weather.

Fin had explained how the procedure worked when she'd first visited The Star and had met the gang. "Ours is but a small operation," he'd said. "But, we all 'ave our parts to play." He'd explained that the boat coming in was painted black with black sails to make it harder for the revenue men, or anyone else, to see it. "There's a spotsman on board who shows a light as the boat comes nearer to shore. On a calm, clear night, sometimes just the spark from a tinderbox is bright enough. Other times, we 'ave to use a lantern. Then I send a signal light back, and make sure the others are ready with the cart and ponies. Dobbin and Tad are the tub carriers," he'd continued. "They unload the boat and put everythin' on the cart. Meantime, William's our batsman. He stands guard wi' a good size lump o' wood to clout anyone who gets in the way."

"Oh my Heavens!" exclaimed Flora, looking at the huge man sat opposite her. "Have you had to "clout" anyone, William?"

William had given his customary small smile. "Not so far," he'd said.

Flora was thankful that Fin stayed shoreside, the whole operation had sounded terribly dangerous to her and she was glad he didn't have to navigate the waters in weather such as this.

The lightning continued to flash and the thunder crashed, cracked, rolled and rumbled with no let-up whatsoever. Flora pulled the blanket tighter to her. At least if he *was* out in the storm, she felt sure that Fin would be safe from the highwayman who would be nothing short of a madman if he was out in it just waiting for a coach to happen along.

Flora lit some candles, picked up her book and hopped back into bed. She knew sleep would not find her again tonight – it was too noisy and she was too worried about how Fin and the others were faring. Flora glanced at the clock on her mantle. She and Fin had made an arrangement to meet at one o'clock today. She opened her book to the last read page and sighed heavily. One o'clock could not come soon enough.

28

Fin had told her they weren't to meet at the chapel anymore – it was too cold and damp now the weather had turned, but it was the only safe place where she could transform from Flora to Francis so she packed a bag and walked Missy out into the woods.

Flora was disappointed to see that the storm had destroyed the building further. The trees, bare of their summer foliage, had allowed the gale unhindered access to the remaining walls and the clearing was littered with more flint and wood than usual. The open doorway still stood and Flora carefully made her way inside. Lacking more roof now, the chapel was lighted inside by the wintry sun. She couldn't help but notice the lack of contraband stacked against the strongest wall at the far side of the building. What did it mean? she wondered. That the shipment hadn't arrived or that Fin deemed the chapel completely unusable now? She very carefully made her way over to the far wall, treading on tiptoe over the wood and flint to retrieve her hat which was wedged under a piece of wood that, in turn, was propped up against the wall. It seemed she would need a new hiding place for this, too – the leather was damp from the rainwater that had seeped into the brickwork last night. She pulled her hair back into a tie and placed the hat on her head anyway, and rode Missy at a canter into Deal.

*

The inn was packed – she could tell even before she stepped a foot inside; the stable yard was almost full with just two empty stalls, and from behind the closed back door she could hear the loud buzz of conversation and laughter. Flora ensured her hat hid her eyes, opened the door and stepped inside.

The four of them were playing cards at their usual table, and she felt ridiculously pleased to see they had pulled another stool to the table. It was empty, waiting for her; for "Francis".

She had never felt a part of anything before now. At home she felt she was considered by her father as nothing more than someone he could marry off; a guarantee that, once wed, the family would continue down the line, his fortune held safe by the next generation, and by Margaret as someone to mother and admonish in equal parts. Here, though, among the common folk, those who spoke as they saw fit, without skirting an issue or mincing their words, she felt at home. The men hadn't yet noticed her, Flora leaned against the wall in what she thought was a manly fashion, and watched them.

William had his pipe in one hand, a hand of cards in the other and a pie in front of him, Dobbin and Fin were talking animatedly and Tad sat with Sukey on his lap, his cards in one hand, the other slowly moving up and down her back from collar to waist and back again.

Flora thought of yesterday, the tea with her sister, Louisa and Clara. She remembered the look of horror on their faces when she had dared speak up for the highwayman and his possible reasons for doing what he had done. She thought back to the talk afterwards of Paris fashion – the latest gowns and hats – and the gossip Clara had brought with her; had anyone seen Sarah Lilley in that dreadful new gown she had bought? The colour was garish and the cut did absolutely nothing for her. And has anyone else heard that Constance Bingham had dismissed one of her maids for stealing some household silver? Flora didn't give a hoot for any of that – she found all of them, even her sister, vapid, their conversation dull and superficial.

Now Dog noticed her and he nudged his way through the crowd, tail wagging, eyes smiling. Flora bent to give him a fuss and let him lead her to the table.

"Ah, here he is," said William. "Shall I deal you in, young Master Francis?"

"Oh, not this time, thank you," Flora smiled, seating herself at Francis's stool.

They were all pleased to see her – Tad said hello, Dobbin gave one of his impish grins and Fin, Fin's eyes lit up like fire beacons on seeing her. Sukey released herself from Tad and with a smile and a gentle squeeze on Flora's shoulder left to bring a tankard with wine in to her.

"What happened last night?" asked Flora. "Surely you didn't go down to the beach."

"We was just talking about it between hands," replied Fin. "It was too wild to go anywhere but we don't know what 'appened to Jacques and Guillaume – the weather would've been fine when they left France, we jus' hope they saw the storm coming and turned back afore it hit."

"I've just come from the chapel," said Flora. "The storm has damaged it further – more of the walls have fallen and there's hardly any roof left at all now."

"Can we still use it?" asked Dobbin, looking serious for once.

"You'll have to see it for yourself to make up your minds."

Dobbin said, "But what d'*ye* think?"

Flora was taken aback. She'd never been asked what she'd thought about something important up till now, her opinion on anything that mattered had never been sought before. She frowned. "I'd say… yes… you probably can… but you'll have to be careful where you stack things."

"That's good enough," put in William now, finishing off his pie, wiping his greasy hands on the belly of his shirt. He checked his pocket watch. "Cards is over," he said, pocketing the deck. "I need to get back to work."

Tad drained the dregs of his tankard and stood with William. "As do I."

Dobbin signalled Sukey for another pint. "I don't."

Fin and Flora got up, too. "Think on what I said, will ye?" Dobbin asked Fin.

A cloud of concern fell across Fin's eyes. "I'll be down later," he said. "But Francis and me 'ave got things to... discuss. C'mon Dog, upstairs."

*

Fin's bedchamber was as neat and tidy as it had been the last time she'd been in it. The bed was made again and there was fresh water in the jug by the wash bowl. She wondered who did for him or whether he did everything himself. She removed her hat and riding coat, and Fin hooked them on the back of the door. Dog wandered over to his blanket under the bed, made a nest, and laid down.

"I have a gift for you," Flora said, digging in her bag and taking out a parcel wrapped in muslin and tied with a festive green bow. She handed it over and Fin gave a frown. "What is it?"

"Open it... oh, carefully! It's probably already a little squashed." She pulled a face. "Sorry."

Fin laid the parcel on his desk and carefully undid the ribbon. The cloth fell open revealing a parcel of rout drop cakes. "Oh," he said, and she was pleased to see a massive smile on his face. "It's them little cake things!"

"I have more." Flora pulled a similarly wrapped package from her bag. "This is for the others – will you give it to them when I've gone?"

"Aye, of course-"

"And *please* make sure Dobbin doesn't eat them all himself!"

Fin laughed. "That I can't guarantee, m'lady." He pulled her to him and kissed her long and softly, his hands on her face. "Thank ye," he whispered. "Come. Sit wi' me, while we talk."

Flora let herself be led by him to the bed and they climbed onto the mattress.

"I missed ye." Fin took Flora's hand in his, running his calloused thumb over the back of it.

"You saw me yesterday," she laughed, untying her hair, using her fingers to comb it out, not realising how beautiful she looked in doing something so natural and simple.

"Aye. But between that time and now, I missed ye."

It was true, he was hooked on Flora like a salmon on a line. Time without her in it dragged. Nothing was as important to him as Flora – he couldn't concentrate on anything, their conversations would replay in his head and he'd see her as she was when they had spoken; dressed as Francis, dressed as Flora, undressed in his bed. He should have been worried about the storm upsetting the smuggling run last light – and it was true he was worried that something terrible had befallen Jacques and Guillaume – but he found he couldn't care less about having no contraband to sell. He should have been worried about his business failing because of the weather and his healing injuries – but he found he couldn't care less about that either. The rest of the world could go to Hell in a handcart – he wouldn't care so long as Flora was with him, and if they both went to Hell with it, well, that would be fine too, anything so long as Flora was by his side.

She leaned over to kiss him, and Fin lost himself in the way her lips felt on his, the way she tasted of the sweet wine she'd been drinking. He felt a stirring down below and moved his hands over her body, slowly untucking her chemise from her breeches. She did the same to him, unfastening his shirt, one button at a time, slowly, as if to make the very act of becoming naked last as long as possible.

She kissed his mouth and then his neck, and her breath was warm and sweet and in between kisses she said, "I've been thinking..."

He ran his hands up inside her chemise, feeling the soft skin of her body, cupping her small breasts in his hands,

"...about becoming with child."

She felt his hands slow and then stop in their roaming over her body, he pulled away and sat up straight, looking at her with wide eyes and his mouth a perfect O.

"Not about *becoming* with child," Flora corrected herself, laughing at the shock on his face, "but rather, how *not* to become with child."

"Oh." Fin relaxed once more and took her hands in his. "I'd love to have a babe wi' you… in fact, I'd love to have about four, but p'raps not right now. M'lady, I try to be as careful as I can," he said. "Though 'tis wi' a great amount of difficulty, I won't lie to ye. But there are other things we can do." Flora raised her eyebrows at him and he moved closer again, kissing the corner of her mouth, moving his lips to her neck, upwards to her ear. "Shall I show ye?" he whispered.

*

They were both laying on their sides, naked in the warmth of the fire in the grate, facing each other, silently enjoying each other's company. Flora was snuggled into a pillow, her hand tracing slow, lazy patterns across Fin's chest and belly and he was propped up on an elbow, his head resting on one hand, his other running slowly up and down Flora's thigh.

"There's somethin' I've bin thinkin' on," he said, lowering his eyes from hers, "an' I don't think yer goin' to like to talk of it."

"Oh?"

"Aye." He took a breath and looked her in the eye. "What will we do when yer Captain returns? What will become of us?"

At the very mention of him. Flora felt her eyes fill with tears and huge droplets balanced for a moment or two on her lower lashes, then spilled over onto her cheeks. It was a question she had tucked into the very far reaches of her mind along with all other thoughts of James, and she had quite successfully hidden those thoughts from herself over the past few weeks. Now Fin had brought them to the fore, and had asked the very question she had been dreading answering all this time.

Fin gently wiped at her tears with a thumb. "Don't cry, Flora. Please."

"I can't help it," she replied with a small sniff, lowering her eyes, distress apparent on her face.

Fin lifted her chin with a finger. "I love ye. Ye know it, aye?" Flora nodded. Her throat ached with yet more tears she was trying hard to keep in. "I loved ye from the moment I first saw ye, back in the chapel." He smiled, sadly. "I thought ye was an angel, did I ever tell ye that?" She shook her head, unable to speak. "I thought I was dying and ye was an angel come to take me to Heaven. And ye are. Ye have."

Now she couldn't stop the tears from falling and she let out a sob, pulling him to her, bunching his hair in her hand, kissing his mouth, his cheek, his chin. "I love you, too," she whispered. "I love you for your kindness, your gentleness and for loving me as I am."

"But the question remains," he said quietly, looking into her eyes, "What happens to us then?"

Flora took in a shuddering breath and sighed it out. "I don't know."

"This Captain, yer still set on marryin' him, then?" And even that was asked gently, softly, with no accusation, although she could tell he was in agony as the words left his mouth.

"I don't have a choice."

Fin nodded in understanding. Resignedly, he said, "Because of yer Da."

Flora looked at the man laying next to her. He'd once asked if she trusted him and she did – she would trust Fin with her life. "No," she replied. "Not because of my Father, but because of my brother."

*

"You're not... shocked?" she asked, after telling him about Stephen.

Fin lay back on his pillow. "Not 'shocked', surprised, maybe." He sat up again. "But if yer brother is happy wi' this other fellow... this 'S', then I think that's what counts. T'ain't a life I'd choose but 'tis love, and sometimes choices don't come into it. Look at us – you, a lady wi' a lady's upbringing an' me, a common man what's nothin' but a boatbuilder."

"And a smuggler," Flora added, smiling.

"Aye, that too. But, I don't understand… why does knowin' this about yer brother mean ye 'ave to wed the Captain?"

"When Stephen wrote to me telling me of 'S', I foolishly took his letter with me to the cliffs to read again." She faltered. "I was so happy for him, so pleased that he had found someone at last. James - the Captain - arrived out of the blue and I dropped the letter. He picked it up and kept it." She looked downcast and Fin knew she was going to say something horrible had come to pass. A shiver went through him. "He told me that if I don't marry him, then he will make sure everyone hears about Stephen and how 'S' is not some lady but rather, another man."

Fin's mouth turned into a hard line and his eyes flashed. "He's blackmailing ye," he said. "Now I know why ye call 'im a pig an' a brute although I could find more fittin' names - bastard, being one."

"There's nothing I can do," said Flora, simply. "If I don't marry him and he does tell people then my Father will lose his business – he might keep the tenant farmers but they too will hear of it and word will spread and his name will be blackened. No one will want to conduct business with him and Heaven knows where that would leave him." She took Fin's hand in hers. "So, you see, although I love you to the very moon and back, and I do, truly, I simply must marry James."

Fin laid back down again, his hand in hers, stroking his thumb over her wrist. She could hear the air catching in his throat as he breathed, could feel him shaking where he touched her, and wondered for a moment if he was crying. She couldn't bring herself to look.

Suddenly he dropped her hand and sat up again. He threw the covers off himself and stood up, walking stiffly to the window, the door, pacing the small room. His eyes flashed and his mouth was a straight line, all softness gone from it.

"Ye Gods, Flora. What will we do?" He looked over at her but there was nothing she could say, so she remained silent. "I'm so, so angry! He's a Captain, in the King's army! He's s'posed to be better than me, and the likes of me, but he ain't. He's a- I can't say the word in front of ye." He spun round again and resumed his pacing. "How can I let ye go off wi' 'im, knowing what he's like? How can I let him wed ye?" Flora dropped her eyes. "I'd kill 'im, but I ain't the murdering type."

"We still don't know for sure that he *will* be coming back," she said. "He might be killed or, or captured," In a small voice she continued, "It's what I'm hoping for above all else."

Fin marched back to the bed and sat down heavily. "Aye, and now I can see why y'said that before." He turned and looked at her. Her eyes were shiny with tears, and the skin around them puffy from crying. Her hair was a mess of curls laying over her shoulders. She had never looked more beautiful. He crawled back into bed beside her and took her in his arms.

"Maybe luck will be on our side," he said.

29

The skies were becoming overcast, threatening rain again, shortening the day even further than usual, and Flora had left on Missy hoping to get back home before it was properly twilight or the Heavens opened, whichever came first. They'd arranged to meet again tomorrow but at the cliffs near St Margarets Bay - if the weather was drizzling or less they planned on taking their horses for a gallop along the cliff path. Once she had left, as he had arranged, Fin went back from the stables to the inn and met with Dobbin, who was propping up the bar, as usual. Thomas poured his brother a beer and the two friends made their way over to their table.

"What's this ye were talkin' about earlier?" asked Fin, moving a stool and making a space for Dog down at his side. "Are ye gone completely mad?"

"Tis not a bad idea, Fin," said Dobbin. "Listen to what I 'ave to say an' think on it proper afore ye say nay."

Fin chewed the inside of his mouth and shook his head at his friend. "Highwaymen? Us? You've 'ad too much beer. Again."

"I always 'ave too much beer and that's the truth of it." He looked earnestly at his friend. "I'm out of money and I can't find any work-"

Fin opened his mouth, but Dobbin cut him off. "Now, wait, afore ye say anythin'. I *know* I drink too much but that's cos there's nothin' else fer me to do! If I worked I wouldn't 'ave time to drink. I've bin lookin' around – there's no farm work this time o' year, I've got no trade and no one'll take me on-"

"'cos of yer drinking-"

"-I know! Ye Gods, will ye jus' shut up and listen. I even

thought about going to sea, as a fisherman, y'know, but remember how it makes me sick? I'd spend more time pukin' than fishin'."

Fin nodded, that much was true.

"I'm all out o' money; livin' on what we make smuggling - but that's all gone now - and anythin' I make at cards."

Fin rolled his eyes. "You never make anythin' at cards, we always beat ye. Even Flora beat ye an' she'd never even played before!"

"Exactly. Anyway, I know you've been struggling too – the weather's not helped wi' your boatbuilding, and I know yer in pain from the sword and gunshot wounds ye got... anyone can see that by the way ye move these days since. I was countin' on that shipment las' night and now it ain't happened. This is a bad winter, with the rain and the gales, who's to say another run won't go awry."

"Tis always a chance we take, ye know that."

"Aye," Dobbin looked downcast. "But now I can't afford to."

Fin was about to take a mouthful of beer, then changed his mind. He studied Dobbin over the rim of his tankard with his eyes narrowed. "T'weren't ye what held up Flora's sister's coach a few weeks since, was it?" he asked.

"No!" said Dobbin, horrified. "But hearin' about it gave me the idea." He finished his beer, thought about ordering another, changed his mind. "It'd be easy money, Fin – I'll be the spotter, back in Dover or Deal, an' keep a look out for any coaches. I'd watch the gentlemen get in the coach, or carriage, so we'll only rob them what looks like they can afford it. Meantime, you'd wait on the road somewhere, hidden, like, and I'd ride back and tell ye which coach and we'd both 'old em up together."

Fin sighed. As a bare bones plan it was all right, he supposed.

"I don't like the idea of robbin' people jus' goin' about their day," Fin said. "Flora's sister was truly distressed after her and her Da got held up." He shook his head. "I don't like the idea of robbin' people at all, truth be told."

Dobbin choked back a laugh. "We're smugglers – we rob off

the government all the bloody time!"

"That's different. Show me a man in Deal, or Dover, or any-where around 'ere, what ain't a smuggler, or what don't buy smuggled goods. Highway robbery, though... if we get caught, we'll hang. It's a hanging offence, Dobbin. No two ways about it."

Dobbin motioned at Thomas for another pint after all, and one for Fin. "You'll 'ave to pay... unless yer Da's feelin' generous."

"Me Da's always generous when it comes to ye... when was the last time y'actually *bought* a pint here, Dobbin?"

"I can't tell ye. But if we do this, I'll pay 'im back every farthin'."

"Good, he'll have enough to buy me a decent burial plot then, for when we've bin 'anged."

"We won't hang." Dobbin sat forward on his stool. "Listen, we'll just do it when we need to, when we've got no money. If the weather's good, we'll still 'ave the smuggling to fall back on. Once spring is 'ere, you'll be boatbuilding more regular again, maybe your injuries'll be better..."

Fin thought. It did make sense, kind of. And it's not like any-one would be hurt – he certainly wasn't going to shoot anyone. The pistols would be for show only – if someone gave them any trouble, a shot into the woods might help them concur.

They had been friends for long enough that Dobbin could see Fin's mind working, and he warmed to his theme. "So, I was thinkin', we'll stop 'em on the Lynch and Gallows Bend-"

Fin put his head in his hands, muttered, "That's irony for ye."

"What d'ye mean?"

"Never mind. All right, so we hold 'em up on The Bend, then what?"

"Then we ride back through the Lynch Small Woods, and get back to Deal through Kingsdown way."

Fin was surprised, Dobbin really had been thinking this through. It still didn't sit right with him, but his friend was right – they were running out of money, perhaps they could just do this for a couple of months, maybe they might only have to do it once or twice depending on what they managed to steal, perhaps the spring would bring better weather and bring him better health.

"We'll need pistols," he said, "And I'm not robbin' any women – if there's ladies on the coach we let it go. And if Flora says nay, I'm not doing it anyway."

Dobbin couldn't hide his surprise. "Flora? Ye'll tell Flora about this?" He went on, only half-jokingly. "Yer henpecked, Phineas. Flora really does wear the breeches, don't she."

Fin shrugged. "I love her - we have no secrets between us. I'll tell her the plan and see what she says."

30

As planned, they met on the clifftop path, Fin on Diamond and Flora on Pudding. For a change, the day was beautiful with skies the colour of lapis, and fluffy white clouds gliding across the heavens. French farm fields could just be made out twenty or so miles in the distance and in the channel ships and boats were each making their way to or from the continent. Save for the seagulls swooping overhead, the clifftop was theirs alone and they drove their horses at a gallop towards St Margaret's Bay.

Flora was enjoying the ride – poor Pudding hadn't had a proper run in weeks, and she missed the size and power of him after riding little Missy for her incognito ventures into town just lately.

On the outskirts of the village they slowed to a walk, and Flora couldn't help but notice that Fin seemed distracted. Had she done something wrong, she wondered.

They walked the horses abreast of each other, Fin quiet and seemingly in a world of his own. He hadn't said much at all since they'd met today and he appeared distant and vague, chewing at his lip, with a constant frown on his face. Flora brought Pudding to a halt and Fin continued on without her, apparently not even noticing that she had stopped. She stayed where she was and watched him walk Diamond on ahead of her, a frown now furrowing her own brow. She had never seen him like this before and it was disconcerting to say the least.

In a world of his own, Fin walked his horse on, wondering how on earth he was ever going to broach the subject that he and Dobbin had spoken about yesterday. He'd hardly slept last night with thinking over Dobbin's plan and worrying about how Flora would react when he told her of it. She wouldn't be happy about it, he knew that for sure. Especially since her Father and sister had been subject to exactly what he was proposing to do. He chewed his lip, still plodding on at a walk, still frowning.

At last Flora trotted Pudding up to him. "What's the matter?" she asked. "Are you angry with me?"

Fin came to with a shake of his head and a smile that didn't quite reach his eyes. "No, never. I, I have something to put to ye but I know yer not goin' to like it." He reined Diamond to a halt. "Let's head back and we'll talk."

The last time he had said almost those exact same words was when they'd spoken of James. She hoped that Fin wasn't going to bring *that* particular subject up again; just the mere thought of *him* put Flora in a black mood and made her feel cross.

"All right. Or shall we sit awhile?" she said.

"The grass is wet."

"I don't care. Do you?"

"At least let me give ye me coat to sit on."

"I have my own. Thank you." She couldn't help but be curt when James came to mind. Flora tried pushing thoughts of her betrothed to the very back of her mind and tried to concentrate on Fin instead. She looked at him closely, felt her black mood lessen and concern for the man she loved take its place. Whatever was troubling him had brought clouds to his eyes. His usually smooth brow wore worry lines and it seemed he hadn't shaved this morning; blond stubble covered his jaw. She took his hand in both of hers. "Whatever is the matter?"

Fin sighed. "As I said, I've something to put to ye, and you're not going to like it."

Whatever could he be thinking of, wondered Flora. Perhaps it was true; he had given more thought to their liaisons, maybe he had decided that things between them needed to end before the two of them became ever more entangled in each other's lives, as if that were even possible. Even though she knew that time would surely have to come, just the thought of it brought with it a wave of light-headedness that made her glad she was sitting down, and caused her heart to plummet to the depths of her stomach. But Fin was talking, and she had missed the first part of what he had said, she had been so wrapped up in her own thoughts and fears.

"- difficult lately," he was saying. "I've bin down to the boat-yard again this morning... the one I'm workin' on - she's still not dried out. I covered 'er over the day after we got drenched, but the wood's still swollen and damp and I don't know when I'll be able to work on her again."

Flora felt herself relax. Boats. That was all. Not James, but boats. She understood why Fin was upset – he was talking of his livelihood after all, but... boats. She felt herself breathe once more. "Soon, surely," she said. "It will dry out soon enough, will it not?"

Fin shook his head, no. "And ye know the smugglin' run didn't happen, again because of the weather." He took a breath, sighed it out. "Times are gettin' 'ard for me, Flora. I need to find somethin' else to keep me goin', to bring the money in – at least until springtime."

Flora had no idea where this conversation was headed. Was he asking her for money? She didn't have much to her own name but what little she did have she would gladly and willingly give to Fin.

He scooched forward on the ground and turned to face her head on, moved his hand so it was he holding hers, tight. "Now, don't say nay right off, let me 'ave my say first but, Dobbin an' me's been talking. He's come up wi' a plan – a decent plan as it 'appens – we're thinkin' of holdin' up the coaches bet-"

"Highway robbery?!" Flora snatched her hand away, covering her mouth in shock."No! Fin, what if you're caught – you'll be hanged!"

Fin took her hand again, stroked the back of it with his thumb. He looked her in the eye, a small smile on his lips. Calmly he said, "We won't be caught. We'll organise ourselves well an' only do it when we 'ave no other choice – maybe twice, three times afore spring, the weather will be better by then."

Flora couldn't believe they were having this discussion. It had only been a matter of days since she'd had the similar conversation with Margaret and her friends, and what had she done then – spoken up for the man who had held up her family's carriage, even going so far as to argue his case, saying how perhaps he had been forced into the situation, maybe it was that or starve and now, here was Fin, telling her he was in the exact same position. Unless… "I could lend you some money, until-"

"No!" Fin looked aghast. "No, Flora. Ye Gods, I would never ask nor expect ye to do that for me. 'Tis my problem, mine an' Dobbin's, and 'tis us what needs to find a solution."

"And this is the only one you can think of? Highway robbery?"

"Aye. 'Tis."

Flora relented, just a little. "You will only do this when you absolutely have to?" she asked.

"Aye. Only then." He smiled. "'Tis a necessity not a vocation. And we'll not be robbin' any ladies, neither – if there's women on the coach, we'll let it travel on."

Flora felt her resolve slipping. What else could she do. Fin seemed to believe Dobbin's plan was fool proof although she suspected that only a fool might think it.

"If ye say no, Flora, I won't do it," Fin said, his hazel eyes boring into her green ones.

"But neither will you take money from me nor be able to survive until springtime."

"Aye, that's about the sum of it." Fin sat up on his knees, squeezed her hand. "I won't get caught, neither of us will."

"Promise me."

Ever the realist, Fin said, "I can't promise ye that. Things 'appen. But, I do promise, *on my life*, that we will be as careful as we can be."

Flora reached forward, cupped his face in her free hand, feeling the day's growth of stubble under her fingers. "You realise, of course, that that promise really *is* on your life." She kissed him, whispered, "So, please, I'm begging you my love, don't break it."

31

It was nighttime and he sat atop Diamond, hiding in the tree-line just back from the road, and watched as well as he could beyond the Lynch and Gallows Bend for Dobbin to ride back from Deal.

It had been many years since Fin had held a gun in his hand, let alone fired one. He and his brothers had been keen hunters when they were younger and had spent countless days in the local woodlands and fields hunting game or setting up targets. Being the youngest, it had usually fallen to Fin to find the things for his brothers to shoot – tree branches, one of his brother's hats, he remembered with a smile, bottles from the inn. Back then, they had used their Da's musket, a temperamental beast with a mind of its own and a tendency to fire to the left which needed compensating for when any one of them took aim. This though, Fin hefted the pistol in his hand, this was a thing of beauty. With a stock of cherry wood and plates of engraved silver, it was a beautiful piece of craftsmanship and when he'd tested it, it shot straight and true. He'd bought plenty of shot and gunpowder – there seemed little point in waving an empty pistol about; even if he didn't intend on shooting someone, at least he could shoot *something* and maybe change the mind of any recalcitrant gentlemen that he and Dobbin held up on the road.

This was an eerie enough place during daylight hours; set down in a dip with the permanent gallows at the side of the road, now, at night, he found it had two purposes; he would be alone out here; fearing the wrath of the ghosts of those who had been hanged previously, no one would lurk in the area unless they had to, and the occasional creak of the gallows frame set to remind him that, if caught, he'd be the one swinging from it soon enough.

The night was cold with a white moon in the sky and mist seeping around at ground level, cutting off Diamond's feet up to her knees. An infrequent breeze moved the leaves on the ground and caused the bare tree branches to move, making him see shadows of people where there were none. He guessed it was around half past ten by now. Dobbin should show at almost any minute. Fin holstered his pistol and huffed into his hands, rubbing them together to warm them and keep the blood flowing to his fingers. He had on a new leather cocked hat which was a perfect fit, and a long woollen overcoat, the latter keeping the cold from his body. At his throat he had ready a mask made of a black kerchief, knotted at the nape of his neck, ready to pull up over his nose and mouth to hide his face.

At last he heard horse hooves in the distance and moved Diamond further back into the treeline just in case, but it was Dobbin on Taffy and he could see their breath misting before them as his friend rode the piebald to meet him.

"Coach is comin'" said Dobbin, bringing Taffy to a halt. "Two gentlemen, dressed in their finest."

For the last time but certainly not the first, Fin asked, "Are ye sure about this?"

Dobbin pulled out his own pistol in answer, swung Taffy round and took up his place on the opposite side of the road. "I'm ready," he called, his voice muffled by the material covering his mouth.

A bare few minutes later Fin could hear the sound of hooves, and some moments after could see the team of four horses pulling the coach, the driver atop the vehicle, the lanterns on the coach casting a yellow glow like cat eyes in the distance. Fin covered his face, raised his arm above his head, looked over the road to where Dobbin was waiting. The coach was only fifty or so yards away now, and Fin could hear the sound of the horses snuffling and snorting, could see their breath misting, could hear the coach wheels grinding as they travelled over the road. He dropped his arm and he and Dobbin each moved from the tree line into the path of the coach. The coachman brought the four horses to a halt, calling out to them, trying to calm them before they became crazed, and fleetingly Fin could see the fear in the driver's own eyes.

Dobbin raised his pistol to cover any move the driver might make, and Fin rode round to the door of the coach. The two gentlemen inside looked scared half to death, each pushing themselves as far back in the coach as possible as though they could force themselves through the back wall of the carriage and disappear into the night.

Fin reached down and unhitched the carriage door. He levelled his pistol at the gentlemen inside. "Stand and deliver," he said, and cocked the pistol ready to fire. "Yer money or yer lives."

32

Flora reached into the very back of her clothing cabinet and pulled out her bag. Since Fin had decided the chapel was too damp and dangerous for her to visit, she had been hiding Francis's hat in her bedchamber. It was unlikely to be found, and if it was it would only be by Molly. No, by far the biggest danger was running into Margaret while carrying it and having to fence difficult questions – why was she carrying a bag? Whatever did she have in it? For a fleeting moment Flora though seriously about throwing it out of her window and picking it up on her way to the stables but, knowing her luck just lately, it would smack Old Bill or Cyrus on the head so instead she clutched it to her chest, crept from her bedchamber, down the stairs, across the hallway and out the front door. So far, so good. She had Willie saddle Missy for her and she left, heading at a trot towards Deal, to The Star.

*

She let herself in the back way as usual, her hair tied back, her hat on her head and pulled down over her eyes and made her way to the usual table. There was no one there yet, except herself. She supposed it was too early in the day for William or Tad to be taking a break and Dobbin, well, he probably was already on his way but stopping off at each inn and tavern between his home and here.

She sat at Francis's stool, her back to the room which by contrast was already busy with customers. A surreptitious glance at the bar showed her Fin's father and brother busy pouring pints and laughing with the patrons. She was pleased to see Sukey making her way towards her.

"Fin's not 'ere," said the barmaid with a smile. "Weather's nice, he'll likely be at the boatyard, I 'spect."

Flora felt herself blush. "Actually, Sukey, it was you I was hoping to see."

Sukey's smile fell from her face. "Sounds serious. Can I get ye a drink afore anythin'?"

"Wine would be lovely." Flora pulled some coins from the pocket of her breeches. "And whatever you drink," she said, handing them over.

"All right. Thank ye. I'll be back soon as I can."

Flora sat, facing the empty stools, staring at the bare wall behind William's seat, knotting and unknotting her fingers, fiddling with the buttons on her coat and finally biting at her fingernails.

She had been feeling strange these past few weeks. Not *ill*, that didn't describe it but, yes, *strange*. She'd have times of feeling queasy and times of feeling light-headed. Some days she had felt so bone tired that she'd occasionally found herself having to take a nap in the afternoon.

Sukey returned carrying two tankards of wine. She sat in Tad's place next to Flora and took her hand. She looked at her, her pretty grey eyes full of kindness. "How many monthly curses 'ave ye missed?" she asked softly.

Flora felt the colour rise in her cheeks again. "Is it that obvious?" she asked.

"Prob'ly only to me, truth be told."

Well, that was a relief, at least.

"Two, perhaps three. I, I don't know for sure... they're not always... regular."

"A bit of sponge soaked in vinegar, that's what ye should 'ave used. Stops things like this from happenin'"

"Really?"

"Aye. But 'tis too late for that now. Now there's nothin' for it but to let nature take it's course."

"Oh." Flora sipped at her wine. She had already known really, in her very heart of hearts. She'd just hoped that, seeing Sukey, giving voice to the worry in her mind would make the worry in its entirety go away.

"Ye'll be tellin' Fin soon?" Sukey sipped at her own wine. Flora only now noticed the girl was still holding her hand. "He'll know soon enough if ye don't," she said, giving that hand a squeeze.

"Yes. Yes, I'll tell him today."

"Why don't you go on up to his room? He'll be back later today for a beer and some pie, I wager. I'll send 'im up."

"I think I will. Thank you, Sukey." The barmaid squeezed her hand again and got up to leave. Flora felt eternally grateful to her for not saying 'It will be all right' or 'everything will work out' because it wasn't all right and everything wouldn't work out – this time she really was in a predicament with no way out. Flora took her wine with her and went up to Fin's room.

*

"Sukey said ye-" Fin stopped mid-sentence and halfway in the door. He came in and closed it quietly behind him. Flora was asleep on his bed, his copy of Gulliver's Travels laying open beside her, her hand a bookmark on the page she last read. He gently removed the book and put it on his desk, his eyes never leaving her for a second. She still had her hair tied back and was laying on her side, curled up like a kitten.

He'd watched her sleep many times before now and usually she had a smile playing on her lips but today there was no hint of a smile and even now there were worry lines wrinkling her brow. He didn't know whether to wake her or not. He removed his boots and laid down next to her, cursing the bed as it creaked under the weight of him.

She stirred, then woke immediately. "Fin?"

"Aye. 'Tis me."

"I was waiting for you. I'm sorry, I must have fallen asleep."

Fin smiled, moved a stray lock of hair off her face. "Aye, ye did that."

Flora fell silent. She had been thinking about how to tell him while pretending to herself that she was reading earlier. Then she had been thinking about it while she closed her eyes. She still hadn't come up with a way. How would he take the news, she wondered. She didn't for a second think he would leave her to carry the burden by herself – Fin was too loyal and loved her, of this she had no doubt.

"I didn't expect to find ye 'ere," he said. "Sukey said you'd bin. She sent ye up?"

"Yes, she did."

Fin looked at her closely, the worry lines were still etched on her brow, and her eyes were clouded with anxiety. She had something to tell him, he was sure of it, and it was not a good something neither, he bet. Perhaps the cursed Captain had returned. Fin felt his head spin and his extremities turn cold. He blinked away the dizziness. There was nothing he feared more than the day she brought him that news. He'd have to ask. He couldn't put it off a moment longer.

"Has the Captain come back?"

"What? No. Not so far as I've heard, anyway."

Fin let out a breath. "Well, m'lady, yer clearly upset about somethin'." He moved closer, holding her to him. "What is it?" he whispered. "What's troublin' ye?"

Flora lifted her head to face him, stroked her fingers over the planes of his cheek, his jaw, moving her thumb across his lips. "Just kiss me," she said, working her mouth into a smile but looking at him with the saddest eyes he'd ever seen. Fin kissed her gently.

"Will you love me?" she asked, freeing her hair from its tie, her hands then roaming over his arms, undoing his neck stock, unbuttoning his shirt.

They undressed each other slowly, between kisses, their hands exploring each other as though for the very first time. He caressed her body, smelling the rosewater on her skin, feeling the softness of her flesh, her small but perfect breasts, the nipples hard under his touch. He kissed every inch of her. The room was quiet - just the sounds of the patrons laughing and talking in the bar below seeped through the floorboards, and the noise of the ever-present seagulls shrieking outside. His hands continued their exploration and he was unaware of the secret she held inside her, there were no outward changes to her body yet. Flora let her hands play over his back, feeling the scars she'd sewn, raised, under her fingertips. She wanted one last perfect time with him before she gave him the news that would change everything, one way or another, forever.

He'd taught her well over the months they had been together and she'd been a keen and willing student – learning how to take pleasure as well as give it. She took him in her mouth, raising her eyes to watch him, not knowing who derived more from this act – he, as he spoke her name, and bit his lip and whispered Oh God or her, knowing she could give him this much pleasure. At last he couldn't bear it any longer and he pulled her away from him, manoeuvring her with gentle hands on her body until she was knelt astride him. Her hair smelled of citrus as it brushed across his face, over his chest. She leaned forward, kissing his mouth between saying his name, between telling him she loved him more than life itself. They moved together and when he almost couldn't take it any more he tried to move out from under her but Flora held fast, said no, and then he really couldn't hold on any longer. She felt his release judder inside her and just watching his face as he poured himself into her brought her to her own climax. Now it was she who threw back her head, bit her lip, her breath coming in uneven gasps.

Eventually, their heartbeats settled into a regular rhythm, they laid next to each other, Flora's head on his chest, their hands entwined.

Fin asked, "Why did ye do that? Why did ye let me…"

Flora took his hand and placed it on her belly. "Because it no longer matters." She moved her head to look at him and he was horrified to see how sad she looked. "We've been careful all these months but it has made little difference, Fin. I am carrying a child."

"A child?" Fin pulled back to better look at her. "Our child? Yer carrying our child?"

"Yes."

She watched, amused even in spite of herself, as Fin's face split in two with the widest, biggest, stupidest grin she had ever seen.

"I'm going to be a father?" he asked no one. Then, "I'm going to be a Da." He kissed Flora on the mouth, laid his head softly against the tiny mound of her belly. She had expected a reaction of course, but certainly not the one she was getting.

"When?" he asked, his hand next to his head on her stomach, as though talking to the babe and not to her. "How far along are ye, d'ye know?"

"Not for sure, but… I think it happened the very first time we… you know. It's still early days though."

"We'll be wed," said Fin, jumping up off the bed, beside himself with excitement. He pulled on his stockings and breeches, still grinning like the local village idiot. "I'll get us a little house, in the middle of town…" Flora watched him, waiting for his excitement to abate, for reality to hit him as she knew it surely would, before too long.

"'Tis always bin a daydream o' mine, since I first met ye…" he was saying now, "…you, me, four babes, in our own place." He pulled his shirt over his head, reached for his neck stock. "I'll 'ave to make more money…" He glanced out the window, at the day's blue sky. "…weather's clearin' lately; boat's almost finished… got another two on order." He hopped up and down on his right leg, pulling his left boot on. "There's a chance o' a shipment comin' in this week… need to get word to Jacques and Guillaume…" Dressed now, he at last took a breath, noticed Flora was still silent. And then the truth hit him like a punch to the stomach.

He sank down beside her where she was, bundled up in his blankets, the wind now knocked from his sails. He took her hand, his eyes now echoing the sadness in hers.

"T'aint goin' to 'appen like that, is it?" he said.

Flora sighed. "It's highly unlikely to, no. All of what you imagined would be a dream come true, but my father and sister will learn the truth of things soon enough and when they do, well, I'll be cosseted away or, worse still, sent away." She paused, playing the scene in her head. "Probably to my Aunt Elizabeth's in Surrey. When the baby comes, I shan't be allowed to keep it."

"But-"

"And even before then, when James returns, my father will have to let him know of the situation."

"D'ye think he'll still… want ye? I mean…" Fin trailed off, unsure how to word his hopes without making their dilemma sound sordid.

"I don't know." Flora shrugged. "Only having met the man three times, and on one of those occasions him blackmailing me, I do not think for a moment that he will just lay down, roll over and forget me." Flora raised a hand to her forehead, trying to massage the headache that was James away. "He's a dangerous man, Fin, and that is what I am most afraid of – he's cruel, vindictive and spiteful. I could tell that from the very first time I met him."

Fin chewed at his lip. "Ye think he'll tell yer Da about yer brother?"

"Yes. I do." Tears filled her eyes, but she wasn't sad now, she was angry. "And that absolutely cannot happen."

"I'm sorry, Flora." Fin took her hand. "If we'd never met-"

"No! Even after everything, I do not regret one single moment we've spent together. I love you, Fin Dawkins, and whatever happens always, always remember that." She sighed. "I just feel that nothing is in our hands – everything depends on what James does and we don't know if he's even coming back."

"The idea of murder is becoming ever more appealing," said Fin.

Flora looked at him, eyebrow raised.

"I woudn't o' course, I couldn't, I'm jus' sayin'"

"If you're 'just saying' then I couldn't agree more. For now though, there is nothing we can do. I just need to hide my…

condition," she placed her hand protectively on her belly, "for as long as possible."

"And I'll make as much money as I can in case he really don't come back." Fin took her hands and kissed each one, then kissed the place where their secret slept. "For now, let's jus' pray on that, aye?"

33

They had sent three thousand troops to the siege of the castle St. Philip on Menorca and barely three hundred had escaped death, disease, injury or capture. Captain James Reed was one of the lucky ones and he welcomed being back on British soil - not least to get away from the dust, the heat and the smell of death and disease that had permeated the garrison on the island. He had taken a day to recover from the arduous sea journey home and was now riding along the Dover to Deal road on his way to Oxney Court, thinking to surprise Flora by turning up unannounced.

He trotted his mount alongside the trees, the branches just beginning to get their new leaf buds, the pigeons cooing in the canopies and the seagulls wheeling and shrieking high above him.

When not engaged in any military work, his thoughts had been almost constantly on Flora during the time he had been away. James conjured her image in his mind for the millionth time; her pretty eyes, her lustrous hair, her beautiful full lips with their defined Cupid's bow. As he rode at a trot, he was vaguely aware of some riders through the trees on his right, but cast the noise of the horse hooves aside as he wondered how far along Flora had come with the preparations for the wedding, whether it was all but organised already and all they needed to do would be to set a date now that he was home. It was now springtime, he expected to be wed at least by the beginning of summer, preferably sooner than that. He hoped she had been kept busy doing all that needed to be done for such an event.

The riders drew level with him the other side of the trees and glancing over, James did a double take and brought his horse up short. One of the riders was unmistakeably his betrothed on her large black stallion, her hair loose and whipping about her head and shoulders, and the other… James's eyes widened in shock and amazement. The other, on a large chestnut mount, hair tied back and wearing a cocked hat was a man. Not a gentleman either, by the look of his dress. The two of them were riding together; he could tell by their easy demeanour. This, he decided, was no chance meeting.

James felt his hackles rise as he watched them together. He bunched his hands into fists around his horse's reins and gritted his teeth.

Part of him wanted to gallop over, to intervene, to find out just what the bloody buggering *hell* she was up to. The two of them seemed oblivious to anything else around them; they appeared to only have eyes for each other but, just in case his betrothed managed to pull her gaze away from the man, James unbuttoned and removed his coat, letting it drop to the ground at the side of the road. If he could see them well enough, there was every chance that, if either of them *did* look in his direction, they'd spot his red coat as easily as a robin in a snowy field. James decided to watch and learn, to stay hidden as best he could.

They knew each other well, that much was obvious; they rode comfortably side by side keeping perfect pace with each other, she in her damned breeches, the outline of her shapely legs visible beneath the buckskin – no wonder the bloody man was enthralled by her – and now they rode their horses shoulder to shoulder, each laughing at something one of them had said.

James was incensed. He gritted his teeth hard enough to make his jaw ache. But he'd wait rather than confront them, he decided. Yes, he'd follow them at a distance, keeping in among the trees – if they continued in the same direction they would be headed to Oxney and then on to Deal. If they carried on riding in the open fields he could keep alongside of them in the trees at the edge of the road at least as far as Ringwould, after that the trees thinned considerably; he'd have to stay back. His body shivered but he didn't notice – it was a cool day despite the bright sunshine, but his rage was serving to keep him warm enough.

He kept alongside of them, hidden in the woodland, as they continued towards Oxney Court. Near the gates to the house but out of sight of anyone inside, he noticed, they stopped. The man swung his horse around so he and Flora were aside but facing one another, then they leaned towards each other. The man placed his hand on Flora's face, tilting her chin towards him, Flora leaned forward, her hand on the man's leg for balance, and then they kissed. Passionately. James's clenched his jaw so hard his teeth ached, and his fingernails, although short, made crescent moons in his palms. He had never felt so furious.

James closed his eyes, his whole body shaking with anger.

It was no good, he couldn't stand it any longer. He kicked his horse forward, breaking through the trees, leaving branches and small boughs broken in his wake. Once clear of the woods, he charged at a gallop over to them.

They looked up in surprise, both wide-eyed and looking fearful, but neither had time to say anything as, at Flora's side, James reached forward and grabbed her by her hair, pulling her from her horse, leaving large clumps of her tresses still entangled in his fist. He left her where she was – dumped on the ground. The man began to protest; shouted something James didn't hear. He made to dismount but James unsheathed his sword and slashed at him with undisciplined strikes, his blade, sharpened only this morning, cutting him across the face, the neck the chest. He saw the wounds gush blood, the wound in his neck spraying blood with each pump of his heart. James watched as the man fell from his horse, heard him groan in pain, saw him collapse, his life blood leeching from him onto the damp green grass.

James opened his eyes and blinked heavily, shaking the images from his mind, and instead of carrying out what he had imagined he sat atop his horse, still shaking from head to toe, and silently seething as he watched the two of them say their goodbyes.

When they were done, Flora turned and trotted her stallion

up the driveway and the man rode on at a walk towards Deal. James sucked his teeth and narrowed his eyes. He'd let him get a way in front before following, keeping him in sight all the while.

Ahead of him, the man crossed from the open field, cut through the trees and onto the main dirt track road. James continued following the other side of the tree line, sometimes losing sight of him but when the trees thinned he would see him again in his workaday buckskin breeches, long woollen overcoat and leather hat.

They were almost out of Walmer and the road became busier with people going about their day. James kept his eyes trained on the man like a hawk on a mouse. Blanking out everything else around him, his sight was blinkered – the man he was following was the only thing that mattered.

At Deal castle the stranger took a left turn and headed to the town. James dismounted and followed him, leading his horse alongside him in between people, carriages and horses, roughly pushing past anyone in his way, never taking his eyes off the man for a moment. Eventually his quarry arrived at an inn called The Star, stabled his horse at the rear and disappeared inside.

James pursed his lips and sucked his teeth. What to do now? he wondered. The man might be in there hours. He looked down at himself. He couldn't go inside, half dressed, his sword at his side and no coat. Neither could he make any enquiries as to who the man was – dressed as he was, even without his coat, it was obvious he was a soldier and... he thought on his next move. No, he didn't want word to get back to the lowly bastard that someone was asking after him; he wanted to find out just who he was dealing with first.

He waited beside the stables, where men came to empty their bladders and the area smelled of human piss and horse shit. A half hour passed, and then an hour, and the man did not reappear. James could bear it no longer – the stench was overpowering, and he was beginning to miss his coat. He mounted his horse and left, heading to the main coast road. And then, just like that, he caught sight of the stranger again – at the beach no less, working on a boat, a mangy cur by his side. James rode slowly past, taking in the man's appearance.

James didn't know anything about boat making but the man looked to be skilled enough; the boat he was working on appeared almost finished and the man seemed to take pride in what he was doing – walking around the upturned craft, running his hands along the wood, using some tool or another to touch up parts that he deemed needed touching up. As for his appearance, he was young, several years younger than James himself, he thought. His hair was dark blond, tied back, curly at the ends. A gentleman he was not, but then he was dressed better than James would have supposed a shipwright would be – his clothes appeared neat and good quality. The Captain watched as the boat-builder pulled a silver watch from his breeches pocket, the sunlight reflecting off the surface for a moment. He was probably a smuggler, James decided. How else could a common or garden shipwright afford such decent clothes and a silver timepiece.

He'd seen all he needed to see, and much more besides. James mounted his horse and headed back the way he had come. So, he thought, not yet wed and Flora was already turning him into nothing so much as a cuckold.

He thought back to his time away, when he had been fighting hard, and starving hungry and the times in between the fighting, when he'd had news of yet another of his troops dying from scurvy, times when all he could think of was coming home to Flora. Times when alone in his quarters he would imagine her there beneath him as he enjoyed la veuve poignet, climaxing into his own hand but imagining himself inside her. It had only been thoughts of seeing and wedding Flora that had got him through his latest duty assignment.

James gritted his teeth once more and trotted his horse back the way he had come, to retrieve his coat, and head for home, all the while formulating a plan.

*

As soon as he was back at the barracks, the Captain called Corporal White and Private Parkin to his chambers. Both men stood to attention in front of the Captain's desk, silent with nerves, wondering whether they had done something wrong – the Captain's reputation as that of a cruel and hard taskmaster was well known throughout the garrison. They both remembered only too well an incident last year when six of their counterparts had each taken a one hundred lash flogging for being drunk in public. The Captain hadn't undertaken the punishment himself but had had each of the six guilty men flog one of his fellows while the rest of the garrison was made to look on and the Captain himself sipped a whisky and ate a sandwich from his place in the front row.

Confusing both men further, instead of reading them the riot act, Captain Reed poured both of them and himself a whisky.

"At ease, soldiers," he said, handing each of them a glass. "You have civilian clothes here?"

Neither men spoke, afraid of giving the wrong answer.

"Are you deaf? You both have civilian clothes here, yes?"

"Yes, Sir," they answered in unison.

"Well good. Then I have a private matter I wish to discuss with you. Come, drink up." Captain Reed smiled at them from across his desk. It was a smile of pure evil and did nothing to put the men at their ease.

*

They had split the shifts between them, twelve hours each, days and nights. Corporal White being the more senior of the two had chosen to operate during daytime hours leaving Private Parkin to the cold and boredom of the night shifts. Their task was simple, the Captain had told them, he wanted them to watch a particular man, a shipwright over in Deal, eight miles away. "I want to know everything about him," the Captain had said, "who he meets, where he goes, what he does. I want to know

173

what he eats for breakfast and when he takes a shit."

He'd described the shipwright to his men, had told them where to find him, which boat he was working on. Their first task was to find out his name. They were to report back daily. He had told them that he believed the man was running a smuggling ring but he needed evidence to support his suspicions. It was up to them to find it. Their duty was to begin immediately.

34

Private Parkin was cold and bored and didn't know which was worse. He had almost lost count of the nights he had stood at this same street corner where he could see both the front and rear entrances to The Star Inn, and so far he had had nothing of any worth to report to the Captain. Over the course of the nights he had kept watch people had come and gone, the stables were full and then all but empty, men had come outside to piss, others to puke, but Private Parkin had seen no sign of the boat-builder. At least they knew his name – Phineas Dawkins. Fin. Corporal White had found that out easily enough, under the guise of needing a boat, along with the fact he lived here, in his Father's inn. People the Corporal had spoken to had not a bad word to say about the man; he had a reputation as a skilled carpenter and a decent man, one that would happily give out coins to those less fortunate than himself. It all seemed a bit *odd* to Private Parkin, all this sneaking around, finding out everything they could about him. The Captain had said it was because he suspected the man of being a smuggler but the Private thought there was probably something more to it than that. However, he wasn't going to argue and would do what the Captain asked. No one in their right mind would want to get on the wrong side of him.

He stood at the corner, hidden in the shadows, blowing into his hands and stomping his feet on the dusty ground trying, and failing, to keep warm. He'd already seen off the advances of several whores during his surveillance and now the appeal of going off with the next one who offered their services was looking more and more attractive, if only to get out of the cold for a short time.

There were plenty of comings and goings at the inn, mainly through the front door, people leaving the premises and returning to their homes. Twice tonight he'd seen wives arrive grim-faced and tight-lipped as they entered the inn and leave moments later all but dragging their errant husbands behind them.

At the rear of the inn only one solitary individual had made use of the stables, then walked around to the front of the building and go inside, presumably to get lodgings for the night.

The clock on the church tower over the way told him it was a quarter to midnight. Private Parkin wondered how he would keep himself warm and awake for the next eight and some odd hours. He began to think of the barracks where at least there would be a fire in the grate. He could imagine standing in front of it, boots off, the flames warming him as he-

The rear door to the inn opened, letting out a shaft of yellow lamplight and the sound of laughter and chatter. Private Parkin straightened himself and moved back into the shadow of the neatest doorway.

A man appeared, walking from the rear door alongside the stables. The soldier squinted into the darkness. The man was dressed in a long overcoat and cocked hat. It was difficult to see if it was the person he'd been sent to watch, but then he noticed the man was carrying an unlit lantern and was turning from the stable-yard towards the road that lead to the beach. This was unusual behaviour. Private Parkin pushed himself away from the wall and began to follow him.

*

"There was four of them, Sir," informed the Private to Captain Reed. "The man you'd have us follow appeared to be in charge. Then there were three others – two tub carriers and a batsman."

Captain James Reed paced his room, taking in this information. He was cross – the Private had had the man in his grasp but had let him go. Why?

"As I said, Sir, there was four of them and only one of me." explained the soldier. "The batsman was built like a bell tower and would have killed me with one blow of the wood he was carrying. Also, Sir, I was in civilian clothes as you advised, and as such I had no weapon."

Captain Reed continued his pacing, barely keeping his temper in check. Of course, the soldier was correct – he could not have arrested Master Dawkins dressed as he was, and as for the batsman...

He pondered the problem. He now knew all he needed to about Flora's beau, he knew his name, where he lived, what he did for a living. None of that information served any real purpose except to satisfy his curiosity. What he really needed was for Master Dawkins to make another smuggling run where he could have his men intervene, catch him red handed, and have him arrested and flung into gaol for the rest of his natural life. No, he no longer needed daytime surveillance of the man, just uniformed soldiers keeping an eye on him for when he undertook his next smuggling run.

Captain Reed at last stopped pacing and turned to face the Private. "You and the Corporal will work together as of tonight," he told him. "You will both wear your uniform and the next time Master Dawkins and his crew bring in their smuggled haul, or undertake any other illicit works, you will arrest him." James stared off into the middle distance, thinking. "Do not worry about the rest of his crew, it is this man I want more than any of them." He looked at the Private, took in his dishevelled appearance after being awake for twelve hours and riding for a further four hours to Deal and back again to Dover. "Go," he said. "Bathe, sleep, do whatever you will but you and the Corporal need to be back at the inn at eight o'clock tonight, in uniform but out of sight. Do you understand?"

"Yes Sir."

"Good. Then you are dismissed."

35

Flora let herself into Fin's room where she found him sitting at his desk, reading a book and finishing off a sandwich. Dog ran over to greet her, tail wagging. She bent to give him a fuss then took off her hat and hung it on the back of the door and shook out her hair. "Fin, I'm frightened," she said.

"Why? What's 'appened?" he asked, immediately on the alert, choking down the last bite of bread.

"Nothing. That's the point. The longer we don't hear any news the more nervous I'm becoming."

"Come. Sit." Fin grabbed her carefully around the waist and pulled her onto his lap. "The longer we hear no news the better for us, surely?" he asked, wiping bacon grease from his hands and face onto a napkin "I've not seen any soldiers hereabouts – if there are any posted at Dover I generally see a few in town, come 'ere to try out the inns for a change o' scenery." Fin took a tress of her hair, played it through his fingers. "If somethin' did 'appen to 'im, would ye even get to hear about it?"

Flora chewed her lip. "My Father and his are old friends. They keep in touch still and, of course, he knows James is to marry me so, yes."

"Then per'aps the battle is still going on and he's still fightin'" He looked her in the eye. "If he was back already he would've made it known, aye?"

"I, I suppose."

"An' if he's bin killed or injured word would get to ye, aye?"

"Yes."

"So, he must still be there."

Flora wriggled off his lap and paced the small room. "But he could come back at any moment and then what will we do?"

Fin caught her hand and pulled her back to him. "We'll deal wi' that when, *if*, we need to. For now we'll jus' carry on as normal."

"That in itself is becoming ever more difficult. Look." Flora untucked her chemise, bunching it up towards her chest. "I have to wear Stephen's breeches on my hips. Unbuttoned."

Fin leaned forward and kissed the small swell of her tummy. "Aye, she's gettin' bigger by the day," he chuckled. "Our angel."

"You're convinced it's a girl."

"Not convinced – hopeful. I'm hoping she will grow in her Ma's image; be beautiful inside and out."

Flora smiled indulgently. "And if it's a boy?"

"I'm still hopeful of the same – that he's a handsome lad with a decent character." Fin pulled her back onto his lap, his hand on her burgeoning belly. "No one's noticed yet?"

"No. I've spent my entire life learning how to avoid my father so I'm not worried about him. I don't think he'd notice anyway – he's always too busy with his rent books to look up from the pages. And Margaret, she's used to my comings and goings. Often our paths don't cross for days at a time." Flora laid her hand over Fin's. "If I'm at home all day I wear a gown with the biggest shawl I can find to cover myself." She gave a small laugh. "I can't say that I am looking forward to hiding under a shawl in the heat of the summer."

"No, I don't envy ye or what yer goin' to have to go through. I love ye for it, though." He kissed her. "I've been busy at the boat-yard when the weather's decent. Almost finished another one so that money'll come in soon. Me and the others took in a large shipment o' tea recently and sent out a fair few bales o' wool." He smiled, feeling the babe beneath his hand moving around, turning somersaults. "The money is mounting up, Flora. If things work out fer us we should 'ave no worries on that score."

Flora tilted his face to her to look him in the eye. "And the highway robbery?" she asked.

"Aye. One more, I reckon. Not yet, in a few weeks maybe. One more an' then no more – it's too riskful. If Dobbin needs to do any more after that he'll be on his own; we've bin lucky so far, I don't want to see how far we can push that luck."

"Good. I hate you doing it." Under their hands, safe in its mother's belly, the baby gave out a tremendous kick. "See," said Flora, "even the babe agrees."

Fin grinned. "Well, I can't argue with the best two ladies in my life, now can I?" His grin faded and he looked serious. "As I say, Flora; one more and that's it."

36

Dobbin had excelled himself this time around with his spotting of four well fed, well dressed gentleman all travelling together from Deal to Dover. He'd stood around the corner from the coach station and watched all four leave the lawyer's office across the street and embark the coach, laughing and talking, with not a clue as to what would befall them four or so miles down the road.

The town hall clock read ten o'clock when the coach pulled away and Dobbin made his way to The Star nearby and mounted Taffy ready to leave, his kerchief knotted at his neck, his pistol holstered at his side. He drove the piebald at a trot through the town, brought him to a canter as he made his approach to Walmer and overtook the coach at a gallop.

This would be the third coach he and Fin had held up and the previous two robberies had gone off without a hitch. Dobbin couldn't believe what easy money holding up coaches made and regretfully wished he'd thought to do it sooner.

They'd had good hauls from the first two coaches – gold watches, coins and a couple of rings – and he'd taken a day to ride into Sandwich where he knew no one and no one knew him, to visit the pawnbroker there.

He headed to the Lynch and Gallows Bend where Fin would already be waiting for him, the night cool and breezy with clouds scudding across the dark expanse, a few stars showing in the night sky and a small silver crescent moon giving just enough light by which to see.

*

Corporal White and Private Parkin followed at a good distance behind Fin on their mounts which had been stabled at The Hope and Anchor acrossways from The Star.

When they had first seen the shipwright leave his home via the stables, they could hardly believe it; night after long night, for weeks, they had stood in almost the exact same spot just waiting for him to make a move, but every day morning time had come around with no sight of him and therefore nothing to report to Captain Reed.

They could tell the Captain was beginning to get upset and disappointed with their lack of anything to report and wondered how long he would keep them spying on the shipwright when absolutely nothing seemed to be happening. Then, tonight, they had watched Master Dawkins leave the stables on his chestnut mare and head, not to the beach front where they had expected him to go, but instead towards the main street, on his way towards Walmer in the direction of Dover.

"Where is he off to?" whispered Private Parkin, a frown on his face. "This isn't the way to the beach."

Corporal White shrugged. "Perhaps he's taking in goods further up the coast."

They followed as far back as they could without losing sight of him, the both of them even more confused as Fin continued along the main road, past Deal castle, through Walmer and down the hill towards Oxney. Here the two soldiers rode on the grassy verge between the road and the treeline hoping to deaden any sound their horse's hooves might make. Master Dawkins never once looked behind him.

Up ahead, the shipwright stopped his horse at the Lynch and Gallows Bend and the soldiers rode their mounts into the woodland behind him, watching in between the tree trunks, trying to keep their horses still and silent.

"I'm going to get a closer look," whispered Corporal White, sliding quietly from his horse, handing the reins to his colleague. "Stay here."

The Corporal crept nearer, cursing the leaves and twigs crunching and cracking beneath his feet.

At The Bend, on the side of the road, Fin felt goosebumps creep over his body. He frowned and looked around him. He could have sworn he'd heard something in the trees behind where he was. Next to him the permanent gallows creaked in the breeze, moonlight shone between clouds that sped along in the sky and made the gallows' shadow grow and fade on the road, but all he could see behind him was trees and all he could hear was the sound of nocturnal animals scurrying around. Perhaps badgers. Then he heard a different noise, as did Diamond. The horse dropped her head and gave out a snort, fidgeting her feet where she stood. "Pay it no mind," whispered Fin, petting her neck, "'tis just the foxes, calling to one another." He checked the time – ten minutes past ten. Dobbin should show soon, he should certainly hear him approaching any time now.

Corporal White crept closer, one careful footstep at a time, his hands on the nearest tree for balance. Whatever Master Dawkins was up to this late at night in the middle of nowhere, it was unlikely to be legal. If they could catch him at it tonight then his and Private Parkin's nights of doing nothing but watching would come to an end and the Captain would be well pleased with them.

Corporal White pulled his spyglass from his pocket and extended it. He didn't think he'd be able to see much with the moonlight coming and going between the clouds but it was worth a try. He aimed the spyglass in Fin's direction, could just make out the shape of him and his horse. Clouds moved away from the moon and in that moment he saw Master Dawkins remove a pistol from its holster at his side. The Corporal lowered his spyglass. He made his way back to his colleague, creeping like a ghost in the night.

"He's got a pistol," he reported to Private Parkin. The Corporal smiled in the darkness. "This is what we've been waiting for," he whispered. "He's going to hold up the Dover bound coach. Fin Dawkins is-"

"Shhh," whispered Private Parkin. "Someone is coming!"

Both soldiers listened. In the distance they could hear horse hooves at a gallop coming towards them on the dirt road.

Corporal White mounted his horse and both soldiers moved as close as they dared to the roadside. In the moonlight they could just make out another single rider heading towards them. When he reached Fin he stopped. The two men were too far away for the soldiers to hear their conversation but they saw the second rider hold up four fingers and nod his head. The soldiers watched as both men took up their positions; one either side of the road. Corporal White checked his watch. It was ten twenty-five. The two highwaymen covered their faces with their kerchiefs and took their pistols in their hands.

They could hear the coach making tracks in the dirt road, could hear the wheels grinding as it made its way nearer to them. Corporal White and Private Parkin moved as near to the roadside as they dared. The coach was almost upon them. They watched as the two highwaymen drove their horses into the middle of the road, directly in the path of the coach. The coachman pulled the four horses up short, one highwayman trained his pistol on the driver, the other, Master Dawkins, made his way to the door and unlatched it. He motioned with the pistol for the occupants to leave the carriage.

"Stand and deliver. Yer money or yer lives."

Both soldiers broke through the trees at a trot. "Hold fast!" shouted Corporal White. "Get back in the coach, gentleman."

The two gentlemen who had made it down from the carriage turned tail and shakily climbed the step to get back inside.

Fin and Dobbin looked at each other, both with eyes wide, both silently asking each other if they should make a run for it, but then the Corporal said, "Phineas Dawkins, I am arresting you for highway robbery."

37

Deal town gaol was every bit as gruesome as they had thought it would be; it was cold, damp, unlit and smelled of piss, human excrement, sweat and other people's desperation. There were three bare walls, one with a tiny, barred window so high that it gave only a view of the cloudy night sky. The floor was also bare, the bars making up the fourth wall thick metal, the key to the lock on the door huge and heavy and carried about the person of the gaoler who sat at a desk in a lantern lit room beyond their cell.

Their pistols had been taken from them on the road and they had been led back to town behind Taffy and Diamond on foot, tied at the wrists with rope and fastened one each to the soldiers who had arrested them. Both had been glad it was nighttime and there were few people around to witness their humiliation.

Anything of any worth had been taken from them before they were thrown in the cell; their boots and hats, coins, Fin's silver timepiece and - what made his heart break the most – the length of black velvet ribbon that Flora had given to him and which he always carried with him in a pocket.

They had shackles around their ankles allowing each one to reach as far as the bars imprisoning them but no further, and neither friend had much to say to the other; the shock at finding themselves in this predicament having stolen all words.

Fin felt tears pricking at his eyes. All he could think about was Flora and the babe – what would become of them now? How would Flora know what had happened, where he was, why he didn't meet her today as they had arranged, at The Star at one o'clock?

Dobbin sat dejected in a corner of the cell. Fin watched him close his eyes and shake his head every so often. Whether this was because he thought he was dreaming a nightmare and a shake of the head would wake him from it, or whether he was just feeling, like himself, disbelief at what had befallen them, he couldn't say.

With little hope in his heart. Fin examined the thick metal cuff around his ankle for the umpteenth time. He moved his fingers along the length of cold iron chain hoping to discover a weak link. And if he did find one, he reminded himself, there was then the cell door to contend with, and then the guard. Fin dropped the chain. As he had foreseen; it was hopeless.

He got to his feet anyway, used all his strength to pull at the chain, hoping to dislodge it from its mooring in the wall. He raised a foot as high as he could, placing it on the wall, trying to give extra purchase to his pulls on the chain but it was to no avail. Angry and disappointed beyond words, Fin let out a yell of frustration that echoed around the cell.

"We could both try," said Dobbin, helpfully. "Maybe the both of us could loosen it together."

"No. It won't move. Many afore us has tried, I'm sure."

"I'm sorry, Fin," said Dobbin. "If I hadn't-"

"But ye did. And I agreed wi' ye." Fin moved as close to Dobbin as he could but there was still feet between them. "I knew the risk, knew this could 'appen." He brushed tears of anger away from his face with the heels of his hands. "Flora's wi' child." he said.

"What?"

"Aye, several months gone. It won't be many weeks now afore the babe comes."

"Fin, I-"

"That's why I don't think this was down to chance, them soldiers catching us,"

Dobbin moved as near to his friend as he could. "What d'ye mean?"

"There's this Captain; James Reed..." He went on to explain

about Flora and the Captain, telling him how she had been betrothed to the man after having only met him twice, how the Captain had then further blackmailed Flora into agreeing to marry him but not telling Dobbin how; he had given his word to Flora that he would never mention Stephen and he would take that secret to the gallows with him.

Fin held a hand over his wrist. He had rope burns from being led to the gaol last night and, although they were the least of his worries, they were still paining him nevertheless.

"I reckon the Captain has been back for some time," Fin said, switching hands, trying to cool the burning on his other wrist. "I think he must 'ave found out, somehow, about me an' Flora and has set his spies to catch me out. So, it should be me apologisin' to ye for getting us into this quandary, not the other way around." He looked his lifelong friend in the eye. "I'm sorry."

Dobbin shrugged, smiled his impish grin that this time didn't reach his eyes. "What will ye do? What will Flora do?" he asked.

Fin slid down to the bare brick floor, his back against the damp wall, his chains rattling as he moved. "I think the question is more what will the Captain do." He pulled his knees up to his chest, rested his chin on them. "What is he plannin' now?"

38

Fin didn't sleep; he spent the night worrying about Flora, thinking over how he could make things any better for her, wondering how the Captain had found out about them. The thoughts went round and around in his head, and he couldn't find any answers anywhere. He and Dobbin knew it was morning when the sky lightened from black to blue though the tiny window above them and the gaoler opened the door and threw in a bucket for them to relieve themselves in. That done, he took it away again and instead handed them a bowl each of gruel and a tankard each of water.

At sometime during the morning, the gaoler announced that Fin had a visitor. For a fleeting moment he hoped it was Flora, then hoped that it wasn't; he didn't want her to see him like this.

At the visitor's request the gaoler brought in a chair and placed it in front of the bars to their cell. Fin and Dobbin looked at each other and frowned. Then they heard the footsteps of heavy boots, saw the bright red coat with the gold brocade, saw the shiny steel sword of the Captain. He silently took a seat on the chair, took out a hip flask from his pocket, unscrewed the cap, lifted it to his mouth and took a swallow.

"They must be... uncomfortable," he said, indicating the shackles with the hand holding the flask. "Cold, I should think. And heavy."

Neither man said anything.

The Captain cleared his throat, gave a twisted smile. "Phineas Dawkins. Fin. I believe we have something, or should I say some-one, in common."

Again, neither man replied.

"Of course," the Captain continued, "Just in case you are confused, I am speaking of the beautiful Mistress Flora Harrington."

Fin found the air catching in his throat just hearing the Captain speak her name.

The soldier smiled. "Spirited, isn't she, with her breeches, big horse and secret liaisons? Still," he went on, taking another swallow from his flask, "being in the King's Army, I am used to breaking men's spirits, trampling them down, taking prisoners... a little girl like Flora will present me with next to no challenge. I will see her kowtow to me before year's end. She certainly won't be wearing damned breeches and riding astride her horse throughout the countryside meeting up with *shipwrights* - she'll be at home, in Windsor, entertaining her lady friends and playing the pianoforte." He stared at Fin, his head on one side. "Did you know she plays the pianoforte?" he asked. "She does, very well, in fact."

Fin felt rage flow through him. He felt hot, then cold, his hands shook. He stared silently at the Captain.

"Do you love her?" asked the Captain now, a simpering grin on his face. "Did you think she was 'the one for you' highwayman?" He chuckled.

Still Fin stayed silent, his breathing shallow, his jaw set, his eyes never leaving the face of his tormentor.

The Captain changed his position, leaning forward towards the bars, lowering his voice he asked, "Have you... fucked her?"

Dobbin sprang to his feet dragging his chain behind him as he stepped towards the bars. "Is she any good? Which does she prefer; to do it flat on her back or from behind, like a bullock takes a cow?"

Dobbin grabbed the bars with both hands, a murderous look on his face. "You bastard!" he growled. "You cunt!"

Fin looked at his friend, shook his head, no. The Captain was after a reaction; he wouldn't give him the satisfaction of getting one, no matter what vile, disgusting thing he said.

The Captain smirked. "I'd been looking forward to breaking her in but no matter – we'll have years to swive and you, well...

sadly, you won't."

He sat back in his chair, took another swallow of whatever he was drinking. "I'm on my way to see the lovely Flora now," he said. "To give her the news that my men, after spying on you for *weeks*, Master Dawkins, have at last caught the highwaymen that have been plaguing the local area. How do you think she'll react? Will she cry, do you think?" The Captain smirked. "I do. I think she will cry, and when she does, I will wipe her tears away."

Fin remained silent. His breath was coming in shallow bursts. Despite the rage coursing through him, he just stared impassively at his visitor.

Flora had been right about the Captain; he was a pig and a brute.

She will hate her life with him, he thought. She will feel as though *she* is in a prison cell. She will spend the rest of her life being miserable. Just the thought of Flora not being allowed to be herself made Fin's own eyes well with tears, but the gaol was gloomy and the Captain couldn't see.

"Your friend here has shown some concern but *you've* not said anything." The Captain got to his feet. "Why? Do you not *care*, Master Dawkins?" All at once he hefted the chair by one hand. "SAY SOMETHING!" he yelled, and smashed the chair against the bars of the cell. It landed, broken, on the floor. Fin and Dobbin just looked at him, both sets of eyes filled with hate.

The Captain muttered something under his breath, most of what he said inaudible. But Fin and Dobbin both caught the name Flora in amongst his murmuring and both felt their hearts lurch. The Captain turned tail and strode from the building.

"Fin…?" began Dobbin once the Captain had left.

"I know," replied Fin. "Ye Gods. Fuck. I KNOW!" He yanked on his chains for all he was worth, throwing himself against the bars of the cell until he had no feeling left in the that side of his body. He shouted and yelled and raged until he had no rage left in him and his voice was hoarse. Then he slunk to the floor, defeated.

39

Flora was dressing in her usual attire for an afternoon spent with Fin; breeches and a jacket. The breeches were getting ever tighter around her. "Soon I'm going to have to give these up, our angel," she said to the babe, "and stick to gowns." At least with a gown she could loosen the corset to accommodate the growing baby. "I'm glad you're almost on your way," she continued. Being with child was a very uncomfortable business and the weather was warming up, which didn't help matters. The child was a lively one; kicking and punching until her ribs hurt, as though she was as desperate to get out as Flora was to have her get out.

And yet, still neither her father or Margaret had noticed.

Margaret had been busy these past few weeks creating guest lists for the wedding and arranging seating plans. She had tried to get Flora to sit down with her on occasion to help but Flora had been true to her word and had flatly refused to have anything to do with it. She had also, for obvious reasons, refused to agree to any dress fittings – the most she had done was to agree to a dress pattern that Margaret had found in one of Clara's catalogues, and state that she wanted the dress to be silver or grey silk, with mother of pearl buttons and decorations.

"I'm not doing anything for definite until I know for sure that the wedding is going to go ahead, that James has returned from the Balearics," she had said.

She pulled a long jacket around herself and checked her reflection in the mirror. She was lucky, she felt, that although the baby was lively she appeared to be small – although her breeches were unbuttoned and resting on her hips, she could still close the jacket over herself.

In the distance she heard horse hooves trotting up the drive and several minutes later a knock on the front door. Shortly after, Margaret walked into her room looking both excited and nervous, her colour high, her hands tying themselves in knots.

"Flora," said her sister, "you'll never guess – your Captain has returned! He is downstairs!"

Flora felt her knees weaken and almost buckle beneath her. She took some staggering steps to her dressing table seat and sat down heavily. A thousand thoughts flew through her mind – he was back; what would happen now? How would she break the news to Fin? What would become of the babe? Was there any way, any way at all, that she could get out of this?

"Are you all right?" asked Margaret. "You look quite pale. I know this must be a shock – Captain Reed appearing after such a time away."

Flora took a steadying breath. "I, I am fine – as you say; it's a shock."

"Change into a gown, Flora. Come downstairs. Here, I will help."

"No! No, it's all right, really. I will manage by myself. Please, go and... entertain him while he waits for me. I'll only be a moment."

Once Margaret had left the room Flora got undressed again and instead put on a green sleeveless gown with a shawl pulled over her shoulders and in front of her.

She couldn't believe he was back. She and Fin had hoped and prayed that this would not happen. Now it had. In a small act of defiance, remembering what James had said the last time she had seen him, Flora pulled her hair into a knot and secured it with her mother of pearl combs.

Shock and disbelief coursed through her veins, making her legs weak, causing her to almost stumble on the stairs. She gripped the banister harder as she descended to the hallway. Jenkins showed her into the sitting room where her father and Margaret were already seated and James stood, his back to the fireplace.

He didn't look any different – he still appraised her with his cold pale eyes as she entered the room and walked on stiff legs to the chaise. But wait, she thought, there *was* something different about him; a glint in his eye, a slight lift to the corner of his mouth turning his smile into a sneer.

"Mistress Flora," he said, stepping away from the fire and taking her hand as she sat. Did she imagine it, or had he squeezed her hand a little more possessively this time?

"I was just telling your father and sister how my men have been busy since our return. Last night, would you believe it, they caught two highwaymen!"

Flora's heart skipped a beat, her eyes widened in shock, her fingers gripped the shawl bunched in her lap. Not Fin, she thought. Please, no. Not Fin.

"Really?" she asked, surprising herself with getting a word out and it sounding steady to her ears.

"Yes, indeed. On the Deal to Dover road. They were about to rob the coach, can you believe it?" He studied her like a child would study a bug under a magnifying glass. Flora felt the colour drain from her face. Fin had been caught. She felt her head spin. Fin would be hanged.

It was then that Flora felt her heart break.

"One is nothing more than a drunkard," James was saying. "The other gainfully employed as a shipwright." James looked to Lord Arthur. "It makes you wonder, does it not, why someone so employed would risk their neck to rob a coach." James shrugged and turned his gaze back to Flora. He smiled his twisted, thin-lipped smile. "I believe you might know him?" he asked, looking even more intently at Flora.

Margaret frowned. "Flora? Know a shipwright? I think you must be mistaken."

James turned to Margaret. "Oh, no, my Lady. There is no mistake. Mistress Flora knows him well, this shipwright-cum-highwayman. His name is Master Phineas Dawkins. You do know him, isn't that right, Mistress Flora?"

Flora took in a shuddering breath, tears brimming on her lashes. "I- Yes, I know him."

"Flora?" Margaret looked both mystified and outraged.

"I've seen them together myself, riding out along the clifftop path," put in James, looking at Flora. "I must say, for a common man he appeared quite the gentleman – accompanying you to the gates of your driveway."

If he'd seen Fin do that, thought Flora, then he would have also seen them kissing; Fin never left her without kissing her goodbye.

Her father looked at her, properly looked at her for probably the first time she could remember. "Is this true, daughter?" he asked. "Have you jeopardised everything for a, a *friendship* with this... man?"

"Oh, Lord Arthur," said James, "Do not worry yourself, Sir; This hasn't changed anything on my part. I still wish for your daughter's hand in marriage."

He does? thought Flora. Why? When he knows, when it's obvious that I care more for another man than I can ever care for him...

"I firmly believe in second chances," James continued solemnly, his hand covering his heart and a steely look in his eye, "I'm sure Flora and the shipwright were nothing more than, ahem, good friends, despite their difference in class." He dropped his hand from his chest. "So, where are you with the wedding preparations, my dear? And, tell me, will your brother be coming?"

Flora blinked in confusion, dislodging her tears, feeling them run down over her cheeks. What was he playing at? What evil plan did he have in store for her now? she wondered. Why mention Stephen, if only to keep her in check.

"Margaret has been busy," she said in a voice not her own. "I believe most of the planning has been done – we were just waiting for you to come back before everything is finalised."

James smiled. "That is good news indeed. The sooner the better, I think.

"Now, Lord Arthur, perhaps we could repair to your study to discuss things further. Oh, and I hear your tenant farmers have done particularly well this year, alongside your shares in the coal mines."

So that was it, thought Flora, for a price her dalliance with Fin would go no further. Now James was blackmailing her father, too. Was there no end to the lengths this man would go?

40

From her seat across the room, Margaret threw her a look of such bitter disappointment and hurt that Flora felt her heart break again and felt a pain like none she had ever felt before rip through her insides. She didn't know what to say so she remained silent, clutching her shawl to her belly, thinking all the while of Fin, how she had to go and see him, had to make sure he was all right – as all right as he could be, under the circumstances. Of course, she had never visited a gaol before, wasn't even sure where in Deal it was. Would Fin be treated fairly there? Did prisoners get fed and-

"I am outraged!" said Margaret at last, steadfastly not looking at her younger sister, her hand hovering over her brow. "How *could* you?"

Flora swallowed hard. "I, I couldn't help it. It wasn't planned, none of this was planned. I just, I just fell in love with him."

Margaret snorted with derision; disbelief still etched into her features.

Flora stood and moved swiftly to the seat next to her sister. "You said before how I can't live life as though in an adventure book, do you remember?" Margaret shook her head. "Well, you did. And for the past year almost, I have been and it's been... wonderful." At last Margaret turned to look at her. Flora took her sister's hand in hers. "Please, listen to me, Fin is-"

"Fin?"

"Yes, the shipwright. Phineas. He's the most sweetest, kindest, loyal man you could ever wish to meet-"

"He has just been arrested for highway robbery. Those traits do not, in my mind, go hand in hand, Flora."

"There's a reason for that. He was doing it for us."

"He was robbing coaches? For you?"

"Yes. Listen, Margaret." Flora winced. The pain in her stomach was becoming worse, coupled now with a dull ache in her lower back. "I know you've had a shock, as have I, but, well, prepare yourself for another one." With this, Flora undid her shawl, placed her sister's hand on her belly.

Margaret snatched her hand away as though scalded. "No," she whispered, at last looking Flora in the eye. "No. Not this as well."

"Yes. And you saying no won't make it go away. Believe me, at the beginning I tried that, too." Flora took her sister's hand again. It felt limp in her fingers.

Margaret looked straight ahead, her mouth a thin line. "I shall write to Elizabeth directly, see if she will have you."

"No, Margaret, I will not be going to Surrey."

"Then you shall stay here, in the house, at all times. Imagine if word got out, if one of the servants spoke out of turn, perhaps." She nodded to herself, a frown now shadowing her face. "Yes, that is what we will do. You shall stay here. I will lock you in your room if necessary."

Despite the situation, Flora gave a small smile. "Margaret," she said, "you can't lock me in my room; I know of at least half a dozen ways to escape – ways I used as a child – and I'll use them again now." She held her bump protectively. "Or kill us both trying." She shifted in her seat. "No, Margaret, *this* is what is going to happen; I am going to Deal to have the child. I have friends – dear, sweet friends – who will help us both when the time comes. But," she gripped her sister's hand, "I do need your help; I need you to wait until you have word that the child is born and then set a date for as soon as possible afterwards for the wedding."

Shock once more covered Margaret's face. "You will still marry the Captain? After having another man's child?"

Flora thought of Stephen, of his secret, of his newfound love in the New World thousands of miles away. "I have to. For a reason I cannot tell you or anyone else."

"More secrets," Margaret said quietly.

"Yes. I am truly sorry but, please, will you help me?"

"He will know. That you've had a child, I mean. The Captain will know."

"Yes, but it will be too late by then."

Margaret stood, wavering slightly on wobbly legs. "I need to lay down. I have a headache and cannot think straight."

"But, will you help us? Will you help *me*?"

Margaret paused on her way out of the room, her hand on the doorknob. She didn't turn around. "Yes," she said. "How can I not – you're my sister."

*

At least that was one thing out of the way. Two, if you counted telling Margaret in the first place. Flora drew in a shaky breath. Her back was really paining her - twinging, like she had overdone something, maybe ridden Pudding too hard, and had hurt a muscle. She pulled the shawl around herself again and got to her feet. Now to see Fin.

On her way to the door she heard voices from her father's study across the hall, the Captain – James – saying no, don't trouble yourself or your staff, Lord Arthur. Truly, I can see myself out. Flora took a quiet step back, about to close the door to the sitting room but, too late, James had seen her.

He strode across the hallway parquet towards her, poked a head into the doorway and looked around. "All alone?" he asked rhetorically. "Splendid!" He walked in, closing the door behind him.

"Please," said Flora, "leave the door open."

James checked the door was latched in place and turned towards her. "Why, anyone would think you don't trust me, dearest."

"I, I," Flora stammered.

"No need to lie." James flicked his hand dismissively. "I know you don't. No matter. Come. Sit." He sat himself on the chaise, patting the seat next to him. Flora walked past him and sat in the chair near the unlit fire. James shrugged.

"I've just had a very productive meeting with your father," he said, "and now I have some business with you."

Flora looked confused. "Business?" she repeated.

James reached into his pocket, pulled out a piece of parchment and unfolded it. "Oh," he said on a laugh. "Wrong letter. This is the one from your brother."

Flora felt her heart leap into her throat. "You haven't said anything have you? You said you wouldn't."

"No, of course not. I gave you my word. Your brother's secret is safe with me, for the time being, anyway." He replaced Stephen's letter and pulled another document from his other pocket. "Ah!" he said. "This is the one."

"What is it?"

"Oh, have a little patience, my dear. I went to see your *friend* earlier today. I must confess, he remained entirely stoic during the whole of my visit. Very admirable, I thought. He loves you, anyone can see that, and I wonder if you love him?" James looked hard at her, his ice blue eyes boring into her. "What, I wonder, would you do to save his life?"

"I don't understand." Flora clutched the shawl to herself, her hands knotting themselves inside the material.

"This, in my hand here, is a pardon, made out to Master Dawkins. It all depends on you, my dearest, whether he receives this or not. Come over here, in front of me."

As though she was floating, Flora felt herself get up and walk over to him, her eyes never leaving his. "Now kneel," he said.

"What?"

"I want you to beg." said James, simply. "If you love him, get on your knees and beg for his life."

Flora knelt. If he was being honest, if he would really spare Fin's life if she begged for it, then this would be the easiest thing she had ever had to do in her whole entire life, she thought. Her whole being was crying out in silence already, all she needed to do was give voice to it.

"Please, please, James, don't let him be hanged," she said, tears already falling from her eyes. "I will do anything," she sobbed, "*anything at all*, if you spare him. Please." Flora took the Captain's hand in hers, kissed it in between words, cried her tears over it as she begged, pleaded and implored. "Don't let him die. I am begging you, James. Please, let him live."

The Captain watched, impassive. "A good show," he said finally, taking a handkerchief from his pocket and wiping her tears from his hands. "Tell me, do you think you could ever love me the way you love the shipwright?"

Flora thought she could never like the Captain let alone love him. After everything he had done, she would be the first to wish him dead, but showing him her true feelings wouldn't help her or Fin. She thought back to happier days, times that she had spent in the company of Fin and his gang, at The Star, playing cards. She thought of the incredulous look the men gave her as she used guile and bluff to win yet another hand, time after time. She put on her game face. "Yes," she said, snuffling in between hitching breaths, "yes, in time, I truly believe I can."

"Then kiss me."

Being sure to keep her body as far from his as possible, Flora stretched forward to plant a soft kiss on the corner of James's mouth. He moved his head so she caught him full on the lips and he took her face in his hands. Flora tried to imagine it was Fin she was kissing but there was no comparison; where Fin was soft and gentle, his mouth on hers always giving pleasure, making her head spin as though she was falling, James's lips were thin and hard and his ultimate goal greed. His tongue was probing and his teeth clashed on hers. At last he broke away.

"Very good," he said, smiling. "Now," he waved the pardon in front of her, "as soon I put the wedding band on your finger, this will come into effect." He took her hand in his. "Nasty place, the gaol. I'm not sure how long the shipwright will survive there, you know. It is probably best if you and your sister get on with the wedding arrangements post haste – we wouldn't want him to die of gaol fever in the meantime, would we?" With this he stood, gave her a bow and left the room.

Flora clambered into the seat he just vacated, her breaths coming in gasps in between sobs. The man was truly deranged – how could he possibly expect her to love him after all he was putting her through? Her life would not be worth living once they were married – she had thought as much before but now she was certain.

Flora got to her feet on shaky legs, the twinges in her back causing her to puff and blow and close her eyes against the pain. She saw the pardon letter in her mind's eye, saw the letter from Stephen in her imagination. Her life might not be worth living but the two men closest to her, both of whom she loved in different ways but with every inch of her being, could go on to enjoy life thanks to her sacrifice. For this she was both happy and grateful.

41

Flora couldn't believe her eyes when she saw the cell where Fin was imprisoned. It was bare and cold and the stench of the place made her gag. She watched him from where she stood, disbelieving, incredulous, holding on to the bars in an effort to keep from falling.

Fin was asleep, sitting on the floor, his back against the wall, chin resting on his chest, legs straight out in front of him. His feet were bare, she saw, with evil-looking iron shackles on both ankles.

She was taken back to almost the first time they had met, back at the chapel when he was injured. Just like back then, his hair was loose and hanging in rat-tails over his face and in his eyes. Flora slumped to the floor on her side of the bars, her very heart hurting at the sight of him, silent tears tracking over her cheeks. Across the other side of the cell, laying on the damp filthy floor, Dobbin was curled up, facing the wall.

"Fin," she whispered. "Fin, it's me."

He came awake instantly, lifting his head, his eyes meeting hers. "Oh, ye Gods, Flora!" He scrambled across the floor on his hands and knees, his chains dragging behind him, scraping across the brickwork. He took her fingers through the bars, raised them to his lips. "Ye shouldn't 'ave come," he said, between laying kisses on her hands. "'Tis no place for ye."

"How could I not come?" she asked, feeling the day's growth of stubble on his face scratching at her skin. "Oh, your poor wrists!"

"They're jus' rope burns. Tis nothin', truly."

"And your feet!" Both looked down. Fin's feet were crusted in blood where the hard metal edge of the shackles had bitten into his flesh each time he moved. He tried pulling them out of sight but there was nowhere to hide them.

"Next time I come, I'll bring honey, and something to wrap them in. Is Dobbin all right?" she whispered.

Fin looked over at his friend. "Aye. Asleep is all – there's not much else to do 'ere." He let go of her hands and cupped her face instead. "I can't believe yer 'ere, ye came."

Over in his corner Dobbin muttered, groaned and then sat up. He looked over to the bars. "Mistress Flora?"

Flora tried on a smile. It didn't quite fit. "Yes, Dobbin, it's me." He crawled his way to the bars in just as bad shape as Fin with bloody feet and the welts of rope burns on his wrists. "Tis good to see ye, my lady."

"You too, Dobbin." Flora sniffed back tears, wiped at her face with a hand. "It is good to see both of you but not like this." She manoeuvred herself into a different position on the floor and Fin noticed the pain in her eyes.

"What's wrong?" he asked, his hand once more gripping hers.

"It's the babe, I think. I've been suffering pains all morning. I think she's on her way."

Fin looked aghast. "But it's not time yet. It's too early."

"Only by a scarce couple of weeks." She moved his hand to her belly. "I don't think she's going to wait that long."

"You need to go to The Star, find Sukey!"

"Not yet." Flora winced again. "I have come bearing news; James has written you a pardon!" She smiled. "Fin, he's going to let you live!" Instead of the happiness she had expected to see on his face there was distrust and, just under the surface, anger.

"A pardon?" he repeated.

"Yes! He says that as soon as the wedding band is on my finger it will come into effect."

"And what did ye 'ave to do to get this pardon?" asked Fin, his jaw set. "Because after 'avin' met 'im I know that, as sure as night follows day, ye'd 'ave 'ad to do somethin'."

Flora dropped her gaze. "It doesn't matter. It is done."

Fin chewed his lip, thinking. "Whatever he made ye do – did he hurt ye?"

"No! No, I swear, he didn't touch me."

Fin considered for a moment, watching her closely. Deciding to believe her, he said, "All right then. An' what of Dobbin?"

Flora cast her eyes downward, unable to bear the disappointment she knew she would see on both their faces. "I'm sorry. No."

Dobbin caught her hand through the bars. "It's no matter, Flora," he said, a kind smile on his face. "There's no one that will miss me anyway, only several dozen innkeepers hereabouts." He chuckled, but it was just noise, there was no mirth in the sound.

Tears fell from Flora's eyes. "Oh, Dobbin," she sobbed. "*I* will miss you." She looked at Fin. "We both will."

Dobbin nodded. "I, I was wonderin'," he said nervously, letting go of her hand and holding the bars instead, "if ye'd do something for me, afore I leave ye both to yer conversation."

"Do something for you? Of course." She covered his hand with her own, squeezed his fingers. "What is it that I can do for you?"

"Aye, well, I wondered if, just once, will ye call me by my name? My proper name, I mean."

Flora barely held back a sob. Tears coursed their way over her cheeks. She sniffed.

"Robert," she said. "Robert Croft, my dear friend, I will never, ever, forget you."

Dobbin looked her in the eye. "Thank ye," he said softly. He moved away, dragging his chains behind him, back to his corner of the cell where he went back to lying on the floor, curled up, facing the wall. Both could see his shoulders shaking as he cried, quietly.

Flora and Fin both brushed their tears away. "This pardon," he said. "Do ye trust 'im to hold true to it?"

Flora took in a shuddering breath. "I don't know. He told my father and Margaret about us – he'd seen us together, with his own eyes, Fin – but he didn't tell them about Stephen and I know he still has the letter; he made a point of making sure that I saw he had it with him."

Fin said, "So once more our lives are in his hands, waiting for 'im to decide what he wants to do wi' us. He's treatin' us like toys, Flora." He reached back through the bars and took her hand again, brought it to his mouth. "I don't want ye to wed 'im, Flora. Ye were right – he is cruel and vindictive. If there is any way ye can get away from 'im, now or in the future, do it. Run away. Run as far from 'im as is possible to run." He shuffled onto his knees, looked at her imploringly. "Yer strong, Flora. Other women might not be able to survive goin' off on their own but ye could. Yer smart an' clever an' brave – ye could do it. I know ye could. Please, will ye promise me that ye'll try."

Flora nodded. Squeezed his hand. "I will," she said. "I absolutely will. I promise. Oh!"

"What? Is it the babe?"

Flora grimaced with pain. "Yes. I need to leave," she said, huffing and puffing, holding her bump, feeling their child wriggle and stretch beneath her hands.

"Go to The Star like we talked about. Find Sukey, Flora. I love ye. Go. Now!"

Without waiting to be told twice, Flora heaved herself up by the bars of Fin's cell and headed for the door, one tentative step at a time.

*

"Yer lucky ye made it 'ere when ye did," said Sukey, busying herself doing something under the covers where Flora lay on Fin's bed.

"Why? Are you... busy in... the inn?" Flora said between huffs and puffs and pains that felt like her insides were coming out. Which, in a way, they were.

"No, I mean this babe is all but born; yer lucky it didn't be born in the street. Or on the stairs."

"Oh my... heavens. Really?"

Another pain came, making her grit her teeth and tense

every muscle in her body. She wished Fin was with her to hold her hand. Once the latest pain had gone she looked around her, reminding herself of where she was. He might not be in the room with her but he was all around her – she could sense him, in the books on his shelf, in the smell of him on his pillow and in his bedclothes; the smells of lye soap, timber and honest sweat. It was comforting and she needed comfort now.

"How… do you… know so much about… having children?" she asked Sukey, trying to keep her mind from the pain.

The barmaid laid a fresh cool cloth over Flora's brow. "I helped me Ma born five of me brothers and sisters," she said. "All of 'em healthy. I know what I'm doin', don't fret, Flora."

"I'm fretting… a little – this one is… early."

Sukey took another look under the covers. "T'aint just early, it's 'ere already! I can see the head. Ye need to push, push for all yer worth, Flora."

Flora pushed. When the pain came, she pushed. When the pain went she huffed and puffed. Then Sukey said, "It's 'ere, it's born," and she felt the strangest sensation of something slipping away from inside her and there was suddenly no more pain and she found she was crying tears of joy, as Sukey bundled the infant who was also crying at the top of its lungs, in a clean linen cloth and handed it to her.

"It's a boy," Sukey said.

Flora looked at the tiny face looking up at her with its blue eyes. It had the cutest nose she had ever seen and the loudest cry she had ever heard.

"A boy?"

"Aye, and don't be frettin' about the blue eyes; they change colour after a few months to what they're goin' to be. He's got all his fingers an' toes and a good-sized pair o' balls, too."

"Oh, my heavens. Well." Flora chuckled, the pain of a few moments ago already forgotten. "I suppose that's a good thing."

"I need to cut the cord and ye need to nurse him 'til I find a wet nurse. 'Ere, let me show ye. And while yer doin' that, I'll get Tad to bring you in your gift from Fin."

The baby sucked contentedly at Flora's breast which, she thought, was also a strange and yet beautiful sensation. "I have a gift from Fin?"

"Aye." The barmaid opened the door and yelled down at Tad who came running up the narrow staircase two steps at a time. "Get the thing," she said.

"The thing?" he repeated. Then, "Oh. Aye, the thing."

Moments later he came back in through the door carrying a crib, placed it at the side of the bed. "Fin made this," he said. "For the babe. He spent weeks doing this, in secret."

Flora felt more tears well in her eyes, slide down over her cheeks. "It's beautiful," she breathed. It was a rocking crib with hearts and the words 'Our Angel' engraved on the head and foot-boards. It smelled of new timber, smelled of Fin.

"Sukey," said Flora, "once the babe is done feeding will you please take him to the gaol, to meet his father."

"You could take 'im yersel' in a day or two."

Flora sniffled. "I don't know if they've set a date for the... you know, for when they're going to... I don't know if Fin's pardon will be honoured - he might not still be there in a day or two. It's important he gets to meet his son."

Sukey took Flora's hand. "I'll leave in jus' a minute. Have ye thought of a name?"

Flora looked down at the infant in her arms. "Yes," she said. "His name is Gabriel Robert Dawkins. Our angel."

42

Flora sat at her dressing table, in her wedding dress, looking in the mirror but not seeing herself. Yesterday had been the hardest day she had ever had to endure in her whole entire life. Yesterday had been a day full of goodbyes.

First, she had gone to The Star where Gabriel was tucked up in the crib his father had made for him, fast asleep, blissfully unaware of the drama surrounding him.

Flora looked down on him, his sleeping form; bottom lip stuck out, eyes screwed closed as though sleeping needed all his concentration.

"Ye can wake 'im," said Sukey at Flora's shoulder. "Say goodbye properly."

Flora sat on the floor and rocked the crib gently. "No. If I hold him now, knowing it's the last time I will, I'm afraid I would never put him down again and you would need to wrestle him from my arms."

Sukey put a gentle hand on Flora's shoulder. "If things don't work out, with Phineas I mean, if we're needed, we will take good care of 'im – I promise ye." Flora reached up, squeezed Sukey's hand. "I know you will. We, Fin and I, couldn't think of anyone else we would rather have raise our angel for us than you and Tad, and we both thank you from the bottom of our hearts."

The baby stirred, smacked his lips and settled back down.

"Ye don't believe the Captain will honour the pardon, do ye?" Sukey sat down beside Flora and straightened the baby's blanket.

"He's arranged the... you know... the..."

"Hanging?"

"Yes. That. He's arranged it for tomorrow, for the exact same time as the wedding."

Sukey sucked in a breath. "Phineas and Dobbin both said 'e was a bastard. He really is, ain't 'e?"

Flora nodded. "He's full of evil games. Everything, everyone, is just a plaything for him to manipulate for his own twisted pleasure and enjoyment."

Sukey pulled Flora's head to her shoulder, feeling her shuddering breaths as she cried silently. "I'm sorry for ye, I truly am."

Flora pulled away, wiping at her face. "At least I, *we*, know that Gabe will be safe; no one knows about him except my sister and she won't say anything – as far as she is concerned, he doesn't exist anyway."

"But he's her nephew!"

Flora gave a small laugh. "Son of a highwayman-cum-smuggler-cum-shipwright. What, pray tell, would the neighbours say?"

"Well, our neighbours will love 'im like 'es their own, don't ye fret. He'll 'ave friends a plenty an' grow up good an' decent like 'is Ma an' Da," Sukey finished.

Flora had laid a kiss on the baby's cheek, light as a feather but heavy with love. "I need to go," she'd said. "I need to say goodbye to Fin."

She'd taken Dog with her as she had several times before. Both were pleased to see each other, Dog laying himself as close to the bars of the cell as it was possible to get without actually being inside.

"Tad will look out fer Dog as well as the babe?" Fin had asked on more than one occasion, fussing the creature behind the ear. Flora set his mind at ease again.

"I hate this waitin' around," said Fin. He had almost a full beard now, blond and untidy, and being locked up for as long as he had been had seen him lose weight. He had a permanent frown on his face from being constantly in the gloom and on sight, Flora barely recognised him as the man he once was.

"They tell me it's tomorrow," he said. "Did ye hear that, is that right, tomorrow?"

"Yes. Tomorrow at one o'clock."

"One o'clock," he smiled, the smile almost lost in his beard. "That's our time. We always met at one o'clock, d'ye remember?"

Flora took his hands. She felt tears running down her face. She'd noticed over the past few times she had visited that he was becoming repetitive, sometimes a little muddled. She didn't know what she could do to help him. "Of course I remember," she said.

"I love ye so much, Flora. So much. I'm sorry it all came to naught."

"Don't say that! Tomorrow you'll be free again," she told him. "In a few weeks, maybe even days, you'll have your strength back, you'll be building boats again, smuggling with William and Tad again. We have Gabriel who will be well cared for and, as soon as I am able, as I promised you, I will leave him – James – I will come back for you and Gabe and we will go somewhere far away where that cruel, sadistic excuse for a man will never, ever find us."

Fin smiled, knowing none of it would come to pass. He wiped her tears away with his thumb, no longer quite so calloused, but softer, from not woodworking for so long.

"Ye got me belongins?" he asked again. "They took 'em off me when we got 'ere."

Once more, Flora put his mind at rest. "Yes, they're all in your room, waiting for you – your watch, some coins."

"And the ribbon?"

"Yes, that too. And the letter you wrote to Gabe."

Fin chewed his lip, nodded. "Good. That's good then."

Flora had sat with him and Dog until the light had begun to fade. They had reminisced, they had spoken of their love for one another, they had talked of Gabriel; who he would look like, what he would do when grown. But they didn't speak any more of James or the wedding or of Flora's future.

And now, here it was, twelve o'clock and here was Margaret knocking on her door and then walking straight in, the same as always, saying, "The carriage is here, Flora. It's time to leave."

Flora got to her feet, took one last look around her bedchamber before she left it, closing the door softly behind her.

*

They drove through a crowd that were all heading to the Lynch and Gallows Bend and Flora could hardly believe what she was seeing. She sat in the open topped carriage next to her father and opposite her sister and watched the people all gathering, heading towards the scaffold.

The soldiers being there she could understand, but there were also men, women and even children, the latter running around, playing hide and seek around their mother's skirts like they were on a day out to the county fayre. Flora felt her heart constrict and rage pulse through her body. She gripped her hands in her lap, gritted her teeth. She wanted to shout and yell and scream at them – how could they treat this event with excitement? How could they bring their children to watch as men were killed in front of them? Flora clenched her teeth harder and stared resolutely ahead of her as the carriage continued at a slow pace towards the church of St. Nicholas at Ringwould.

*

They still wore their shackles and were tied at the wrists with rope, and when they were brought outside to embark the closed prison cart with the barred windows, both Fin and Dobbin stumbled and raised their arms to their faces, the brightness of the day hurting their eyes. Both stood for a moment, breathing in the fresh seaside air, looking up at the blue sky, listening to the sounds of the town around them; the streets alive with horses, vendors, women chattering, children laughing, people going about their daily business. The soldiers let them take it all in for a moment then opened the rear door to the cart and assisted each man to climb up the steps and get settled inside.

Neither of them spoke – neither could think of anything to say; there wasn't anything to say, not anymore. Once they were both safely inside, the soldiers locked the door behind them and the cart made its way towards the scaffold at the Lynch and Gallows Bend.

*

The church of St. Nicholas at Ringwould was packed, mostly full of her relatives; uncles, aunts and cousins she rarely, if ever, saw. Flora didn't see them now – she was just aware of a sea of faces swimming before her eyes, all turning to look at her as she stepped, one slow footstep at a time, up the aisle towards the alter and him – James.

He was smartly attired as always, in his dress uniform, his black boots gleaming, sword at his side. His red coat with the gold brocade and buttons would have made him stand out from the rest of the crowd even if he hadn't been the only person standing, waiting for her.

Flora felt her nerves overcome her the nearer she stepped towards him. Her heart was racing; beating in her throat. Her hands and feet felt cold as ice and her legs shook, threatening to spill her on to the ground.

Five minutes, she thought, ten at the most, and Fin would be free.

She had done as James had bid, she had got on her knees and begged for his life, surely after that he would stick to his word.

Flora took another step forward.

Just ten minutes more.

*

James watched her walking towards him – she looked breathtaking in her silver grey gown, light from the candles that illuminated the church reflecting off the bodice which was decorated with mother of pearl. Her hair, as he preferred, was loose, and her curls bounced on her shoulders as she stepped ever closer to him.

He couldn't believe the day had finally come when he would make her his wife, and he was already looking forward to tonight, when there would be just the two of them and he would make her his alone. He patted the pocket where the pardon letter lay, feeling the parchment crackle under his fingers.

She was almost next to him and her father let go of her arm, handed her over to him and took his place on the front pew. James took Flora's hand in his, noticing the icy feel of it under his own burning touch. The reverend cleared his throat and began the service.

*

The prison cart rumbled along the road from Deal towards Walmer, throwing Dobbin and Fin against the walls, against each other, making their chains rattle. They drove through the town, down the hill from Walmer and eventually came to a stop at the Lynch and Gallows Bend.

Already Fin could hear the crowd outside, those come to gawp at their misfortune, most of them saying they deserved all they were getting. The guards stepped down from the driver's seat and Fin and Dobbin heard the door to the cart unlock. Fin grabbed Dobbin's hands, like his, tied at the wrists. "My friend," he said. "My dear friend."

Dobbin looked over at him, his hair in his eyes, his eyes shiny with unshed tears. He gripped his hands back. "Farewell," he whispered hoarsely. "'Til we meet again."

They were helped from the cart by the guards, their legs weak from nervousness and lack of recent use. Fin thought the shackles felt heavier than ever around his ankles and each step he took was a torment. He saw people jostling each other to get a good look at them, some spat, others threw things; rotten vegetables, fruit gone bad. He hardly felt the missiles as they landed, but in his shackles, a guard's hand under his arm, he shuffled his way towards the gallows soaked in putrid juices and spit, and all the time he was thinking of Flora, conjuring her image to his mind.

He climbed the scaffold steps, a guard guiding his way, Dobbin following mere footsteps behind. The nooses swung in the breeze and Fin was taken to his spot above the drop, the rope – thick and heavy – was placed carefully around his neck, under his chin. Fin gazed out at the crowd, at a hundred or more Flora's all looking at him. The guard tightened the noose around his throat. Fin smiled, and closed his eyes.

*

"I, James Peter Reed, do take thee Flora Anne Harrington..."
Five minutes thought Flora. Just five minutes.

*

"...til death do us part, according to God's holy ordinance; and thereto I plight thee my troth," Flora finished. The words were just words, not even that, they were just sounds, meaningless to her. The new gold band on her finger glinted in the candlelight, reflecting the colours from the stained-glass windows all around them.

"I now pronounce you husband and wife," finished the Reverend. With a smile at James, he said, "You may kiss the bride."

"The pardon," said Flora, as James leaned in towards her.

He moved away again, his hand in his pocket, pulling out the parchment, unfolding it inch by slow, painful inch. "I just can't take the risk of you running off to be with him, my dear," he said, tearing the paper in two, then in four, in front of her eyes.

"No!" Flora breathed, watching the pieces float lazily to the floor. She looked back up at James, shaking her head, breaking away from his grasp on her arm, turning and running back down the church passageway, unaware and uncaring of the looks of disbelief and amazement from the people seated in the church.

Flora ran down the aisle, out the door and into the churchyard. Without stopping for breath, she turned right, crossing the road, heading into the woods.

Behind her people got to their feet, whispering, murmuring, looking to each other for an explanation of what they had just witnessed.

James followed her down the aisle at a brisk walk, elbowing the guests out of his way. "Bring me a horse!" he yelled, but no one had come by horse alone, only carriage, and he ran to the nearest one, near the lychgate, struggling with fingers numb with anger to unharness the beast. At last the horse was free and he mounted it bareback, pulling the length of rein shorter, kicking the creature to make it follow Flora into the trees. But the woodlands here were thick, with not much room to manoeuvre between trees, and the branches were low and overhanging, swiping at him as he tried to ride through them. At last he gave up, turned the horse around and made his way back from where he'd come, thinking to take the road instead, to beat her to the gallows where she was surely headed.

*

Flora ran as fast as she could through the trees, the low branches snagging in her hair, tearing it out by clumps. "I should never have trusted him!" she cried, freeing herself from the branches, gulping down air, running again. It was obvious to her now that James had never had any intention of letting Fin live. Twigs whipped her in the face as she scrabbled through them, thorny stems scratched at her arms and ripped holes in her gown.

All she could think of was Fin. She realised it was too late – it was gone one o'clock – he would not be saved, but if she could only be there, if hers could be the last face he saw…

The trees thinned before her and between the trunks she could see the crowds ahead; the soldiers in their red coats standing guard, the ordinary folk beginning to head back to town. Scratched and bleeding, her gown in tatters, she came to the edge of the woodlands, breaking free of the trees. Ahead of her, through the thinning crowd, she could see the scaffold. She could see Fin - dear, sweet Fin - hanging, lifeless, by his neck. She stopped, stood stock still; there was no reason to run anymore.

James made it back to the road and threw the horse into a gallop, barely hanging on to its back. He kicked at the horse's sides, trying to make it go faster than it possibly could. When he was almost directly opposite the Lynch and Gallows Bend Flora came running out of the trees. Before he had a chance to slow the horse she stood, stock still, only feet in front of him.

James tried to stop the horse in its tracks. He pulled the reins up short, but this was a placid carriage horse; unused to being ridden. Blinkered, it was suddenly aware of an object in front of it and it reared up on its hind legs, its forelegs frantically waving in the air. One of its hooves caught Flora in the head, knocking her down then, frenzied, the horse bucked and reared again, throwing James to the ground and trampling Flora where she lay, bleeding in the dirt.

James crawled over to her. She looked a mess with her gown shredded and her arms and face faring no better. He put his fingers to her neck, hoping to find a pulse, but knowing it was futile. Visions of what would never now happen played across his mind – there would be no dinner parties, no piano recitals. Friends and colleagues would not look upon his breath-taking wife with envy in their eyes, wishing they too had a woman so beautiful. He wouldn't have a chance to make her his, after all.

He got to his feet. A crowd had begun to gather around them – stragglers from the spectacle across the road. There were whispers; "What happened?" "Who is she?" "Is she all right?"

James ignored them all. He pulled his gaze away from his wife's crumpled and beaten form, from the blood pouring from her head and pooling in the dirt on the ground. He turned around, watched for a moment as the men took the body of his rival down from the gallows. He looked down at himself, saw how his boots were scuffed, his coat covered in dust. James brushed himself down and walked away.

43

First everything was red, and then it turned black.
Sounds that had been muffled turned to silence.
The pain went from intense to no pain at all.

When next Flora opened her eyes, through the mist she saw him – Fin, a smile on his face, love in his warm hazel eyes, holding out his rough, shipwright's hand to her, come to take her with him.

The End

Author's note

Most anyone who, like me, has lived in the Dover or Deal area of Kent has heard the stories of the Grey Lady (sometimes called the White Lady) who haunts the road at Oxney Bottom. Not much is known about her origins, or why she feels tied to Oxney. A highwayman is also said to haunt the same area. His origins have been traced back to one Thomas Saperg, the youngest son of a Deal innkeeper who was forced into highway robbery by circumstance and was hanged in chains at the Lynch and Gallows Bend aged thirty-six.

The Lynch and Gallows Bend has not survived – the layout of the main Dover to Deal road having been altered over the centuries.

There really was a massive raid on the Deal smugglers on the night of October 31st 1781 and one man, wielding a mattock iron, was "considerably injured" while clambering over a wall in a bid to escape.

The original Oxney Court house with its tower and crenellations was destroyed by fire during WWI and then left to rot until the 1980s when it was bought, raised it to the ground and a new property built on the plot.

Read on for the first chapter of the sequel to The Ghosts of Oxney Bottom, All for a Tear due out in 2022.

The Atlantic Ocean

1803

Chapter 1

For not the first time during the past four weeks, Gabriel Dawkins wondered if he was doing the right thing in travelling to America. Below deck, he was surrounded on all sides by the mournful noises of his fellow passengers moaning, sobbing and whimpering. The cries never let up no matter what time of the day or night. And the smells, ye Gods, the smell of rot and disease, unwashed bodies and tar ate into his nostrils until it was all he could taste, even during the times, like now, when he went above board and looked out at nothing but the vastness of the ocean surrounding him.

He stood at the quarterdeck and watched the indigo waves rolling on endlessly, hitting the hull of the Isobella, churning up the icy cold salt spray. The spray hit the skin of his arms and face and made him feel alive once more after hours of being cooped up with a hundred or so others below deck. Around him sailors undertook their tasks, shouting orders to one another, and the sails of the vessel flapped in the wind while the masts creaked and groaned, and the wind whistled through the rigging. He turned slowly, his eyes on the horizon. There was nothing out here, nothing at all to see. Today the sky was an azure blue, the sun a bright yellow orb in the sky and there were no clouds. They were still too far from land to spot even a bird. Gabriel took in a big breath of salty fresh air, turned and made his way back below deck.

He negotiated the slippery wooden steps carefully, and once down them did his best to step over or around the puddles of seawater and puke on the deck floor. They were supposed to be swept down daily but this rarely happened. He could count on the fingers of one hand how many times he'd seen a sailor with a broom down here since they'd set sail.

It took his eyes took a few moments to adjust to the gloom and he picked his way cautiously past the other passengers and headed toward the rear of the ship. He'd known the journey would be rough, had anticipated a degree of seasickness among his fellow travellers, he'd even expected there would be a shortage of rations at some stage into the voyage but not after a mere four weeks, and he hadn't expected the rations that were left to be as rotten as they already were. These days the bread was mouldy more often than not or worse, infested with weevils, the potatoes had eyes and the meat was so salty that it made you crave water even though the water was rank.

He squeezed past a group of three men standing near the berths, they too stank – of stale sweat, illness and something else... perhaps desperation, and Gabe was mindful to avoid looking them in the eye or brushing against them as he passed.

It was dim below deck – a few lanterns hanging from the timbers here and there cast a mean glow and threw long shadows. There were no portholes on this deck and the lanterns were lit all day and all night. People stood in the aisle or lay on their berths doing nothing, for there was nothing to do. Those that were ill tossed and turned on their seaweed stuffed mattresses, or slept, when they weren't puking. Gabriel found his own berth and climbed in. The man opposite gave a weary smile and pointed at his face. "How is it?" he asked.

Gabriel touched his fingers to his mouth, feeling the scab there at the corner, and smiled back. "I'll live."

Yesterday, the blow had come out of nowhere, a complete surprise. One minute he was sitting on his berth trying to read the next, the punch caught him square on the jaw, rocking his head back, making his teeth rattle in their sockets and the hunk of bread he had been holding was ripped from his hand.

Gabriel had shaken his head and blinked hard, trying to clear his vision. Through blurry eyes he saw the thief walk away without so much as a backward glance. The man in the berth opposite climbed out and shuffled quickly through the puddles on the floor over to him. "Are you all right?" he worried. "I didn't see it coming or I would have warned you."

Gabriel smiled through a split lip, licked the blood from the corner of his mouth. "It's nothing," he replied. "Though we're only a few weeks into the journey – I s'pose there'll be more o' that 'appenin' the longer we travel."

"They can buy more rations on the quiet from the stewards," the stranger had said. "But I suppose stealing it is a great deal cheaper." He had held out his hand. "I'm Henry Atkins."

Gabriel had shaken hands with him and introduced himself.

Like most of their fellow passengers, Henry was leaving England behind to start a new life in America. He was travelling with his wife and small child but the mother had been struck down with whichever disease it was that was now rife on board – an illness that started off with a headache and fever and went on to develop into sickness, aches and pains, a persistent cough and a rash. A few people had already succumbed completely, and their bodies had been dumped overboard with little to no ceremony. Gabriel could hardly believe it the first time he'd seen it. Two sailors had descended in silence on the dead, they'd wrapped the body in the thin blanket that was included in the price of the berth, had secured it with rope and then hauled it up the narrow steps to the open deck where it was slung overboard. He'd seen it from the open deck, too – the ship's chaplain saying one or two words before the body was thrown into the icy depths. It had made him feel sick to his stomach.

"How's your family?" Gabriel asked his neighbour. Henry raised his eyes to the berth above him where his wife slept fitfully in between bouts of coughing. "Not good," he answered. "Getting worse as the days roll on. I just thank God that the boy here shows no signs of it as yet."

Gabriel took in the small child sitting at his father's side. His eyes were wide below his blonde fringe and his jaw was clenched shut. He looked like he was trying very hard not to cry.

Gabriel felt a kind of affinity with the child. It was highly likely that his little family would be torn apart by their journey's end and that a voyage that had started out with his mother, father and himself would end with just his father and him. Perhaps not even that if they were unlucky. Gabriel patted the mattress next to him, smiled at the boy. "Come 'ere."

The boy looked up at his father, who nodded. He slunk over, looking wary.

"What's your name?"

The boy looked at him. He'd been right – there were huge tears balanced on his lower lashes and his eyes were shiny with trying to hold them back. "Michael," he whispered.

Gabe smiled. "I'm Gabriel," he said. "But people back 'ome used to call me Worm." The boy blinked, dislodging the tears that slid down over his cheeks. He brushed them away with a pudgy hand and looked up at him. "Worm?" he asked, disbelievingly.

"Aye. Can ye guess why?"

The boy, Michael, shook his head.

"Because when I was about your age-"

"I'm six."

"Aye, well, when I was about six, I was always wriggling into places I had no right to be in." Michael stared at him. "Once," continued Gabe, "I climbed into an empty ale cask and couldn't get back out. I was there for ages afore anyone noticed I was missing

223

an' came to look for me."

"What did you do?" asked Michael, looking a little less upset.

"Listened. I listened to all the goings on around me. I 'eard smugglers talking about their hauls of wine, gin and lace, 'eard them tellin' where they'd hid it, I 'eard women gossiping wi' other women, and children, like me, playing."

"Why didn't you call for help?"

Gabriel frowned. "It was… interestin'," he said. "Hearin' what other folks was up to. Also, I knew as me Da wouldn't be 'appy wi' me for gettin' in somewhere I shouldn't 'ave. Again."

Michael wriggled further onto the berth. "How did they find you?"

"I fell asleep, curled up in the bottom o' that ale cask like a kitten. My Da's dog sniffed me out eventually."

Gabriel thought back to the day, remembered being woken from his uncomfortable slumber in the bottom of the smelly ale cask by Dog whining beside the barrel. He could hear his claws tapping on the wooden floor, could hear him snuffling and woofing quietly as he paced back and forth, could feel the barrel move ever so slightly as Dog brushed up against it. Gabriel wriggled himself onto his knees and then stood up. As well as the sounds of Dog he could hear his Da calling for him. He stood up on tiptoe, his eyes reaching just above the cask top and he called out. "I'm in 'ere!" His Da strode across the room and looked down on him with a resigned look on his face as he reached in and hauled young Worm out of his prison by his armpits. "What the devil are ye doin' in there?"

"Hidin'."

Tad Walker had stood the boy on his two pins beside him. "One day, Worm, you'll wriggle yersel' into a whole lot of trouble," he'd said.

Still in the past, thinking of his Ma and Da he conjured up an image of them in his mind. He could see them at the coach station that unseasonably hot, sunny day six weeks ago as they all waited for the coach to carry him off to Plymouth to catch the packet ship The Isobella.

"I still don't understand why it is ye want to go," Tad Walker had said for at least the fiftieth time by Gabe's reckoning. "Yer travelling halfway across the world when ye 'ave no guarantee the man is even still there!"

It was an argument they'd had countless times and Gabe shook his head in exasperation. "He was still there two years ago," he countered. He'd written to the British Army asking the last known whereabouts of Captain James Reed, and had told an outright lie to get the information he needed. It wasn't something he was proud of; he had not been brought up to lie but in order to get them to take him seriously, he'd said that he had reason to believe that the Captain was his father. The Army had written back that the Captain had in fact been promoted to Major but had left the Army and was living in Millbrooke, North Carolina. "And what will ye do if ye find 'im?" Tad continued, "Beat 'im? Kill 'im? And all fer what – ye can't change the past, Worm."

No, it was true, he couldn't change the past. His parents – his real parents – were both dead because of the man he was crossing an ocean to track down. His father, Fin Dawkins, arrested by him and hanged by his neck when Gabe was only a few days old and his mother blackmailed, somehow, into marrying the man he now sought, then trampled to death under his horse's hoofs all on the same day. No, he might not be able to change the past, to bring his parents back, but he wanted with all his being to set eyes on the man he felt was responsible for their deaths, he wanted with everything he had to have that man apologise to him, to ask forgiveness, even just to shed a tear.

And now here he was, on board The Isobella, almost all his most prized possessions – his father's pistol, his mother's velvet hair ribbon among other things - packed into a holdall and used as a bolster for his thin pillow in the tiny berth on this godawful vessel. Gabe sighed and shook his head to clear the memories. While he had been remembering, the boy had left his side and had climbed into the berth next to his father.

The older man's face was a picture of worry, his eyes raising to the berth above each time his wife gave out a hacking cough and then jumping to his feet to check on her each time she fell silent. Gabriel was glad he was making this journey alone and only had himself to worry about. He untangled his long legs, crossed at the ankles, and swung them up into the berth. He'd been lucky so far; a little bit of seasickness when they'd first set sail until he'd found his sea legs, but no symptoms of the disease running virulent throughout the ship.

His Ma – well, Sukey Walker, the person who he called his Ma, the one who, alongside her husband, Tad, had raised him from when he was only a few days old – had been so worried for him when he'd said about embarking on this journey. She'd tried to put him off with talk of shipwrecks and pirates, tales of Indians waiting on the other side of the world to kill him. Now she pulled her last card.

"Are ye sure you're not jus' doin' this because of… ye know," she'd said, taking him by the arm, looking into his eyes.

Gabriel's blood ran cold. *"Gabe, I'm sorry…"*

"You can say her name," he'd replied, gruffly. "Anna. And no, ye know that's not the reason." Tad shot her a look and shook his head. Sukey's eyes filled with tears. She was defeated. She'd pulled him to her in a bear hug, having to stand on tiptoe to speak in his ear. "We'll never see you again," she'd fretted. "Ye'll never come back, once ye get there."

He'd tried to set her mind to rest – he certainly had every intention of coming back to England once his journey in America was over. He'd told them both he was coming back, back to set another thing straight. He may be a common man raised by common folk, his father may have just been a shipwright and a criminal, but his mother had been a Lady and he was the family's sole heir. His American adventure was only the first leg - once he was done in the colonies, once he'd found Major James Reed and had held him to account, he fully intended to return to England – he had a birthright to claim.

Printed in Great Britain
by Amazon

66804102R00137